The Waking of Willie Ryan

The Waking of
Willie Ryan

John Broderick

THE LILLIPUT PRESS
in association with
THE JOHN BRODERICK COMMITTEE

Published 2004 by
THE LILLIPUT PRESS
62–63 Sitric Road, Arbour Hill,
Dublin 7, Ireland
www.lilliputpress.ie

First published 1965 by
WEIDENFELD & NICOLSON
20 New Bond Street
London, W1

A CIP record for this title is available from
The British Library.

ISBN 1 84351 049 9

The Lilliput Press receives financial assistance from
An Chomhairle Ealaíon / The Arts Council of Ireland.

Printed by Creative Print and Design Group, Middlesex

Foreword

JOHN BRODERICK, whom I knew slightly, was an awkward customer in the literary Ireland of the 1960s. He had high critical standards and an acerbic style in which to express these standards, which he was not afraid to do, often at the expense of his colleagues in the writing trade. He was a heavy drinker and homosexual. While the first of these traits was par for the course in bohemian Dublin the second was unquestionably a handicap, especially in the days before decriminalization. A passionate lover of the Roman Catholic Church and its ritual, he also loathed and excoriated its dishonesty and hypocrisy in sexual matters.

Born in the large Irish midland town of Athlone, he inherited a prosperous bakery business and lived in some style in a large villa on the outskirts of the town. His wealth gave him the opportunity to travel, but not even this could compensate for the narrowness of Ireland, which he found stifling and provincial, and eventually he moved to the Augustan city of Bath where he died from the effects of drink and loneliness.

Not surprisingly in the circumstances, his books never received the attention or the critical acclaim they deserved during his lifetime. His reputation has however been kept precariously alive by a small group of admirers in his home town. Virtually unique among his contemporaries, John Broderick ruthlessly exposed the truth of the social and sexual life of pre-Vatican Two Ireland.

The Waking of Willie Ryan in particular is a masterpiece.

A brief summary of the action of the novel demonstrates just how courageous Broderick was in selecting his subject matter. The book was published in 1965, well before revelations about clerical sex abuse, the acknowledgment of the horrendous abuse of children at State institutions, the Bishop Casey scandal, the X Case and the release of real figures concerning Irish abortion had exposed the reality of subterranean sexual activity in Ireland and the calculated hypocrisy with which this was concealed.

The novel opens with an elderly lady, Mrs Whittaker, stopping her car to avoid a hen and discovering a flat tyre. When she has remedied this problem she takes a rest, drinking in a view of the midlands with its special atmosphere of bog, river and mountain beautifully evoked by Broderick. Then she notices the figure of a white-haired man gently catching and cupping in his hands a falling leaf.

The old man's name is Willie Ryan and his history is disclosed gradually throughout the novel. First a victim of his brother Michael's precocious sexual advances (this brother now having become a shambling queasily hypocritical successful businessman largely thanks to the shrewish energy of his wife) he then falls in love with a more sophisticated neighbour, Roger Dillon. Ironically Willie only reluctantly accepts the sexual side of this relationship as the price he must pay for that love. Eventually he becomes part of a circle of similar young men surrounding the more promiscuous Roger. Inevitably it is the most outrageous of these who blows the whistle, causing a scandal that brings matters to the attention of the local priest, Fr Mannix. Willie and Roger continue to meet in secret, although the strain tells heavily on Willie, driving him to an overindulgence in drink.

Clumsily trying to mend his fences with his sister-in-law – who herself has had a crush on Roger Dillon, which adds the sharpness of jealousy to her spiteful nature – he tries to kiss her. She sees an opportunity to dispose of her unwanted brother-in-law, cries rape and Willie is hunted out of the way to a convenient mental institution. That this was a common occurrence in Irish life in the twentieth century when troublesome relatives were labelled insane and tucked out of sight is confirmed by firsthand accounts like that of Hannah Greely's autobiography *Bird's Nest Soup*. Willie's love affronts conventional society and must be extinguished or hidden away.

At the opening of the novel Willie has unobtrusively slipped out of the asylum after twenty-five years incarceration and made his way home to die, in a rather pathetic detail removing his shoes as he passes through his own village so as not to arouse the suspicion of his former neighbours. His nephew Chris affords him shelter and once it becomes clear that he is not in fact mad and probably never has been, the family are left with a problem. To save face they attempt to make him perform his religious 'duty'. They enlist the help of Fr Mannix, still active in the parish. The core of the novel becomes the battle between Willie and the priest. It becomes clear that there is a double edge to the title of the novel because at the end his family feel that he has not had a decent Wake at all, whereas in the light of his own comment that he has been dead for twenty-five years, the entire novel constitutes an account of a protracted but unacknowledged Wake.

It is a tribute to Broderick's mastery that he does not make a monster out of Fr Mannix, who is seen as very human indeed, complaining of being 'poisoned' by all the tea he is given by his parishioners and who accepts being bitten by bitches both human and canine as part of his job. But he is no match for Willie, who demonstrates the truth of Fr Mannix's own observation earlier in the novel that 'men die as they live'.

Over the whole novel hangs the pall of provincial respectability. An earthy, decent girl, Susan, who enters Chris Ryan's life with honesty and vigour, gives us a realistic view of the Mass they decide to hold in the house: 'In a sense they don't believe anything at all. It's just that it puts the seal of respectability on things.' This could be a verdict on the whole society revealed in the novel. Willie is expected 'to make peace with the Church' not, you may note, make peace with God. In the midst of all this Willie's Joycean 'non serviam' stands as a lonely instance of integrity. He refuses to go to confession although it could be argued that at the end of the novel he makes a secular confession to, and is absolved by, the sister of the man he loved, in a reversal of Evelyn Waugh's sentimental description of the deathbed conversion of Lord Marchmain in *Brideshead Revisited*.

Outwardly Roger Dillon conformed and the priest believes that he won that particular battle. But in a wonderful reversal of fortune the ailing Willie takes control of the situation and intimates to the priest that Roger's confession was as insincere as Willie's own attendance at the farmhouse Mass has been. Frail and elderly, Willie has an intellectual and emotional strength that makes him master of the situation.

There are some wonderful minor characters like Miss Pinkie White with her servile interest in the aristocracy and British royalty and the good-hearted asylum official Mr Halloran. There is also a delightful bitchiness about some of Broderick's descriptions, such as that of Mary Ryan: 'unlike most goitred women she never wore scarves, and always affected rather low-cut frocks'. Broderick has his knife firmly stuck in Mrs Ryan and treats us to a

4

glimpse of her enjoying a little episode of nose-picking when nobody is about to see.

He catches also the landscape in deft phrases such as 'there was a frosty ring around the moon and the river glittered like an oiled blade'. There is a controlled and organic symbolism in the book that supports and strengthens the impact of the writing. For example the smoking chimney in the restored farmhouse appears to symbolize the natural forces that cannot be extinguished by 'respectability' and it is significant that this smoke coils into the room at the very moment of Fr Mannix's defeat. Similarly the chiming of the drawing-room clock at the end of chapter two becomes an objective correlative for the fragility of the outward respectability but insidious materialism of the Ryans: 'The little ormolu clock whirred under its glass dome and prepared to strike the hour. The six silvery chimes broke the silence of the room like a coin tapped gently against the window pane.'

That such a book was written at all in the 1960s is astonishing. That its author should have been from the Irish provinces is little short of miraculous. The reissuing of this remarkable volume is welcome but long overdue and I hope it may be followed by the republication of the entire canon of Broderick's works.

DAVID NORRIS

This story takes place before the Liturgical Constitution, promulgated at the Second Session of the Vatican Council, was adopted by the Catholic Church in Ireland.

J.B.

'The Law worketh wrath; and where there is no law, neither is there transgression.'

ST PAUL (ROMANS IV 15)

ONE

MRS WHITTAKER braked to avoid the white hen. The car dipped and swayed gently as she guided it to a halt by the grass margin on the far side of the road. She put on the hand-brake and got out. The hen was now perched on top of the ditch, its small reptilian head red as a sea snapper at the end of a rigid neck. Mrs Whittaker started to chase the hen into the field to make the road safer for the next motorist; but then she saw the soft front tyre, and turned back to the battered old Ford.

She got out the jack, took off the tyre and examined it anxiously. She could find nothing embedded in the worn rubber and sighed with relief as she straightened up to give her aching back a rest. She looked at her watch. Half-an-hour to spare before her appointment at four. It rarely took her more than ten minutes to get into town from this point, except on a fair day.

She got out the pump and began to work briskly in spite of her back and the rheumatic pains in her knees. Her small, blotched hands gripped the handle firmly; as she worked she found herself breathing in time with the expelled air. When the job was done she did not straighten up immediately but leaned on the handle for a few minutes with her eyes closed.

'Thank God that's over,' she said, placing a hand on the back of her hip and levering herself up cautiously.

She leaned against the bonnet to recover her breath, and looked down on the scene below. When she had time Mrs Whittaker often stopped at this spot to admire the view. Here the road ran along the top of one of the few hills in that flat district: the middle of the great central plain of Ireland. She never tired of the sight of the plain stretching away for thirty miles to the horizon. Except for the short blue line of the Slieve Bloom mountains, there was no part of it that did not end with the sky. The wide strips of colour into which it was divided varied with the seasons. The water-meadows, green in the spring and gold in the summer, were a muddy silver in the winter when the mighty Shannon overflowed its banks for a mile on either side. The bog, which eternally strove with the river for mastery of the plain, began where the meadows ended and swept away to the south, barren, sinister, brooding; purple in summer and autumn, black as a night-beast in winter, golden only for a brief time in the spring when the whins flowered for a month before their burning.

Already at the end of October the river was swollen and dark; and the hazy sky blurred the rim of the horizon. Mrs Whittaker shook her head as if she were awakening from a light doze, and began to gather up the tools. When she had locked them in the boot she wiped her hands with a country-woman's gesture on the back of her hips. Peering along the way to see if any traffic was coming, for she was parked on the wrong side, she saw a man coming up round the turning beyond which the road ran down the eastern slope of the hill into the town.

Half-way between the parked car and the turning a gate led into the farmhouse of Michael Ryan, whose wife Mrs Whittaker was going into town to meet. From where she stood the old woman could see the long low front of Summerhill, one of the few two-storied houses in that district to remain thatched, with its small windows looking out through the ivy like eyes through a tousled mob of hair. Inside the gate stood a great beech, already half consumed by its own tongues of flame. And beside the wall the stranger was standing, looking in her direction. Mrs Whittaker, who knew everybody in the district, narrowed her eyes and stared. The man backed slowly against the wall under the shelter of the big beech. A car came round the bend and roared past, the blurred-faced occupants glaring at the Ford parked on the wrong side. Mrs Whittaker got in, started up and drove along to the Summerhill gates, where she stopped again with a jerk and a little angry intake of breath, for the white hen had reappeared on the ditch and was about to make another clucking swoop on the road.

The old woman got out painfully but firmly and made for it.

' Shush! ' she hissed, flapping her hand in front of her. ' Shush! You and your soft tyre! '

With a frightened squawk the hen scrambled over the ditch and disappeared. A little appeased, Mrs Whittaker turned round and looked across the road at the stranger by the gates. Although she could not make out the man's face clearly, it seemed to her that he had a thick shock of white hair. The beech tree shaded the upper part of his body; but Mrs Whittaker could see a pair of thick dusty boots, the ends of coarse grey trousers, and a small white hand, supple and beautifully shaped, twisting a button on his coat. He seemed completely unaware of the car and its owner. It was this detachment, even more than his facelessness and the white coiling hand, that made Mrs Whittaker linger on the roadside peering at the stranger. It was a dull day, and there was no sound between them except the mouse-like rustle of the dead leaves slipping through the branches of the tree.

Suddenly Mrs Whittaker caught her breath. The white hand, so strangely contrasted with such coarse clothes, stopped twisting the button and reached out towards her. But the man was not beckoning. He was holding out his hand to catch a leaf, which had detached itself from one of the branches of the tree, and was fluttering to the ground, changing colour in the dappled shade from red to purple, until it rested on his palm, light and yellow as a brimstone butterfly. The stranger covered it with his other hand, touching it as gently as a blind child fondling a doll. Then he turned slowly away through the gates, and up the curving avenue to Summerhill.

Mrs Whittaker got into her car and drove off, talking quietly to herself in the manner of those who spend a lot of their time alone.

'Is Chris home yet?' asked Michael Ryan.

'No,' said his wife without looking round from the mantel-piece, where she was winding a little ormolu clock. 'Why?'

'No why. I just asked. Did you see the paper anywhere?' He picked up a magazine from a table, flicked through it and left it down again.

'It's in the breakfast room, where you left it this morning.' Mrs Ryan picked up the glass dome from the arm of the chair beside the fireplace. She did not replace it over the clock, but stood clasping it against her breast, tapping the paper-thin glass with her finger-tips. 'Is there anything particular in it?'

'No, no. I just wanted to have another look at the Dublin market, that's all. Dolan's traveller was telling me that sultanas are going to fall.'

'But you haven't bought the Christmas fruit yet, have you?' Mrs Ryan replaced the dome carefully over the clock.

'No.' Her husband looked at the tea things on the table in front of the sofa: the Crown Derby cups, the silver kettle, the Carrickmacross lace – an important visitor. Crumbs from the madeira cake lay on the off-white carpet like pollen from a broken flower. Then he glanced up and was startled to find his wife staring fixedly at him in the mirror above the mantelpiece. Like many people who have lived together for many years they had ceased to look directly at each other for any length of time.

Mary Ryan turned away quickly and touched her smooth hair with the back of her wrist. It showed little trace of grey; and she wore it brushed back severely and tied in a bun at the nape of her neck. With her large brown eyes, angular body, elongated hands and thin yellowish face, she looked like an El Greco figure.

'Did you want to see Chris?' she said, sitting on the arm of the chair. She had a habit of twisting her mouth at the corners and blinking her eyes rapidly.

'No, no.' Her husband rubbed his plump hands together. They were small, but ill-shaped; and of that unnatural chalk colour which one sometimes sees in those who come from generations of manual workers, but who have themselves done no physical labour for many years. He was several inches shorter than his wife; round and smooth and pink-cheeked from good living, and with a head of thick white hair. 'I was just wondering if he was home yet. It's nearly tea-time.'

Mrs Ryan looked at the clock.

'It's half-past five. He never comes back until half-six.'

Ryan sat down on the sofa and broke off a piece of madeira cake, which he began to crumble between his fingers.

'Did you have someone for tea?' He moistened a finger on his tongue and picked up a few crumbs of cake.

'Mrs Whittaker. She came about the jumble sale for the ISPCC. I had to give her a few things, some cardigans of my own, and that blue shirt of yours that's frayed at the collar. Also some shoes.'

'How is she?' Ryan licked his fingers again and wiped them on the white handkerchief in his breast pocket.

'Quite well. Her rheumatism is getting worse, but she doesn't complain much. She's a nice old thing.'

She stood up and walked over to the window, switching on a pink-shaded standard lamp as she went. The light was failing. Outside the garden was already wrapped in the pigeon-winged haze of an October afternoon. A neon sign in the cinema at the end of the road touched the sky with a metallic pink. Mrs Ryan felt the sill of the large bow window with her fore-finger for dust.

'She got a soft tyre on the way in. Just outside Summer-hill.'

13

Ryan did not reply. He lit a match and watched it burn to his fingertips before he threw it into the ashtray.

'Kathleen is out there with Chris, isn't she?' he said at last.

'Of course she's out there with him,' snapped Mrs Ryan, turning from the window and narrowing her eyes. 'She's out there every day now, as you know perfectly well.' She clasped her hands in front of her breast, and began to speak in an entirely different voice: girlish, gushing, the words stumbling over one another excitedly. 'Oh Chris, bring me too, won't you? I love cows. I'm only at home in the country.'

The distortion of her face and voice disappeared as suddenly as a tic.

She came back and stood with her back to the fireplace: legs planted wide apart, hands clasped on her flat rump in a masculine stance which did not become her. With her exaggerated bone structure she was one of those women who cannot strike an attitude without risking the grotesque.

'A lot she knows about farming, brought up in a hovel, and all belonging to her working in the factory.'

'Well, you'll have to get used to her, Mary. He's going to marry her. And after all her people are not so bad. I remember when they had a nice little business of their own. It's not her fault if they went down in the world.'

'A lot of no-goods. I don't suppose she's got enough to buy herself an outfit, leaving her job the minute she became engaged. I can see Chris forking out for the wedding, along with all the other expenses. That is, if it comes off.'

'Well, at any rate you won't have to have her here with you.'

Mary Ryan was staring over her husband's head at a gilt-framed portrait of a woman in eighteenth-century costume, which hung on the wall facing the fireplace.

'When I think of all the girls he could have in this town,' she went on in a low, almost dreamy voice: the voice of real anger. 'Look at Susan Carroll, two pubs and an hotel, and a

14

nice refined girl into the bargain. Mad about him too, as every-body knows.'

'Mary,' said her husband softly, clasping his hands between his knees, and rubbing his stubby thumbs together.

Mrs Ryan looked down with blinking eyes at the top of his gleaming white head. She unclasped her hands from behind her back, and grasped the edge of the marble fireplace with one of them. The other hung by her side, the fingers separated, curled and stiff like the claw of a dead bird.

'Yes?' she said in the same low tone.

'Mary, I had a phone call this morning . . .'

He broke off and both of them looked towards the window. In the silence of the room, broken only by the crackle of coal and the tick of the clock, they could hear quite distinctly the sound of running footsteps on the gravel of the avenue. They were sharp and rather unsteady. They listened until they ceased, waiting for the doorbell to ring. Ryan made to get off the sofa; but his wife motioned him back with a masterful gesture.

'Imelda will answer it,' she snapped. She crossed to the door and switched on the main light. The large, richly furnished room sprang into life about them, with its winking crystals, its gleaming tables laden with silver and cut glass, its pictures, mirrors, and many-coloured cushions. Mrs Ryan hurried to the window and pulled the curtain cord, shutting out the darkening trees with a little velvet sigh.

'Is it Willie?' she said quickly.

'Yes.'

'Why didn't you tell me at lunch?'

'I didn't want to annoy you. After all they may have traced him by now. They don't know where he's gone.'

'He's here.'

'What!' Ryan jumped up. 'Where is he?'

'In Summerhill, I think. It was something Mrs Whittaker said when she was here.'

They spoke rapidly in low voices, their eyes turned towards

15

the door. Suddenly it was thrown open, and a young woman came stumbling into the room. Her low forehead was streaked with perspiration; she was panting; and her large dark eyes were staring wide.

'Kathleen!' exclaimed Mrs Ryan. The girl made no reply, but looked from one to the other, swallowing hard between her gulping breaths. Mrs Ryan walked past her and closed the door sharply. Then she walked back to the fireplace and peered at the girl through flickering eyelids. Ryan took the intruder's arm and led her to the sofa; but she did not seem to notice him. When she spoke she addressed herself to the older woman.

'Oh, my God, Mrs Ryan, thank God you're here,' she sobbed, closing her eyes and clasping her hands in front of her mouth.

'What on earth . . .'

'Where is Chris?' asked Ryan.

'He's still at Summerhill. He's in the house. I got a lift back into town. I couldn't stay, I told him I couldn't. I was terrified. I knew there was something going to happen this afternoon. I sensed it.' She flung back her thick black hair with a side-way toss of her head.

'What happened?' demanded Mrs Ryan harshly. 'Is Chris all right?'

'It's your brother, Mrs Ryan.' Kathleen covered her mouth with a hooked forefinger, so that speech was muffled. She stared at the older woman for a few seconds and then turned impulsively to her husband. 'I mean it's *your* brother Willie, Mr Ryan. He's come home, out of the asylum. He's out in Summerhill. Chris is with him. That's how I managed to get away. I told Chris I'd tell you.'

'My brother,' said Ryan in a toneless voice. He stood looking down at the girl with his hands hanging limply by his sides.

'What sort of joke is this?' snapped his wife.

'It isn't a joke,' cried Kathleen, throwing out her arms in a wild gesture. 'I saw him I tell you.' Her voice rose hysterically.

'Stop acting, Kathleen,' said Mrs Ryan in a quiet voice. Then she turned to her husband and went on briskly: 'He must be sent back at once. Go and ring them up. If we act quickly it may be possible to get the whole thing over quietly.'

Ryan hesitated, his soft mouth quivering, his toes turned in, and his shoulders hunched as if to ward off some blow: the posture of a semi-defiant schoolboy.

'Hurry, Michael.'

Upright, with stiffened body, her small head tilted back, she watched him leave the room, touching the chairs and tables with his fingers as if he were seeking some kind of mute support from them. Only when the door closed behind him did Mary Ryan relax. She sat down on the sofa, took up one of the striped satin cushions, punched it on her knee, and put it back in its place without leaning against it.

'You realise, Kathleen, that this is entirely a family matter. I expect that it will be cleared up quietly and without any fuss. I suppose it's too much to expect in a town like this that some word won't go round. But for your sake, as well as ours, I hope you won't speak of it. You understand what I mean?'

'Oh yes, Mrs Ryan, of course. I wouldn't dream . . .' the girl leaned forward, holding out her hand in a timid gesture. But Mary drew back a little and turned away, flickering her thin nostrils with her knuckles. She could smell the heavy feminine odour of musk, which always disgusted her when Kathleen came too close to her.

'Who gave you the lift into town?' she said coldly.

'A stranger. A traveller, I think.' Kathleen's voice was sullen. As always when Mrs. Ryan repulsed her friendly overtures she felt the blood rising from her breast, colouring her neck and cheeks: a reaction over which she had no control, and which always increased her discomfiture.

'I hope you didn't say anything to him. Those commercials . . .'

'Of course I didn't. Do you take me for a fool?'

Mrs Ryan stood up, fingering the heavy rope of pearls about her long neck with its slight goitre.

'You're overtired and excited, Kathleen. I think you'd better go home and lie down. After all, as I said, this *is* a family affair.'

Kathleen jumped to her feet so quickly that she twisted on her high heels and had to clutch the arm of the sofa to prevent herself falling. When she straightened up her cheeks were crimson.

'I'm not going to leave this house until I find out if Chris is all right,' she exclaimed. 'God knows what that man might do. I heard . . . I was told . . . I mean . . .' her bluster wore itself out, and she was left plucking nervously at the leather belt of her red woollen dress.

Mrs Ryan looked down at the cheap stiletto-heeled shoes and smiled; a smile which almost transformed her face, ironing out the habitual twitch at the corners of her mouth, and steadying her flickering eyelids. It made her appear younger, even vulnerable, and about to say something pleasant. Instead she said:

'If you're so worried about him, why did you run away?'

'I didn't run away. I wanted to tell you about it.'

The two women faced each other: one flushed, confused, impotently angry; the other pale, composed, smiling.

'And you left your coat behind you.' Mrs Ryan twisted her large sapphire ring slowly about her finger. Kathleen looked at it with dull intensity.

'I shouldn't have left,' she said in a flat voice. 'But I'd heard about him being, well, violent. But it wasn't that that frightened me, it was something about him . . .'

'That's enough.'

Something in the older woman's tone, a genuine note of pain caused the girl to look up in surprise. Mrs Ryan's eyes were closed, and her mouth was tightly compressed. She had pulled off her ring, and was holding it between her thumb and forefinger. Suddenly, the thin gold circle twisted like a live thing between the tips of her fingers, and fell on to the lambskin hearthrug. She did not seem to notice it but opened her eyes and stared through Kathleen. But with the toe of her shoe she was prodding the pile of the rug, like a child burrowing in cool sand on a hot summer day.

Kathleen bent down and picked up the ring quickly and gracefully; no longer clumsy and unsure, now that sympathy had taken the place of resentment. She cradled the ring in her palm and offered it to Mary with a shy smile.

Mary took the ring, and looked away as her cold fingers touched the warm, damp young flesh. She slipped the sapphire back in its place with a brief nod of acknowledgement, and began to rub her hands slowly against the waist of her black dress. Kathleen turned away to a small Sheraton half-table that was placed under a convex mirror on the wall facing the window. The mirror, powerful as a magnifying glass, threw her square-chinned face with its bold vulgar colouring into sharp relief against the richly glowing room behind her, gathered up and compressed within the ornate frame like a stage setting. She turned away quickly as Michael came back into the room.

'Well?' asked Mary, her fingers pressed against the swelling in her neck. Unlike most goitred women she never wore scarves, and always affected rather low-cut frocks.

'They're coming. When they couldn't find him near the place they guessed that he'd made for home. People usually do, they say.' His chalky hands flapped against his thighs.

'When did they leave?'

'About an hour ago.'

'Then they'll be here any minute.' Mrs Ryan sat down and held her hands out to the fire. The blue veins stood out like pencil strokes on the crinkled skin. She scratched her ankle with the heel of her crocodile shoe.

Kathleen looked at Ryan anxiously.

'What about Chris?' she said. 'He's out there alone with . . .'

19

'Chris will be all right.' Michael looked at the back of his wife's head. 'His uncle will do him no harm.'

'But I heard . . .' Kathleen stopped short, biting her lip.

'You hear a lot of things in this town,' went on the old man quietly. 'It's a mistake to believe all of them.'

The girl followed his gaze and turned towards Mrs Ryan. But she remained silent, staring into the fire. She was so still that they both watched, tense and fascinated, as her fingers, extending stiffly before the glowing coals, slowly folded back into her palms like the petals of some insect-eating plant, and her thumbs closed upon her fists.

The little ormolu clock whirred under its glass dome and prepared to strike the hour. The six silvery chimes broke the silence of the room like a coin tapped gently against the window pane.

⁌ ⁌ ⁌ 3 ⁂ ⁂ ⁂

CHRIS RYAN reached up and took down his pipe from the wooden ledge above the chimney-piece. Although he was six feet tall he had to extend his hand above his head to get it. A range had been set into the big open fireplace, and ash from the burning turf drifted down between the bars to settle on the hearth in a little heap that shifted gently under the shower like sand at the bottom of an hour-glass. The young man took out his pouch and began to press tobacco into the bowl with his forefinger.

He stopped and looked down at the pair of sodden boots set before the range to dry. They had begun to steam.

'It's no good drying your boots, if your socks are wet too, Uncle Willie,' he said in his deep, slow voice.

Willie Ryan, sitting in the corner between the table and the range, raised his feet in their thick grey socks and held them up to the fire. He cocked his head sideways and looked at them, pursing his blue lips, and screwing up his narrow slanting eyes. He shook his head.

Chris lit a match which immediately went out. He lit three more, threw them away, drew on his pipe and looked down again at his uncle's feet.

'And it's no good trying to dry them on you either,' he went on. 'Now, take off your socks and warm your feet properly, or you'll get your death of cold. I have another pair in the press. They may be a bit big for you, but they'll be better than what you're wearing. Come on now.'

Willie wriggled his toes inside his wet socks and shifted in his armchair. His thin body moved with a curious lithe, sinuous grace within his coarse tweed clothes. Then, his tongue protruding between his lips like a child performing a difficult exercise, he began to peel off the socks. Chris held out his hand for them; but Willie shook his head and stuffed them behind him at the back of the chair. The young man went to the door and took down a towel from a nail.

Tiny sounds filled the big low-ceilinged kitchen: the soft settling of the blazing turf-sods, the ticking of the alarm clock on the window ledge, the creaking of the chair as Willie bent over his purple-veined feet.

Chris left the towel on the arm of his uncle's chair, and lit another match. The naked electric bulb hanging from the ceiling behind him threw his giant shadow with hunched shoulders and fingers prodding his pipe on to the far wall: a reflection of a stranger playing a tin whistle.

Willie Ryan paused and looked up at his nephew. The young man was puffing his pipe calmly, staring into the fire with large unblinking eyes, a lock of fair hair falling over his forehead. His tweed jacket was old but well-cut, and unlike his uncle's did not imprison his body, but was moulded by it. The cloth clung to his powerful shoulders and muscular arms; and although his pockets were stuffed with letters and papers they emphasised rather than concealed the slimness of his waist and hips.

The old man reached out and touched one of the matches on the flagged floor with his toes. He seemed absorbed in studying it, his long thin foot arched forward like a dancer, his narrow white hands coiled back under the arms of his chair, so that his wrists protruded like fingerless stumps from his frayed sleeves. But he was not staring at the matches: he was listening, peering sideways from under his lids at the door leading to the hall.

Chris looked down and saw the towel lying untouched on the chair.

'What is it?'

Willie started and looked up. His face, which had been in shadow as he sat huddled in his chair, was suddenly fully

22

exposed to the harsh glare of the bulb. In spite of his snow-white hair, and the hollows in his temples, he had preserved a startling, even a shocking youthfulness. His pale skin was unlined, fine, clear and taut. The features were blunt and mask-like, with wide nostrils, thick lips, and brown almond-shaped eyes. Raised now, drained of shadows, with eyes puckered against the light, the young-old face was tense and watchful, the lithe body stiff as the rough clothes which enclosed it.

' What is it, Uncle Willie?' said Chris.

' Is there somebody in the hall? I thought I heard a sound.'

Chris walked across the kitchen with his slow, indolent tread and opened the door. The hall was dark except for the tiny red glow of the Sacred Heart lamp.

' No, there's nobody there.'

' I thought maybe it was Mary.'

' Mary?' Chris frowned, puzzled. ' No, it was Kathleen. She's gone home a long time.' He closed the door and leaned against it with his hand on the knob. In the shadowed corner beside him something moved and took shape with a sleepy grunt.

' Down Toby,' said Chris to the collie, who, wakened by the draught, had raised its head and began to beat its tail on the flags. The dog sneezed and collapsed again on its inert flanks.

' Why was she crying? Was she afraid or something?' Willie insisted.

' But that's an hour ago. She didn't know you when you came in and took fright or something. Sure, you wouldn't want to pass any heed on what women say or do.'

He came back to the range and looked down at his uncle's feet. Slowly and stealthily Willie withdrew them and hid them under the chair, unaware that a match had stuck to his damp toe. Chris stooped and took up one of the boots from the hearth, tapping the sole with the stem of his pipe.

' How in the name of God did you get your feet so wet?' he asked with a frown, the heavy wrinkle between his dark

23

brown eyebrows dilating his nostrils. With the shadows of the fire playing over his bent head he looked older and heavier.

Willie took his feet out timidly from under the chair, raised them a few inches from the floor, and studied them as if they belonged to somebody else. Then he noticed that they were throwing a shadow on the opposite wall. He crossed his ankles and wriggled his toes.

' Look,' he said, pointing to the wall, ' a butterfly. Isn't that nice?'

Chris nodded and smiled. Willie stood up and linked his hands together with waving fingers. A great shadowy butterfly fluttered against the whitewashed wall.

' That's very good, Uncle Willie. Can you do a rabbit?'

' Yes, yes. And a camel too and all sorts of things. I used to be always doing it long ago in here. Wait now until I try again.'

But before he could adjust his hands to continue the shadow-play he stopped dead. Chris looked at him enquiringly, and then again at the door to the hall; but his uncle seemed to have forgotten him. He was staring at the back window. Suddenly, with a lithe and graceful step, his white toes flattening out on the flags, he hurried over to the back door and flung it open. The night air blew into the kitchen, and the collie raised its head again and pointed its muzzle in the direction of the wind.

Chris looked anxiously after his uncle; but Willie did not go out. He stood in the doorway, one hand cupped behind his ear.

' Come back from there. You'll get your death in your bare feet.'

Willie raised a finger to his lips.

' Ssh. Do you hear him?'

Chris went to the door and looked out into the rustling shadows. Already since summertime ended it was pitch dark at a little after seven.

' What is it?'

Willie pointed to a line of sycamores behind the outhouses. The yard was filled with the smells of manure and hay; and the heavy underarm scent of milch cows. But high up in one of the trees a thrush was singing, the thin whistling notes cutting the silence as sharply and vividly as a chink of moonlight through velvet curtains.

'Listen. They start singing every year about this time.' Willie stepped into the cobbled yard and looked about him. 'About the end of October or the beginning of November. I used to be always waiting for them.'

'It's stopped now, Uncle Willie. Come on in.'

But Willie was staring across the yard, his thin hands held up in front of his chest.

'Oh, look out there. It hasn't changed at all. And there's a hunter's moon. I used often to think about it.'

Far off below him the endless plain stretched. A few clouds floated across the great yellow moon; and the river glimmered and glowed, now silver-grey, now dull bronze, as the cold light dimmed and brightened over it. The water-meadows were pale; and the bog, black against the purple horizon, seemed to breathe like some immense crouching animal in the swaying light.

Chris looked over his uncle's shoulder, and saw the swollen river and smelt rain in the wind. He took him firmly by the shoulder and led him back into the kitchen, closing the door behind them with his elbow and the heel of his boot.

'Sit down there,' he said firmly, putting the old man sitting in his chair, and picking up the towel.

Willie looked up at his nephew and smiled uncertainly. Chris was frowning, beating the towel gently against his leg. Willie sucked in his lower lip and began to whistle in imitation of the thrush: an uncannily accurate sound which made Chris raise his heavy eyebrows in surprise.

'That's fine, Uncle Willie. How did you learn to do that?'

'I could always do it. And the blackbird too, and the chaffinch. I learned how, because the spring starts in November when the thrush begins to sing, and there's many a thing still growing at the end of October, and so nothing ever dies. I don't know how it is but I could never do the curlew. Maybe it's because they're always crying of death.'

Chris knelt down and began to rub his uncle's feet with the towel. Willie grasped the arms of his chair and stared at the top of his nephew's blond head. He seemed about to touch it, but hesitated, and the white wasted hand fell back and coiled about the carved arm-rests again.

'Did you take your shoes off?' asked Chris, looking up enquiringly.

'When I was coming through the town last night I took them off for fear anybody would hear me.' Willie's voice was simple and matter-of-fact and held nothing of the quivering undertone of emotion with which he had talked about the thrush's song.

'But it was pouring rain last night, Uncle Willie,' exclaimed Chris, resting his buttocks on his heels, and balancing himself expertly but somewhat painfully on his toes. He spread the towel on the floor and lowered Willie's feet gently on to it.

'Yes, it rained a lot.'

'Where did you sleep?'

'In Harney's down the road. Is there nobody living there now? Half the roof is in, and not a soul anywhere.'

Chris steadied himself with his fingers on the floor and looked up. His handsome, somewhat fleshy face was grave. The old man's hands fluttered weakly against the arms of the chair, and he blinked his eyes rapidly, moving his head from side to side to avoid his nephew's gaze.

'The old people died, and the son went off to England. I have the land.'

'Many's the good night I had in Harney's long ago. They were great neighbours. It was queer to see the roof fallen in. I was wondering all night if I was in the right place.'

Chris smiled and patted his uncle's knee, before hoisting himself to his feet. His bulk shut out the glare of the bulb; and

Willie's slanting eyes opened wide like a cat in the shadows. He tucked his warmed feet under the chair and stared up quietly at the tall young man.

' Well, you're all right now, Uncle Willie,' said Chris gravely. ' You're at home.'

' Didn't you say your name was Christopher?' asked Willie suddenly, after he had watched his nephew take up his pipe from the table and get out his matches again.

Chris nodded, dropped the lighted match and stamped on it. Then he put down the pipe again and took up the teapot. A bright red cabbage rose flamed through a network of cracks in its side. ' I think we ought to have another cup of tea.'

' Christopher,' repeated Willie, smiling and nodding to himself. ' That's after my mother's brother. He died when he was twenty. But you're like my Uncle Mick that went to America and became a priest. You're a real Ryan.'

Chris put down the teapot and looked down at Willie's bare feet. Then he went out through the hall and came back a few moments later with a pair of brown socks.

' You'd better put these on now or you'll get cold.'

He rinsed the teapot with water from the bucket under the table, and threw the leaves out on the back door. The collie, wakened by the draught and the chink of china, uncoiled and walked sheepishly towards the fire. Chris poured more water from the bucket into the kettle, and set it on the range before going back to the table to cut more bread.

' You must be Michael's boy,' said Willie, looking up with a sock poised over his upturned toe.

Chris nodded and went on cutting the bread.

' Have you any brothers or sisters?'

' No. I'm sorry I haven't anything but bread and jam, Uncle Willie, but I don't take my meals here.' He went to the range and poured hot water into the teapot. ' You see we left this house when I was four or five, and went to live in the town. Mammy's brother died and left her his business, and Daddy gave up the farm and went to look after it. Well, he didn't really give up this place, he always kept it stocked, but we haven't lived here for a long time.' He held the teapot between his palms and whirled the water inside slowly. He was frowning again, his heavy lower lip thrust out. 'But I don't care for business much, and I spend most of my time out here running this place. I like the land.'

Willie looked around the low-ceilinged kitchen with its high dresser almost empty of china, its gaping mealbins, its couple of bentwood chairs; no curtains at the windows, no oleograph of the Sacred Heart over the hearth, no smell of freshly baked bread and buttermilk. He leaned forward and pointed to the hearth.

'There used to be a settle-bed there,' he said.

Chris opened the back door and threw out the warm water from the teapot. He came back to the range, took down the canister from the ledge and threw in a lavish fistful of tea. 'Oh, there's a bed in one of the rooms upstairs. I sleep here sometimes when one of the cows is calving or something. You can have it tonight.'

'My mother died in the settle,' said Willie. 'She couldn't breathe in her own room so we brought her down here.' He leaned his jaw on his fist and stared into the fire. 'I thought I'd die there too. I didn't want to die in that place.'

'Don't talk like that, Uncle Willie. You're not going to die.'

'Oh, yes,' said Willie quietly, 'I'll be dying now shortly.'

Chris swung round and prodded the collie with the toe of his boot. 'Get out of my way, Toby,' he growled. 'Do you want me to break my neck?'

'Poor Toby,' Willie put out his hand. 'Come here to me.'

The dog sidled across and licked his wrists. The old man pulled its ear gently and ran his fingers over its soft yellow flanks and belly.

'Toby is a bitch,' said Chris, putting down the teapot on the table. 'But I called her Toby because that was the name of the last two dogs I had. She's good with the cattle, the rogue. Here, give me your cup.'

28

When his tea was poured Willie held the cup against his chest and looked down into Toby's lazy brown eyes.

'Our dog was always called Toby too. And I see this Toby is going to have pups.'

Chris swung round from the table spilling tea on his boots.

'Christ God, no!' he exclaimed. 'I didn't know that, the old bitch.'

'Yes indeed, in about a fortnight I'd say.' Willie patted Toby's head and chuckled. 'Life goes on.'

⁴⁴⁴ 4 ⁴⁴⁴

THE GATES were elaborate: an intricate pattern of scrolls, fleurs-de-lis, and other flowers of the forest of the imagination hammered in iron. In the glare of the headlamps Farrell stared up at this masterpiece of the blacksmith's art for a moment before opening it and allowing the blue Ford to drive into the avenue. He closed the gates carefully, meticulously, with a touch of reverence before getting back into the car with Halloran.

'Boy,' he said in an awestruck voice, 'those gates cost something.'

'A local version of Buckingham Palace,' said Halloran, sliding into gear and moving off along the smoothly raked gravel from which every October leaf had been carefully removed.

Farrell pocketed the comb with which he had been repairing the damages done to his fine fair curls by the wind, and looked about him, sitting up primly with rigid shoulders and legs as close together as a jack-knife.

'Some money here, Peter. That's a gorgeous house. I wouldn't mind living in a place like that. That's what I call gracious living.'

Halloran said nothing. At the end of the curving avenue under the great yellow moon, he saw an ugly Victorian villa with rough-cast walls, tricked out with tiny balconies, turrets and weather-vanes. A wide terrace of mass concrete had been added to the garden side of the house, and an uneven line of auction urns cluttered the balustrade like headless ghosts. On one of the balconies a peacock huddled against the wall, his tail swaying in the wind. The headlamps swept over a huge lily-pond, which once might have stood at the end of a noble walk, and which was now sunk in the middle of a small lawn broken up by triangular flowerbeds.

' Surely this isn't Willie Ryan's place,' said Farrell.

' It's his brother's place.'

' Boy, he must have some money in the bank. Will you look at them stone lions outside the front door? They're like something in a museum.'

Halloran stopped the car beside the black Wolseley parked at the bottom of the steps.

' I wouldn't be surprised if they had a coat of armour in the hall,' he said, opening the door and squeezing his massive bulk out of the driving seat. He was a huge man with a close-cropped head of greyish-red hair, cauliflower ears, a battered pock-marked nose, puckered blue eyes and a small humorous mouth. He groaned, heaved back his shoulders and expanded his chest.

Farrell pattered round the bonnet and waited for his colleague, clearing his throat softly like a singer preparing to break into song. His beady eyes missed nothing: the coloured glass panels surrounding the door, the coach-lamps on either side of it, the stone gorgon's head affixed to the wall above it.

Halloran mounted the three steps between the lions; but before he could reach for the bell Michael Ryan opened the door and motioned them inside.

' My name is Halloran. This is Gabriel Farrell.'

' Pleased to meet you, sir,' said Farrell, snapping off a glove and extending a small, red hand. Ryan took it limply.

' Won't you come in and meet my wife?'

' Is he here?' said Halloran.

' No, he's out in another house with my son. I'll tell you about it.'

As Farrell followed them into the drawing room he took in the hall. No coat of armour; but a stag's head, a rug-chest of fumed oak, and an oil painting of Pope Pius XII framed in gleaming gold leaf. Gabriel cleared his throat behind his fist and walked more delicately than ever.

Mrs Ryan rose to greet them. She bowed her head as Michael

31

introduced the two men, and sank back into her chair without a word. Halloran and Farrell left with no instructions stood awkwardly inside the door; the big man slowly turning his hat in his huge fists; Farrell counting the room with sidelong looks. Michael pulled out a couple of tiny incidental chairs from either side of the door and asked them to sit down.

'Have you had tea?' asked Mary after a suitable silence, during which they all avoided one another's eyes, and Farrell's gaze flickered from object to object.

'Yes, ma'am, at the hotel.' Halloran put down his hat on the carpet between his big brown boots.

There was another silence during which Mary stared into the fire, plucking at her pearls, and Michael grasped the back of a chair and tapped it gently against his plump belly.

'Perhaps you'd like to smoke,' she said at last.

'No thanks, ma'am,' said Farrell, his rigid face contorted by a smile. 'We don't smoke.'

'I suppose my husband has told you where he is.' Mary passed her hand over her forehead and sighed.

'Yes.' Halloran looked at Ryan. 'Will your son stay with him in the house until we get there?'

'Of course.' Mrs Ryan turned quickly and spoke for her husband. 'I don't know what we'd have done without my son. He stayed with him in the house and sent us a message just a short time ago. My husband would have gone out, but we were expecting you. Unfortunately there is no phone in Summerhill, which is in the country.'

'Would you care for a drink?' said Michael suddenly, pushing the chair away and going to a Chinese cabinet in the corner. He took out a bottle of whiskey and three glasses.

'I won't have anything, Mr Ryan, thank you very much,' said Farrell with a quick glance at Mary, who was frowning at her husband. 'I'm a Pioneer.'

Michael poured out two stiff whiskeys and looked at Halloran.

'Water?'

32

' Please.'

' Michael, I don't want to hurry these men, but Chris must be waiting . . .' Mary pushed herself forward and sat poised stiffly, on the edge of the armchair, gripping her knees.

' You needn't worry about him, ma'am,' rumbled Halloran, accepting his glass with a nod of thanks. ' Willie – I mean Mr Ryan – is quite harmless. He wouldn't hurt a fly.' He raised his glass and grinned at Michael. ' Slainte!'

Michael swallowed half the whiskey in one gulp. He choked, closed his eyes and shook his head.

' What do you mean – he wouldn't hurt a fly?' Mary stood up and went to the table where her husband had left the whiskey. ' He must have changed a great deal.' She took the bottle and left it back in the cabinet.

' When have you seen him last, Mrs Ryan?' asked Halloran mildly.

Mary closed the door of the cabinet and put her two hands on the glass top.

' What has that got to do with it?' she said without turning round. ' I remember him before he went away.'

' I often meant to go and see him, but somehow I never did,' said Michael, wiping his damp eyes with his handkerchief. ' I suppose I should have.' He gulped down the remainder of his whiskey.

' Some of them like to have visitors, some of them don't,' said Farrell, crossing his legs, and putting his fingertips together. ' If they have a deep trauma visitors don't do any good. I was reading . . .'

' I've been twenty-five years in the asylum,' broke in Halloran, looking at Mrs Ryan's back over his glass. ' I came the same year as Willie. He's a strange man, but he's not any stranger than many that are outside. I don't think he's capable of violence.'

Mary turned and picked up her husband's glass as he left it on the table. She glanced at Halloran briefly, before opening the cabinet again and replacing the glass.

'You've never had trouble with him?' said Michael, plucking at his lip.

'Never,' said Halloran. 'I suppose you could say that he lives in a world of his own, whatever that means. But then, don't we all? I think I know him better than any of the other inmates. He keeps to himself a lot, although of course he plays the banjo and sings at the concerts and that sort of thing. But we've never had any trouble with him.'

'Of course conditions are very different now with all the new treatments,' said Farrell, looking at Mrs Ryan with his contorted smile. 'Psychiatry is doing wonders.'

Mary gave him a nod and looked at her watch. Farrell, who was now completely in tune with the situation, consulted his watch, and gave a sidelong glance at Halloran's half-full glass.

'Of course he's not normal, Mrs Ryan,' he went on briskly. 'He's disassociated.'

Halloran cleared his throat with a thunderous rumble and sipped his whiskey before saying:

'Sometimes I ask myself what's normal, and what's abnormal. I wonder if it isn't a question of getting a reputation. If you establish yourself as normal it's extraordinary what you can get away with. On the other hand if you get a reputation, something can be read into the most harmless actions. After twenty-five years you stop making snap judgements.'

'Very interesting.' Mary looked at Farrell with raised eyebrows. 'But people don't usually get a " reputation " as you put it, without doing something. My brother-in-law was committed for good and proper reasons. It may be that owing to treatment he's behaving himself, but I can tell you there was a time when he didn't.'

'Will you have another?' said Michael.

'Not at the moment, thanks.'

Michael went back to the cabinet and poured himself another large whiskey. Mary looked at Farrell and frowned.

'Do you think you ought to go out to the house? I'm worried about my son.'

Farrell cleared his throat and looked at Halloran. The big man finished his drink, picked up his hat and stood up.

'Yes, I suppose it's the only thing to do.' He put down his glass and looked at Michael, who was pouring water into his whiskey. 'Can you tell us how to get there?'

'Miss O'Neill, a friend of my son's, is in the house . . .' cut in Mary quickly. 'She can show you the way. My husband is too upset to go. I'll call her.'

She left the room, leaving the door open behind her. Halloran pushed it to with a quick jab of his elbow and looked at Ryan with puckered eyes.

'Do you think I ought to see him?' said Michael helplessly.

'That's up to you, sir,' replied Halloran quietly.

'I don't know, I don't know. I'd like to see him.'

'It mightn't do any good. I suppose he has nobody to look after him.' For the first time Halloran looked about the over-furnished room, his small mouth set in a grim smile.

'No, you see my mother died.' Michael gulped his whiskey and looked at Farrell. 'Does he ever speak about us?'

'No,' said Halloran, staring at the chandelier. 'He was always very quiet, and since his heart attack two years ago he's even quieter. You were informed of course.'

'Yes, yes,' mumbled Michael, looking away. 'I was going to go, and then they told me he was out of danger.'

'Sometimes he sings,' put in Farrell, giving Michael the benefit of his twitching smile for the first time. 'He has a lot of little things in French. It entertains the other men, and of course it's good therapy.'

'He always had a good voice. He learned those songs from – ' Ryan broke off and gulped whiskey again—'well, from a friend of ours. He was always a little strange, different, you know, from the rest of us, but . . .' his voice trailed off, and he looked down at his slanting glass.

'What exactly happened, Mr Ryan?' asked Halloran bluntly. 'There are records I know, but I've lived with him for twenty-five years.'

35

'It's a long story.'

'Your wife spoke of violence. I find that hard to believe.'

Michael turned away with a clumsy gesture of his free hand.

'My wife will tell you. Ask her. She knows all about it. I don't want to have anything to do with it. It wasn't my fault.' He sat down on the arm of the sofa and began to drink his whiskey with both hands.

Halloran took the car key from his pocket and handed it to Farrell.

'Here, you drive this time, I'm tired.'

Michael suddenly lifted his head and drew in his breath as if he were about to speak. But before he could say anything Mary came back briskly into the room.

'Miss O'Neill is waiting in the hall. Naturally she's very upset and nervous. I hope you will arrange it so that she doesn't meet him. She can come back in my son's car.'

'Don't worry, ma'am,' said Farrell with a little bow. 'We'll see to all that, you can be sure.'

Michael drained the last of his whiskey and stood up a little unsteadily. He made a gesture towards Halloran with his empty glass.

'I . . . I hope there won't be any trouble. If there's anything I can do . . . my only brother . . . Willie . . .' He put down his glass and began to fumble in his inside breast pocket.

'There won't be any trouble with Willie, Mr Ryan,' said Halloran with his hand on the door knob.

Michael took two five pound notes out of his wallet, and lurched across the room to offer them to the big granite-faced man at the door.

'Here, give him something, will you? Is there anything he asks for?'

Halloran took the notes and folded them neatly.

'Well, I did hear him talk about a guitar,' he said slowly.

'A guitar!' burst out Mary, opening her eyes at Farrell.

'Get it for him,' mumbled Michael, laying his hand on Halloran's sleeve. 'If you haven't enough there, write to me and tell me the price. Get him whatever he wants.'

' I'll do that, Mr Ryan. Come on, Gaby.'

The Ryans stood still for a few minutes listening to the voices in the hall, waiting for the door to close. When it did they both came to life, like sleepers awakened by a sudden noise; indirectly, with blurred movements, also like sleepers, who have not yet succeeded in co-ordinating their reactions. Michael blundered towards the cabinet, moving with a heavy dragging step, his fat buttocks swaying, his fingers fumbling with the gold watch-chain stretched across his belly. Mary watched him silently, her mouth slightly open, her dark eyes hazy with weariness.

Suddenly she snapped to attention.

' You've had enough to drink, Michael,' she said sharply, snapping her fingers irritably. ' You've been drinking all afternoon.'

Her husband took out the bottle, and poured himself another glass with slow, half-drunken deliberation. He leaned an elbow on top of the cabinet and held the glass under his nose. He sniffed it lovingly.

Mrs Ryan stared at his broad back for a second. Then she lifted her hands and shook them in front of her as if she were settling lace ruffles at her wrist. It was a little gesture she always made when she was tired as well as angry. And she never made it in public.

' I hope he gets that guitar,' said Michael in a maudlin voice.

Mary squeezed her eyes and clenched her fists to control herself, before she replied in a soothing tone:

' Yes, I hope he does. I'm sure he will too. Now go and lie down, and I'll make you a nice hot drink later. You've had a tiring day.'

' He had a guitar long ago when we were young. I remember in the big meadow in the summer nights we'd all gather together, and he'd sing in the dark. Nobody knew what he was singing about, but that didn't matter.'

'Nobody ever knew what he was singing about,' snapped Mary, with a sudden return to her former taut manner: eyes blinking, mouth twitching, fingers coiling crisply about her big sapphire.

'Yes, that's right, Mary,' muttered her husband, lurching towards the door. ' Nobody ever knew.'

5

MRS RYAN stood in the middle of her shop, holding a bunch of keys in her hand, and listening to a commercial traveller.

'A very substantial discount in view of the fact that my directors think on my recommendation that the volume of the business and the good name and extensive distribution of your firm merit a closer consideration and a gesture of esteem on our part which I recommend personally, and . . .'

'Quicker delivery next time,' snapped Mary, her eyes raking the big supermarket with its rows of dizzily-coloured tins and packets, and its four white-coated assistants.

'Precisely, precisely, I couldn't agree more. A complete re-organisation is being effected which in the short-term view has led to some slight disruption of our distribution is now in full spate but in the long-term view will lead to a wider and more extensive . . .'

'I'll see the accountant.' There was a cobweb in the corner over the jams. Mrs Kearney was washing the rubber with a light hand. The Reilly girl must be made to wash her face properly, and keep her white coat white, especially when Ryans were paying for it. On the stand in front of them the traveller's cordials were not moving fast enough, discount or no discount.

'A complete new window display service based on the most modern Scandinavian techniques . . .'

'Could you call again later in the day,' said Mary, not asking, ordering. Above the plump little man's shoulder she had a view of the street. Too early for traffic, too late for the children running to school, it was almost empty. A white-clad arm hanging up a side of beef in the butchers opposite; three shutters down from Morgan's pub window, three more to go; a diminishing trail of dried cow turds in the middle of the road; Father Mannix walking past, silver-handled cane, black shadow, speck of white; hands, face – three red blobs; the whirl of bicycle wheels and long skinny legs in black stockings, Mrs Keegan, two weeks a widow. And in front of the door, Chris's stationwagon drawing up.

'Good morning,' Mrs Ryan nodded briefly to the eager young man who suddenly crumpled up, his padded shoulders sagging, his nicotine-stained nails digging into his briefcase, discoloured teeth biting his wet lower lip.

'It was a blunder, Mrs Ryan,' he stammered, picking up his order-book from the top of his own slow-moving cordials.

Mary Ryan looked at him with cold eyes. Her face was ashen, and her mouth twitched angrily.

'You have blundered out of your own book, young man,' she snapped, and turned to meet her son. They did not speak, but walked together to the office door at the back of the shop.

The private office of Kieran McDonogh & Co Ltd, Wholesale and Retail Grocers, Wine Merchants, Coal Importers and General Hauliers, was not gleaming like the shop: it was merely functional. A small space with a worn pink carpet, an old-fashioned roll-top desk against the grimy wall, a leather swivel chair, a green Whitfield safe which reached to Chris's shoulders, and an equally tall filing-cabinet. The only decoration was one of the company's own calendars: a reproduction of Millet's 'The Angelus'. Two modern tubular chairs struck a slightly frivolous note.

Mrs. Ryan had walked through the shop briskly, her elbows against her ribs, her angular body erect, carrying herself with something of the lean inflexibility of an upright oar. But once inside the office with the door closed on the world and on her staff, her body softened and sagged. She dropped the keys on the desk, sat down on the swivel-chair with her back to Chris, and pressed her wrists against her temples.

'Chris, where have you been?' she began in a tired halting voice. 'I didn't close an eye all night. Your father is in bed.

He started drinking yesterday, and you know the way he is when that happens. I had to open the shop this morning to put some sort of face on things. Because they're all watching, they all know. What on earth made you stay out last night?'

Chris was standing at the window looking down at the yard below: a vast concrete space bounded by bottling sheds, stores, garages, checking-rooms, fuel-oil tanks. One of the trucks was loading coal; another was unloading wheaten meal. The drivers stood leaning against a wall, smoking. A man in a white coat hurried across the yard with a bundle of yellow invoices in his hand.

'I gave a message to Kathleen. Didn't she give it to you?'

'Yes, she did. I didn't know what she meant, and neither, I think, did she. She was very excited, even hysterical. I sent her home.' She sighed and rocked her head in her hands. 'It's so hard, so difficult. I thought it better to send her out with these men than to let your father go. And when those awful men brought her back and she told me that you were staying out there alone – Oh Chris, Chris, what has happened at all?'

Chris turned away and sat down in one of the chromium chairs.

'I couldn't send him back, Mammy. It wouldn't be human.' He took his pipe out of his pocket and tapped the empty bowl against his palm.

The phone rang. Mrs Ryan picked it up.

'McDonoghs. Yes, yes. Oh, Mr Jackson, hold the line a moment please.' She picked up a pencil and pushed a note-pad into position with her elbow. 'Yes, Mr Jackson. Two tons on Thursday. Yes, it's English coal. No, you can't beat it. Yes, yes, yes. Yes. Yes. Yes. No. Good. Mmm. Mmm. Well do remember me to her won't you? I agree rest is absolutely essential. Yes, indeed. Oh, certainly, Thursday morning without fail. Good morning, Mr Jackson, and thank you very much.'

She left down the receiver and picked up a house-phone.

'Keane? Mr Jackson of Cullogh wants two tons of Bryanston's on Thursday morning. And before I forget, while it's no business of mine what you do when you leave here, such as not going to your duties and so on, that's your own business, I went into the girls' dressing room a few days ago, and found one of them reading a certain filthy book whose name I won't mention, but your name was written on it. Now that girl is only sixteen, and to give a book of that kind to her is downright evil. If I hear of any more of that sort of thing you'll go, Mr Keane, and without a reference. Is that quite clear?'

She slammed down the phone, and drummed her fingertips on the desk. Chris put his pipe back into his pocket and smiled to himself. He scratched his armpit and waited for his mother to speak.

'When are you going to send him back, Chris?' She said at last, mildly, almost pleadingly.

'I don't know, Mammy. He wants to stay.'

'Did he say that?'

'More or less. He said he didn't want to die in the asylum. He walked home forty miles, and came through the town with his boots off for fear anybody might hear him. And one of the attendants told me he had a coronary two years ago. I didn't know that. It would be awful to send him back after that.'

Mrs Ryan sighed again, and turned the chair round slowly to face her son. Her sallow face was strained, and her eyes were screwed up in an effort to prevent the nervous blinking which grew worse when she was upset. But she was attempting to smile; her small head tilted affectionately sideways, her body slumped and relaxed.

'Chris, child, I know how you feel. I know how good-natured and kind you are. But you mustn't be too soft. I know the whole thing is terribly sad and pathetic. What way do you think your father and I feel about it? But these things have to be faced. Willie was sent away for very good reasons. It's very painful to have to recall all this after so many years. It has completely upset your poor father, and what way do you think I was last night, thinking of you alone in that house with Willie. And all I know about him.'

Chris folded his arms across his chest and looked at the ground. His heavy eyebrows were drawn together, and his wide mouth was set. He made no reply.

'How did you manage last night?' his mother went on in an even softer tone. 'There's only one bed in the house.'

'I gave him the bed, and slept in the chair in the kitchen. He was no trouble. When I woke up this morning he was making the tea.' He raised his head and looked at his mother. 'There's nothing the matter with that old man, Mammy. He's as harmless as a child. I could see that myself, I'm not a fool. But one of the attendants, the big fellow, told me the same.'

Mrs Ryan covered her goitre with her hand and leaned forward.

'Chris, child, you've been brought up very different from a lot of people. You're too trusting. You think everybody is as straightforward as yourself. But the world isn't like that . . .'

'I'm not a child.' Chris's voice was harsh and he ran his fingers through his thick fair hair in exasperation. 'I'm twenty-five years of age.' He paused and suddenly grinned. 'Ten years younger than poor old Fred Keane. What would you do if you found me reading *Lady Chatterley*?'

'Oh, Chris, really!'

'Well, I have read it.'

'It seems to me that everybody in the town has, except me.' Mary settled herself firmly on the sloping leather of the worn chair. 'However, I'm not going to have the shopgirls reading it during working hours.'

Chris laughed and stood up.

'That's the real sin, isn't it?'

Mary touched her goitre again and shrugged.

'I'm not quite as simple as that,' she said indifferently.

Chris pulled open the filing-cabinet and ran his hands over the yellow folders. The crisp sound was magnified in the silence of the dingy little office.

'You should have let those men take him back last night. In the long run it's the only thing that can be done with him, and he'd be happier. Now, it's going to be more difficult. And of course the whole town knows. I could sense it as I came in this morning. I could see it in the faces of the staff.'

Chris shut the drawer slowly and turned round.

'What exactly happened about Uncle Willie, Mammy? It's not the sort of thing you ask strangers about, and neither you nor Daddy have ever talked about it.'

Mrs Ryan drew in her breath sharply, closed her eyes, and expelled the air slowly with a little groan through her open mouth.

'It's something that you try to forget, Chris.'

'Yes, that's exactly what's happened, isn't it? We've forgotten Uncle Willie for twenty-five years, refused to think about him, avoided any responsibility.'

'No, Chris,' said his mother patiently, 'we have not forgotten him. But what could we do? Nobody wants to have a relative in the asylum. He wasn't put there for fun, or for any reason except that he had to go.'

'What happened, Mammy?'

Mary covered her face with her hands. Only her mouth and nose were visible as she spoke, haltingly and with an effect of great weariness.

'I'm very tired, Chris. All my life I've worked hard to build up this business – I and your father have worked – to build it up for you. It was bad enough to discover that you didn't want anything to do with it, that it'll all end with us. And that won't be long now. Neither of us ever tried to force you into it. When you said you wanted to farm instead of taking over this place, we didn't stop you, did we?'

She dug her fingertips into her temples, stretching the already taut skin.

'Willie was always impossible,' she went on. 'He never fitted in anywhere. He was always well treated by us and by your grandmother. It was his own fault that he ended up

44

where he was. It was all due to his own folly and wickedness.'

' I find it hard to believe that old man is wicked.'

Mary snatched her hands away from her face and clasped them convulsively.

' Yes, Chris, wicked. Wicked and vicious. Oh, I don't want to bring up all that again after twenty-five years. Try and be sensible. There isn't anything you can do about Willie.'

The young man's face darkened angrily.

' For God's sake, Mammy, stop treating me like a child. If you won't tell me I'll make it my business to find out elsewhere.'

' Willie seems to have made quite an impression on you. He was always good at getting round people. His sort always are.' Mrs Ryan's body, which had become pliant and supplicating as she pleaded with her son, grew taut again, and her shoulders stiffened.

' He struck me as a harmless and pathetic old man,' said Chris, ironing out a wrinkle in the faded carpet with the toe of his boot. ' And don't forget that we all did rather well out of him. If he hadn't been sent away Summerhill would be his. I have it now, and surely the least I can do is give him a roof.'

Mrs Ryan stood up. She pressed her clenched fists against her stomach as she faced her son.

' I was waiting for that one,' she said bitterly. ' I can see that you have been listening to talk, the usual dirty gossip. Well, let me tell you that Willie's mother signed over the place to your father long before anything happened. Five or six years before, in fact. She was left a widow very young, and she had to work and slave to keep that place going with no man to help her. And she didn't want to see the place going to rack and ruin, with Willie spending his life drinking and singing and making a fool of himself. I never made a penny out of Summerhill, and neither did your father. There wasn't anything in it – Willie had seen to that. And when my brother died and left me this shop there wasn't much here either at the time – it was only a hole in the wall. Anything we have we worked hard and long for. For you,' she concluded, unclenching one fist and stretching it out rigid and trembling towards her son.

Chris, who had been staring at the floor with his hands in his pockets and his big shoulders hunched, looked up and shook his head.

'No, Mammy, you did it because you enjoyed it. Let's be honest about that anyway. Of course parents work for their children; but they work for themselves too. And you love business, every minute of it. You've said so yourself, often. I don't. But I'm lucky. I'm able to live the life I want to live. In Uncle Willie's old home. I think I ought to do something for him. It's horrible to think of him being sent back to a public asylum.'

His mother turned away and began to shuffle papers on the desk.

'You've always resisted us, Chris,' she said in a plaintive voice. 'I don't know why. I don't understand it. Your father and I have done our best according to our lights. Maybe they're not your lights, but I don't think we can be blamed for that.' She paused and held up an invoice short-sightedly before her nose. It was pale blue, and it caught Chris's eyes as effectively as if she had waved a coloured scarf above her head. 'I don't understand why you want to keep this man, when you know perfectly well that neither your father nor I want it, and that every hour he's kept makes it harder for us all. You won't even take my word for it that he's a dangerous, violent lunatic . . .'

'In twenty-five years he hasn't done a single thing which . . .'

'He was under control. That's the whole purpose of having people like that in institutions.' Mrs Ryan turned the blue invoice upside down, and continued to study it as attentively as ever. Chris took a step forward to see if it was now right-side up; but his mother moved a little and hid the paper from his sight.

'But the attendant told me that the doctor in charge would let him out at once if he had anybody to take him.'

'That big bruiser is very free with his opinions. I suppose Willie got round him too. Did he say anything about Willie going to Mass or attending to his duties all these years?'

'I didn't ask him.'

The blue invoice appeared again over Mrs Ryan's shoulder. It was shaking, and with her head turned away she was no longer pretending to read it.

'You don't seem to have asked him much. Well, your father did make enquiries about that down the years. It was the chief thing that we were interested in, considering the sort of life your uncle led. He has never been to Mass or confession since he was a young man, and he didn't change his ways in the asylum.'

'Surely to God that wasn't why he was sent away!' Chris burst out.

'Of course not.'

'Had it anything to do with you, Mammy?'

Mary crumpled the blue paper in her fist, and let it fall on the desk. She did not reply. In the silence the invoice, loosening in its tight ball, crackled faintly. Then the phone rang again.

'Mammy, can I bring him in to see you?'

'No, Chris. You won't bring him into my house.' Holding her hand to her forehead she took up the phone. Chris hesitated for a moment, and then walked out of the office.

⤙⤙⤙ 6 ⤚⤚⤚

MISS PINKIE WHITE leaned against the doorpost.
Beyond the broken wall at the end of O'Neill's backyard, the
vacant lots stretched down to the river, which ran behind Miss
White's knees. Her waist was level with the horizon, where the
dark lowering bog met the sky; her long skinny upper body was
framed against the grey clouds.

'Dark goings on up at the Hall,' she said in her thin piping
voice. 'Oh, my back!'

'You poor thing,' said Mrs O'Neill, pursing her lips as she
poised her brush over the tin of water-colours on the kitchen
table.

'A touch of pastel blue,' went on Miss White, leaning forward a little, and screwing up her raisin eyes as she considered the lampshade which her next-door neighbour was
painting. Then with a smooth agile movement of her snake-like
body, she transferred her shoulder from one side of the door
to the other. Nobody had ever seen her standing upright. She
leaned her way through life. No wall was far enough away for
her to make for when stopped in the street by an acquaintance;
no door safe from her sharp shoulders.

'I never heard of blue roses.' Mrs O'Neill dipped her brush
firmly in the red, and applied it savagely to the shade.

'It's the Queen Mother's favourite colour. Besides there's
such a thing as artistic licence you know. Did you see the
lovely full page colour portrait in this month's *Women's
Times*?'

'I did not.'

'I'll lend it to you if you like. I have a copy left over in
the shop. It's Mrs Hamilton's, but as you know she's gone to

her daughter in England for a late holiday. Just in time for the re-opening of Parliament. Such a colourful ceremony to see, don't you think? I love the Queen.'

Mrs O'Neill shifted her massive bulk in her chair and looked at the kitchen table heaped with water-colours of summer gardens and Connemara mountains; pieces of *petit-point* for the nuns' bazaar; woollen scarves and socks for the friars' jumble sale; and two pink cardigans for the parish raffle. All around the gaily coloured oddments lay squalor: the unwashed breakfast things in the sink, the grime embedded in the brown linoleum, the damp streaks in the red wallpaper. She raised her enormous eyes and looked at Miss White over the parchment shade.

'What did you say about the Queen Mother?' she said.

The agile spinster's thin mouth twitched, and with a swift serpentine scoop of her body she twisted her way round the doorpost and leaned against the wall inside.

'Which Queen Mother did you mean?' She took a scrap of paper from her pocket and a pencil from behind her ear and jotted down a few lines swiftly. 'Just a thought,' she went on, raising her sharp nose and gazing dreamily at the oleograph of the Sacred Heart over the range. 'It often comes to me like that, often in the middle of the night.'

Mrs O'Neill looked at her red-tipped brush thoughtfully.

'I mean to say was it a portrait of the Queen Mother that was in the *Women's Times* or was it blue roses?'

Miss White put back her pencil and paper and flattened herself against the wall.

'Well now,' she said briskly, 'as I said, I'll bring it in to you and you can see for yourself. The most beautiful delicate blue ball gown, just like a poem. But what really strikes me is the association of ideas. I'm shocking interested in that, aren't you? I mean to say the whole of literature is full of it. A portrait of the Queen Mother in the *Women's Times*, and immediately I think of Mrs Ryan. That's my private name for her, you know. It's very naughty of me, but then I simply can't stand pretension.' She narrowed her two little raisin

49

eyes again and squinted down at Mrs O'Neill's thick coils of blue-black hair.

That large lady raised a pudgy hand languidly and dipped the tip of her brush in an eggcup of water.

'All the same,' she murmured thoughtfully, 'blue roses are a bit much.'

'And so are the goings on up at Ryans,' squeaked Miss White. 'Who do those people think they are anyway? The Windsors? Upon my word I don't know how you can stand it. After all the O'Neills are a very old family, in the town. Quite one of our oldest families I always heard my father say, and if he didn't know nobody knew. But these people are nothing, simply nothing.'

'Well, now, I wouldn't say that altogether.'

'I would. Of course I know you can't stop young people going about together nowadays in the most unsuitable circumstances, and Christopher Ryan is quite a civil young man. I mean to say he has some manners. A looking glass is not necessarily a mirror to him. But the parents . . .' Miss White stopped and closed her eyes, allowing her body to slump against the wall, so that she looked as if she were hung on a peg to dry.

Mrs O'Neill looked up from her red roses. Her great eyes with their heavy lids gazed dreamily out of the door. The sullen sky was knife-grey, the river cloudy, the immense black plain still as death under the motionless clouds. She sighed and turned back to her table, her eyes resting affectionately on the blue Connemara mountains and the brightly daubed summer gardens. She dipped her brush in the eggcup again and applied it to the red.

'They're very nice people,' she said in her low sulky voice. 'Hard-working and respectable. And you can't say they haven't got on well.'

Miss White sniffed and rubbed her undulating shoulders against the wall.

'New rich. The very worst sort of set. Look at that vulgar house they have. It's a wonder they haven't it hung from top to bottom with lace curtains. Mountains falling and dung-hills rising, that's what I say. And as for getting on well, everybody knows that the Queen Mother's grandfather – if he was her grandfather – came into town with a bag on his back, and set up that huckster's shop down the street. When she came into it there wasn't enough in it to buy salt for your porridge for a week. That's why she married Mick Ryan, so that she'd get his money from the farm to set up properly. Everybody knows that, and more than everybody.'

'I never bother my head with things like that,' said Mrs. O'Neill, throwing the thickened water from the eggcup into the grate, and refilling it from a jug at her elbow. 'Besides, the Ryans are an old family in Summerhill, I often heard my husband say so. Nothing can be said against them.'

'Except of course the lunatic brother who has just broken out of the asylum, and landed home on top of all of them. That's a nice counter-tongs as they say in France. What does Kathleen say to that?'

'Every family has its crosses,' said Mrs O'Neill comfortably. 'Kathleen and I said a rosary for the poor man last night. I suppose he's been sent back by now.'

Miss White's thin lips curved up at the edges, showing her pointed teeth, and she opened her small eyes as wide as she could.

'Do you mean to say that you don't know that Christopher intends keeping him at Summerhill?' she said with a high whinnying giggle. 'Can it be possible that Kathleen didn't tell you? Or doesn't she know?'

Mrs O'Neill, whose brush had been hovering over the red, miscalculated and dipped it into the blue instead. She looked at the purple tint, and carefully drew an unnecessary butterfly over the red rose. Miss White watched and waited.

'That's her business,' said Mrs O'Neill at length. 'Now that you mention it she did say something. I wasn't listening much.'

'A nice prospect for Kathleen, I must say, marrying into a house with a lunatic. Would you do it?' She slid along the wall and took up her former place in the doorway. The tiny kitchen grew a little darker.

Mrs O'Neill made no reply. She merely chuckled fatly as she plucked one of her own long dark hairs out of the end of the brush.

'Chris is a nice boy,' she said slowly. 'I'm very fond of him. Indeed, to tell you the truth I'm fond of the whole family.' She looked up, her soft yellow face placid and smiling. 'It's a lovely thing to see Kathleen and him together, they're that much in love.'

'Ha.' The sound was like the twanging of a wire.

'For all I know they may have this thing fixed up among them.' The fat woman lifted a lazy arm and brushed a stray hair off her low forehead, which was startlingly white in contrast to the rest of her face. 'And anyway, isn't it a charitable thing to give a home to a poor harmless old man with one foot in the grave? It's just the sort of thing Chris would do. Oh yes.'

'If he was all that harmless,' snapped Miss White, drawing herself up with one of her supple, snake-like movements. 'It's a wonder they kept him in a common asylum for twenty-five years. And all the money they have.'

'Well now, that you mention it, I did hear Chris say that he was very happy where he was, and didn't want to be moved. I suppose he just got lonely and wanted to come home. After all, he's very old.' Mrs O'Neill completed the purple butterfly, and drew back with brush poised to admire it. 'The nuns will love this,' she murmured.

'He's sixty-one, two years older than Mick. They may have him on their hands for years, God help us all.'

'The ways of God are strange, surely,' crooned Mrs O'Neill.

'And the ways of men too.' Miss White's shoulders dipped and swayed against the doorpost as she grew more heated. 'It's a wonder Kathleen hasn't heard from Christopher since he decided to take the old man out. Wasn't it the night before last that he arrived home? Well, Christopher and the Queen

Mother had heated words yesterday morning, and in the afternoon he went over to the asylum to sign him out. And now I hear he has had another bed brought out to Summerhill, and intends to stay there. If you ask me Kathleen has a big problem on her hands.'

Suddenly the leaning body stiffened, the small head was thrust backwards through the doorway, and a long yellow finger was held up in front of the hollow chest. Mrs O'Neill looked up and blinked lazily.

' The bell,' said Miss White. ' Somebody in the shop. I must fly.' And she slithered out. Mrs O'Neill waited for a few minutes listening to the hurrying footsteps on the concrete path of the yard, the scrape of the gate leading on to the lane, and then the slightly dimmer sound of Miss White's gate as she hurried back to her newsagents shop next door. Then she heaved herself slowly out of her armchair and waddled across the cluttered kitchen to the door which led to the hall and the parlour.

' Was that Pinkie I heard in the kitchen?' asked Kathleen as her mother came in. She was sitting on a chair behind the castor-oil plant in the front window. In the street outside a race of giants walked by on their afternoon business. The little house was old; over the years the street level had been raised; two steps led down into the hall: a watcher in the front parlour looked out on a world of thighs a foot higher than his own.

' Yes.' The huge woman with the gypsy face sat down on the first chair available, as was her habit.

' What was she doing? Spouting about poetry as usual, I suppose.'

' She had a thought,' replied her mother, holding up her paint-stained fingers, and gazing at her blankly, ' about blue roses.'

' God!' Kathleen stood up abruptly. ' I suppose that means another poem in the local rag next week.'

Mrs O'Neill licked a finger daintily and wiped it on her skirt.

'Well,' she said slowly, a faint gleam of malice lighting her dreamy eyes, 'she sells a lot of their papers. Besides the poems are always good for a laugh. I wouldn't be surprised if she took up painting next. It's plain to be seen that she's mad jealous of mine.'

Kathleen looked around the cluttered room, at the feeble water-colours on the walls, the embroidered cushions on the horsehair sofa, the paper flowers in the Belleek vase on the mantelpiece, the electric light shade decorated with shamrocks. For almost two days she had sat in this room, waiting for Chris to call, listening to the fat ticking of the grandfather clock in the corner, sole legacy of better days and a bigger O'Neill establishment.

She turned aside to the little folding table by the wall and took up the library book she had been reading. *Forty Years at Court* by the Marchioness of Malahide, lent to her mother by Miss White to improve her mind. She flicked through it idly in time with the muffled tick-tock in the corner. Then she turned and looked out on the window.

A red coat passed, tightly draped about an enormous backside. A pair of blue jeans strode past it. Puddles on the roadway splashed softly under blurred wheels. Heels tapped bluntly beyond the closed world heavily draped in yellowing lace.

Mrs O'Neill yawned, lifting her hand as far as her enormous bosom in a token gesture of politeness.

'What was she saying?' said Kathleen sharply. 'She was a long time.'

'Until the bell rang. Round one for today. Well, she was talking about the Ryans, like the rest of the town at the moment.'

Kathleen sat down again and studied her nails.

'It appears that Chris has taken the notion that his old uncle is as sane as himself, and intends keeping him at home in Summerhill. Nice for you, I must say, to have a lunatic in the house.' She plucked a feather from her skirt, watched it drift on to the green linoleum and then put her small foot with its swollen ankle on top of it, as if she were stamping on a dying wasp. ' That is, if you *are* marrying into it.'

The clock ticked on plumply. Kathleen continued to study her nails attentively. Her mother folded her hands and let them fall limply into her lap, like tubes out of which air was escaping. She closed her eyes for a long moment and then opened them slowly to look at her daughter. In the street a car braked with a muffled shriek of tyres.

' Where did Pinkie hear all this?'

' Where does anybody hear anything in this town? I suppose she heard it from the Ryans' maid, or from some of the girls in the shop, or from some of the people round Summerhill. Anyhow she seems to know, and you don't.'

Kathleen looked at her mother with tightened lips. She locked her fingers together and rubbed her thumb against her palm.

' It won't be long until I do,' she snapped.

' An upsetting crowd the Ryans, the whole lot of them,' said Mrs O'Neill placidly, settling a hairpin behind her ear. ' I could never stand the sight of any of them. But pride hath a fall. In the old days when your grandfather had his shop he wouldn't have looked the side of the road any of them were on. Or sat in the same seat in the chapel. Now of course you'd think they were the royal family or something with the way they carry on. Mountains falling and dung-hills rising.'

' Don't be silly, Mammy.'

' And now where are you? I always said you shouldn't have given up your job when you got the diamonds from Chris.'

They both looked at the big ring on Kathleen's engagement finger.

' Maybe the old man isn't so bad, only a little soft. There are lots of people like that hanging about. Besides, he might be useful on the place.' Kathleen twisted the ring and stared out past the lace curtains. A blue skirt swung by.

Her mother chuckled softly.

' In the name of the Father and the Son and the Holy Ghost,' she murmured ironically.

Kathleen sprang to her feet.

'I'll have to see Chris,' she exclaimed. 'At once. This is too serious to leave up in the air.'

'I think,' said her mother softly, 'I'd see the Queen Mother, as Pinkie calls her, first. Unless I'm very much mistaken she's not too pleased with your boy-friend at the moment. And she holds the purse-strings. Charity, as they say, begins at home. Yes, if I were you I'd see Mrs Ryan first.'

Kathleen searched her mother's soft impenetrable face. But the huge brown eyes were fixed on a water-colour of the lakes of Killarney that hung on the opposite wall.

'But be careful what you say to her,' went on the chocolate-cream voice. 'It's a touchy subject with her. After all, the old boy tried to murder her.' She turned her vague eyes from the dreamy daub and smiled at her daughter affectionately. 'Or so they say.'

'I'll go up this very minute.'

'Put on your heavy coat and scarf, alannah. There's a 'flu going in the church. The town is rotten with it.'

Kathleen took down her coat from the peg in the hall and hurried out. Mrs O'Neill returned to her fond contemplation of her work on the wall. Then she heaved her mountainous body out of the chair and padded back to the kitchen to wait for her husband to come home from work and do some cooking.

⟨⟨⟨ 7 ⟩⟩⟩

FATHER JOHN MANNIX tapped his breviary on his knee.
It was a habit he had. His great white-maned head, red face and
thick lips seemed to promise an ample stomach; but in fact his
waist was trim and his long legs were spindly. He wore thick
grey hand-knitted socks and elastic-sided boots.

'Are you sure you won't have another cup of tea, Father?'
asked Mrs Ryan anxiously.

'No, thank you, ma'am,' replied the priest in his deep
plummy voice, his breviary lying idle as he spoke.

'Well, as I was saying, it's a great worry to all of us,' went
on Mrs Ryan, her eyes resting on her husband's face as he sat
on the edge of the armchair opposite, clasping his knees and
staring into the fire. His teacup lay untouched on the small
table beside him: an indication that his hands were still too
unsteady after two days of heavy drinking to risk raising it to
his lips. Occasionally he shivered and shot a sly glance at the
priest from under his eyelids.

'Um,' said Father Mannix.

'There's nothing in the world we'd rather do than take
Willie home, but . . .' she flung out her hands in a gesture of
helplessness. The priest began to tap his knee again. The little
thud, rhythmic and slightly menacing, affected Michael's
nerves. He grasped his knees firmly with his trembling hands
and turned to the visitor.

'What should we do, Father?' he asked hoarsely. His smooth
pink face was blotched, and his eyes were swollen and blood-
shot.

The breviary was still. Father Mannix cleared his throat and
looked up at the clock.

'It's hard to say. What do the hospital people say?'

Michael looked at his wife. She stood up and brought his teacup back to the silver tray on the table behind the sofa where the priest was sitting.

'I've only been talking to the two attendants who came for him. One of them spoke well of him, the other had his doubts.' Mary poured the cold tea carefully into the slops bowl. 'It was always like that with Willie. He could charm anybody he liked, and then . . .' She put the cup down sharply on the tray.

'But have you been talking to any of the doctors?' asked the priest.

'We . . .' The Ryans began to talk at the same time, and then fell silent; Michael turning to the fire, his wife making her way back to her chair. Tap tap tap went the breviary.

'Well, actually, we haven't,' said Mary, settling her skirt about her knees modestly. 'But Chris went over to the asylum yesterday . . .'

'And?' The breviary was still as Father Mannix lifted his face and fixed Mrs Ryan with his glittering china-blue eyes.

'We haven't seen Chris since,' Mary's voice faltered and she plucked nervously at her skirt. 'He's staying out at Summer-hill.'

'But your brother-in-law is still at Summerhill?'

'Yes, Father,' said Michael. 'Willie is still at home.'

'I see. That would seem to suggest that the doctors gave Chris a good report, and allowed him to take his uncle out, doesn't it?'

'Doctors are often wrong,' said Mary mildly.

'Indeed yes,' said Father Mannix with sudden enthusiasm. 'Do you know, a friend of mine, a classmate at Maynooth, was examined by a top specialist in Dublin on a Thursday, told he was a hundred per cent, and dropped dead on the altar the following Sunday. Only fifty-four years of age, God rest him.'

'Amen,' said Mary making the sign of the cross.

'The Lord save us,' muttered Michael, hunching his shoulders and gripping his knees more firmly.

They discussed sudden deaths for some time. Father Mannix grew so expansive on the subject that he took his breviary off his knee and left it down on the sofa beside him.

' It just shows you,' said Mary, shaking her head, ' that you can't ever be prepared enough.'

' Ah well,' said the priest, ' God is good.' He took up his breviary and began to tap again. Then he stopped abruptly and they both waited for him to speak. ' But a curious thing happened about this friend of mine that I was telling you about, Father Brian Milligan. Before he went out on to the altar that Sunday, a death notice was left in the sacristy for him to read off the pulpit. He gave it to one of the altar-boys to put on the pulpit. Now he died before the sermon, and that notice was never found.' He paused and raised a finger, looking from one to another of his rapt listeners. ' And nobody died in that parish on that weekend, except Father Milligan.'

' God protect us all,' said Michael, looking up at the ceiling.

' Did the altar-boy remember the person who left it in?' asked Mary.

Father Mannix snorted disgustedly.

' Altar-boy! You ought to know what these youngsters are like, ma'am. No heads. All he could remember was taking it from a strange man he had never seen before.'

' Well, that was one man was prepared to go anyway, in spite of the doctors,' said Mary piously. ' It just goes to show you.'

' People die as they live,' whispered Michael.

' You never said a truer word,' said the priest, slapping his sharp knee with his breviary. ' In all my experience I never witnessed a deathbed conversion yet. A man that shuts God out of his life, will shut him out of his death too.'

They sat for some minutes looking into the fire. The little clock whirred and struck the half-hour. The gentle thud of the prayerbook accompanied the strokes. Then Mary drew herself up and turned towards Father Mannix, her hands joined before her breast.

'And that, Father, is the real reason why I asked you to call this afternoon. You have, as usual, put your finger on the real thing that's worrying us. Well, it's like this – I don't know whether you know it or not – but yes, of course you do, I suppose everybody knows – Willie never went to Mass or confession since he was a young man. And he didn't go all the years he was in the asylum.'

'That wouldn't say that he's insane,' said the priest sharply. 'Lots of people turn away from their religion. It's our duty to pray for them.'

'Sure, we have ourselves worn out praying,' exclaimed Mary passionately. 'Isn't that right, Michael?'

Her husband nodded and held out a shaking hand towards the priest.

'I've had hundreds of masses said for him over the years,' he said in a whining voice, 'and not a bit of good.'

'No Mass ever goes to waste,' Father Mannix tapped his stubby fingers impatiently on his breviary and frowned.

'Oh yes, Father,' cut in Mary with a sharp look at her husband. 'If they haven't done him any good they'll do it for somebody else.'

'How do you know they haven't done him any good?' said the priest, opening his dazzling blue eyes wide, and raising his bushy white eyebrows.

'I didn't mean that, Father. It's just that he's still as bad as he ever was. There isn't a shred of Christianity in him. He's a complete pagan, and always was.'

'Dear me,' said Father Mannix, pushing himself forward to the edge of the sofa, 'I had no idea it was so late. I'll have to go.' He paused, leaning his weight on his fists and directed a sharp glance at Mary. 'By the way, how is Kathleen O'Neill taking all this? Are she and Chris agreed on giving a home to your brother-in-law?'

'Do you think they should, Father?' asked Michael eagerly.

'If the doctors say that he's cured I should think it's very much up to Kathleen. After all she's marrying into the place.

A good girl. I believe she's taking a great interest in Summer-hill. It's nice to see a young girl nowadays anxious to settle down on a farm. All most of them want is to get into the factory or go off to England.' He heaved himself up from the low sofa, tucked his breviary under his arm, and slid his red hands into the sleeves of his jacket. He stared into the crackling fire for a few moments while the Ryans stood awkwardly waiting.

'Is that English coal?' he asked suddenly.

'Yes,' said Michael.

'No,' said Mary.

Father Mannix took a hand out of his sleeve and gave it to Mary.

'Goodbye now, and God bless you. Goodbye, Michael.'

'I'll see you to the door, Father.'

Mrs Ryan took up the poker and stoked the fire savagely while she waited for her husband to come back from seeing the priest to his car. When he did, she flung the poker on the fender, and turned to meet him.

'Why in the name of God did you say that was English coal!' she burst out. 'Don't you know perfectly well that he can't stand the sight of anything English?'

Michael flapped his hands weakly, and shook his head. His plump jowls quivered like jelly.

'Ah, sure I didn't think, I was that upset. I don't know what way I am.'

'I'm not surprised,' snapped his wife.

Michael sat down and took out a large handkerchief with which he began to wipe his sweating palms.

'Well?' he said, avoiding Mary's eyes and giving his full attention to the roaring fire of English coal.

'Well, all I can say is that we should have known better than to ask that old fox about anything. Did you ever see any-thing like the cuteness of him!'

'Didn't I tell you that?' replied Michael with some heat. 'Sure, you couldn't get a straight answer out of that man if it was to save your life. I knew well it'd end up like that.'

'Did you give him any money at the door?' Mary leaned forward hands on hips, and searched her husband's flushed face.

'Did I what?' blustered Michael. 'Is it me give that fellow money! Isn't it enough that we have to contribute to every sale-of-work, bazaar, and jumble sale in the whole county without giving him any more?'

'The Church is all changed.' Mary pressed her fingers against her temples. 'They have no use for anybody now except the working class that they can ride roughshod over. It's a different proposition with people like us, and they know it.'

'Well,' said Michael smugly, 'I told you so.'

'Will you shut up! Haven't I enough on my mind without listening to you. Did you notice the sly way he brought Kathleen into it? The nerve of him! Only for I didn't like to, I'd soon tell him where to get off. Who does he think he is anyway? Ten minutes late every morning saying Mass, and the rest of the time playing golf and bridge!'

'And a big Mercedes car. Wouldn't you think a Morris Minor would be good enough for him, and all the people that's starving in the country?'

Mary twisted her head from side to side stiffly, as if she had a crick in her neck.

'Oh, yes, the O'Neills and the likes of them are the only sort the priests want now. That and marriage. Marry, marry, marry, and have ten children – that's all they want. And they don't care who marries who. It's disgusting, that's what it is.'

'Ah, sure, I know,' said Michael soothingly, 'everything is half Communist now, even the Church.'

'You'd think at least he'd take some interest in Willie's soul. It isn't as if he didn't know. Wasn't he a curate in the half-parish beyond Summerhill at the time? Don't tell me he didn't know about Willie's goings on. After all, that's what I asked him out for. I thought he'd see at once that it's crazy to expect a man like that to settle down.'

Michael gripped his knees firmly and looked up at his wife timidly.

'Ah sure, maybe he will, Mary. He's old now, and the wild days are over. Why else would he come home after all these years?'

Mary Ryan sat down slowly and turned her face away from her husband. She began to weep, silently and without a shudder. She held her face in her hands and rubbed the tears into the flesh of the cheekbones. Michael looked at her out of the corner of his eye; then stood up and looked about the rich room helplessly. The satin cushions gleamed and the chandelier glittered; the velvet curtains, still undrawn, framed the darkening October afternoon. At the end of the garden six bare poplars were as quiet and still as a line of old men at a funeral. A few soft-stemmed roses hung from the standard bushes below the terrace. In the triangular beds begonias still bloomed fatly. Beyond the poplars the lights of the town began to wink; and the purple back of the great bog arched against the horizon.

'Don't cry, Mary,' said Michael Ryan uncertainly. He drew himself up, and clasped his trembling hands. 'I'll tell you what I'll do. I'll get the friars to say a Mass. They say a lovely one, at least ten minutes longer than anything you'd get from Father Mannix or his curates, gabbling away like ganders. Yes, that's what I'll do, and if that doesn't pull off the hat-trick, nothing will.'

⟨⟨⟨ 8 ⟩⟩⟩

KATHLEEN STOPPED in the middle of the path a few yards from the Ryans' gate as the black Mercedes drove out. She turned aside quickly and looked across the wall into the garden of the next house, a red-roofed villa called 'Lavender Gate'. The priest's car purred along behind her on its way back into town.

An autumn stillness settled about her. The six Lombardy poplars which divided the Ryans' garden from 'Lavender Gate' were grey in the milk-blue light. The veins of the Virginia creeper stood out on the pale plaster walls of the villa. Leaves like blobs of dried blood littered the short avenue. A small shaggy Sealyham came running round from the back of the house to bark at the girl leaning over the wall. Kathleen turned away and walked back quickly towards the town.

Greetings exchanged in the narrow streets seemed to linger in the damp air like falling leaves. A flash of half-curious eyes, a ripple of laughter, an automatic baring of teeth indicated that the dark-haired girl in the cheap red coat belonged to the place. Cars hummed and rattled about her; children screamed; women huddled in twos and threes on the paths grew silent and stared after her. Then, fingers crooked before eager malicious mouths, they took up the ritualistic gabble again. October rose like a ghost from the pavement at the end of the lanes leading down to the river: dim, bundled figures walking there waded knee-high in blue-grey vapour. There were pink streaks like half-healed weals in the cold face of the sky. At the end of the main street beyond the semi-detached villas the country began, slashed with the curving scimitar of the river, and stretching flat to the horizon at the end of the earth.

Kathleen quickened her pace and hurried out of the watching town on to the Summerhill road. She began the gentle ascent too fast, and was out of breath by the time she reached the turning on top of the hill out of sight of the roofs of the town.

She sat down on a stone and stared out over the great plain on which the dappled shadows were falling. She slapped her tired ankles and pressed her fingers into the calves of her legs. A cold damp wind blew along the sodden road. She turned up the collar of her coat and walked on.

Inside the Summerhill gate, in the shadow of the big beach, she wiped the mud of the road off her shoes in the coarse grass. Chris's wagon was parked at the gable end of the house. A spiral of smoke rose from the tall chimneys. Toby came out and waddled forward barking. Then, scenting a friend, crept towards the girl, her back legs tucked under her, her head twisted apologetically.

Kathleen walked into the house with the bitch rubbing herself against her legs. The tiles in the hall were wet, and damp streaked the walls. She turned into the kitchen and stopped in the doorway.

Stripped to the waist, Chris was washing himself over a basin in front of the range. The muscles in his egg-brown back rippled as he bent over the soapy water, gurgling and humming to himself. He had tied a towel about his waist, and his shirt and vest were thrown on the old armchair in the corner. Kathleen stood watching him for a few minutes, wiping the perspiration off her upper lip with her forefinger. Chris splashed his face and straightened up; untied the towel and covered his face with it. He turned round rubbing his eyes vigorously. Soap suds flecked the soft fair hair on his chest and arms. Kathleen turned away abruptly into the hall and looked out the door for a few minutes. When she came back he was wiping his hands and arms, and peering at her through eyelids smarting with soap.

' Hullo,' he said with a grin. ' I was getting ready to go in to see you.' He stretched the towel over his head and began to rub the back of his neck.

Kathleen went over to the window and looked out on to the yard. A thin, white-haired figure was walking by the stables, touching the walls with an outstretched hand, like a blind man feeling his way.

' You might have come in sooner,' she said in a sulky voice.

' I was busy,' said Chris curtly, crumpling the towel in one hand and rubbing his chest and under his arms. ' I didn't have time.'

' You had plenty of time if you wanted to. As it is I had to walk all the way out here.'

' A two mile walk never did anybody any harm. It'll do you good.' He reached for his vest and slipped it over his head.

In the yard Willie grasped the half-door of one of the stables and leaned in, his white head disappearing in the darkness. Like a child peering over a wall he kicked the bottom of the door with his toes.

' Anyhow,' went on Chris in a muffled voice as he slipped his arms into his shirt, ' what have you been doing? Talking things over with my mother, I suppose.' He undid the buttons of his pants and settled his vest and shirt about his waist. After a moment he buckled his belt and reached for his tie.

' And if I did?' Kathleen had taken off her scarf and was holding it stretched out between her hands.

' It would be very natural. Women usually get together over these things.'

' As a matter of fact I haven't been talking to your mother. I intended to, but I came out here instead.'

' That's my girl,' said Chris lightly, turning away and peering at himself in the shaving mirror on the window ledge behind the armchair. He opened his mouth and examined his strong white teeth before he began to brush his yellow hair.

' Is it true that you've taken out your uncle, and are living out here at the moment?'

Chris stopped brushing his hair, stripped his teeth again, and rubbed them with the back of his finger.

'Mm, yes.'

'Are you in earnest, Chris?'

'Of course I'm in earnest.' He plucked some loose hairs from the brush and smiled at the girl, who had turned around and was staring at him with wide, unbelieving eyes. 'By the way, you haven't met him yet. He's out in the yard at the moment. You'll like him.'

Kathleen threw down her scarf on a chair beside her and looked at her engagement ring. The diamond glittered as it caught the light of the naked bulb over her head.

'How do you know I'll like him? You haven't given me much of a choice. You might at least have talked this thing over with me.'

Chris reached for his tweed jacket and slipped into it, heaving his shoulders and pulling down the cuffs of his white shirt.

'You didn't wait to talk about it. In the meantime I was busy. Do you want your tea?'

'No, I don't want tea. Do you expect me to come and live in a house with a man who's been over twenty years in an asylum for assaulting your mother?' Kathleen straddled a little as she spoke with raised voice.

Chris sat down in the armchair and clasped his hands between his open legs.

'So that's what you're afraid of?' he said with a short laugh.

'Of course I'm afraid. Wouldn't any girl be? Be sensible, Chris.' Kathleen glanced across her shoulder into the yard; but there was no sign of Willie.

Chris punched his palm with his fist.

'All right, I'll tell you. Willie didn't attack my mother in the way you think. He didn't strike her, or try to knife her or anything like that.' He looked up at Kathleen gravely. 'He kissed her.'

'Kissed her!' Kathleen's voice rose shrilly. 'But that's even worse.'

'No, it isn't. Not the way Willie tells it, and I believe him.' He got up, walked back and forth across the kitchen a few times, and then rested one thigh on the edge of the table and swung his leg in and out under it. 'He knew that my mother disliked him. He used to try and amuse her by singing little songs and clowning for her, but that only made her worse. Then one day she gave out to him – here in this kitchen – and he went up and kissed her.' He stopped swinging his leg and looked down at his brown polished shoe. 'It was a childish thing to do. I suppose she thought she was going to be attacked or something, anyhow she began to scream. And then he lost his head. He shouted at her that if she didn't stop, or if she told anybody what had happened he'd kill her. He was terrified. Perhaps they both were. Most of the ugly things in life can be traced back to fear.'

Chris put his hands in his pockets and smiled at Kathleen, who was staring fixedly at his motionless foot. 'But you have nothing to be afraid of.'

Kathleen raised her eyes and looked at the smiling face of the big man lounging against the table.

'So you're going to take Willie's part against your mother, are you?' she said slowly. 'Because that's what it means.'

Chris lifted his thigh from the table and stood up.

'Did I take her part against you?' he asked quietly. 'Would you like me to do that?'

'Oh, I know well I'm not wanted. I'm not good enough.'

'Don't be silly, Kate,' said Chris gruffly, tapping on the table with his knuckles. 'We're giving a home to a harmless old man who wants to spend his last years here. It would be very easy to send him back and forget about him.'

'I didn't say that . . .' protested Kathleen hotly.

'But that's what you're thinking. You just don't want to be bothered with him.' He looked at Kathleen quizzically, his thick brows drawn up in an inverted V over his nose. 'Oh, for God's sake take off your coat and sit down. You're just making a scene.'

Kathleen flushed angrily and clutched her coat tighter about her.

'I will not sit down, and I am not making a scene. It's all very well for you to play the good Samaritan, but a lot of other people have to suffer for it.' She slipped off her engagement ring and held it in the palm of her hand. 'Chris, when I took this from you, it was you I wanted and only you. Is there anything wrong about that?'

'You've got me.' The young man came over and circled her neck with his hands, forcing her head back so that she was staring up into his face. Slowly, gently, he increased the pressure of his thumbs and forefingers, until the girl's face grew flushed, and her eyes began to harden. 'Haven't you?'

She waited passively, her whole body seeming to hang from his joined hands. The ring slipped from her nerveless fingers on to the flagged floor. Suddenly he released her and turned away abruptly. Kathleen backed against the wall and pressed her body against it. She made a tiny sound, half-sob, half-sigh. The blood drained from her face and her slack body hardened.

'No,' she said in a hoarse whisper, 'I haven't got you, and now I know I never had at any time. Maybe you're sorry for this old man. Maybe. But that's not all of it. What you really want is to get your own back on your family. Charity begins at home, Chris.'

'This is your home, Kathleen.' He was standing in front of the fire with his back to her, his shoulders raised, his thumbs crooked in his trousers pockets, fingers tapping his thighs.

'I don't think it is going to be my home. I don't think I want to be used, like that old man out there, to prove your independence. I didn't see it because I wanted you and not your family. Well, there are plenty of girls in the town just as unsuitable as I am. You won't have any difficulty in fixing yourself up with any of them. And they won't mind Willie. After all you're a good catch.'

She picked up her woollen scarf and shook it angrily before throwing it about her neck.

Chris turned round quickly. They stared at each other for a few moments. Then the young man laughed, a short mirthless snort through the nose.

'Is there a woman in the world who believes in anything?' he said bitterly.

'Women are realists, Chris. They have to be. It's a man's world, as they say. The least you might have done was asked me before you did anything about Willie. No one likes to be taken for granted. It isn't as if this is an ordinary case. There's nothing ordinary in giving a home to a man whose . . .'

'So you want me to get rid of him.'

'I didn't say that either. It's the way you've done things that I can't understand, and it frightens me. God knows I've nothing to be grateful to your mother about. But she is your mother after all. The least you could have done was talked to her about it, and try and get her to understand.' She knotted her scarf about her neck and walked to the door. 'I don't believe you give a damn about Willie, any more than you give a damn about anybody else,' she flung back at him.

'In short, it'd be OK if I let you and my mother manage the whole thing, just to show me that you both own me.' Chris took a step forward, and the bulb threw deep shadows on his pale angry face.

'Well, you own Willie now.'

Chris was about to reply when he stopped short and looked at the back door. Toby raised her head and gave a short token bark. Willie pushed the door open with his shoulder. He was holding something in his hands; something brown and furry from which blood dripped slowly on to the floor. Toby whined, raised her long nose and sniffed. Willie went over to a stool in the corner and sat down, laying the dead rabbit gently on the ground at his feet.

'I'm afraid it's dead,' he said looking at Chris. 'It was caught in a trap in the big meadow and its back leg is crushed.'

He looked down at his bloodstained hands. 'It was still alive when I got there, but I was too late. It's a pity.'

Toby was edging forward towards the dead body, her nose twitching.

'Get back, Toby,' commanded Chris, shoving the bitch aside with the sole of his shoes. 'It's one of those bloody Hannigans from down the road. They're always setting traps. I told them if I caught them at it again I'd summon them. Suppose one of the calves got trapped. Here, Uncle Willie, wash your hands in the basin.' He looked across his shoulder at Kathleen, who was standing in the doorway, staring down at the rabbit and the thin trickle of blood oozing from its body. Willie stood up and stepped across it, holding his bloody hands in front of him. He stopped when he saw Kathleen, and looked uncertainly at Chris.

'This is Kathleen O'Neill, Uncle Willie. I was telling you about her.'

Willie smiled and nodded his head, then hurriedly plunged his hands into the basin of water in which Chris had been washing himself. The young man picked up the rabbit by the ears and went out the back door. Toby lumbered after him with eager twitching ears.

Willie straightened up and reached for the towel. He turned round, wiping his hands, and smiled shyly at the girl. But she was not looking at him. He followed her gaze and saw the diamond ring glittering on the floor, near the little pool of blood where the rabbit's body had lain.

'Oh,' he exclaimed, throwing away the towel, 'what a lovely ring! Is it yours?' He stooped down and picked it up, holding it in the light between his thumb and forefinger.

Kathleen took a step forward into the kitchen. Her face was white and strained, and her eyes had an ugly puffy expression.

'No,' she said in a low voice, 'it's Chris's.'

Willie raised his eyebrows and bit his lower lip.

'Is it?' he said wonderingly. 'I never saw it on him.' He slipped the ring on his little finger, and crooked it admiringly in front of his face. As he looked at it he closed one eye, and encircled the other with his fingers.

'That's the way they do it in the jewellers,' he said, screwing up his mouth and allowing his head to sink down into his shoulders. While he was playing this little pantomime, Chris came back. He looked at his uncle with a frown.

'What are you doing, Uncle Willie?' he said sharply.

'He found your ring on the floor,' said Kathleen. 'He wants to give it back to you.' She turned back into the hall and disappeared.

Chris strode over and held out his hand for the ring. Willie slipped it off and gave it to him.

'I got a ring in a cracker once,' he said sadly, 'but it was only glass.'

'So is this,' replied Chris grimly, as he put it in his pocket. He hurried into the hall, but Kathleen was already walking down the darkening avenue. He shouted after her, but she did not turn. After a minute's hesitation at the door, he muttered an oath, and turned back into the kitchen. Willie was kneeling down mopping up the blood with a wet rag.

'Jesus Christ,' swore Chris, running out into the yard, and banging the door violently behind him.

The old man started, straightened up and looked about the harshly lighted kitchen with the bloody rag in his bone-white hands. Then he got to his feet and dipped it in the soapy water of the basin which turned from blue to purple.

TWO

‹ ‹ ‹ I › › ›

ON HIS DAY OFF Halloran drove over to see Willie. As he turned his secondhand Volkswagen in on the Summerhill gate he saw Willie coming along the avenue in his old tweed suit, but with a muffler about his neck. Halloran stopped the car and opened the door.

'Hullo,' he said, 'get in and we'll go for a drive. But I want to have a pump first.'

Halloran squeezed himself out of the tiny car and stood up, pressing his hands into the small of his back with a grunt of satisfaction. He walked stiff-legged across to the tree, and disappeared behind it. When he returned his gait was more supple, and he swung his arms like a soldier on parade to limber himself up.

'I was never made for the likes of these cars,' he said ruefully, as he prepared to fold himself back into the driver's seat. 'We'll have to get out and have a walk somewhere.'

'Right,' said Willie, pressing himself against the door to make room for his companion, whose enormous bulk made the little car look as if it had been built around him like a shell.

'Look at that chestnut tree over there, Peter,' said Willie tapping on the window as the car reversed through the gates. The tree stood in the middle of the field at the side of the house, its great dome-shaped crown outlined against the lowering sky. The outer leaves were still green; inside it was a mass of autumn gold, and looked as if it were lit up by some unearthly light. 'It always used to go off like that. Even on the darkest days you'd think the sun was shining through it.'

Halloran slid into first and started off down the road away from the town.

' Were you expecting me?' he asked.

' Yes, I thought you might come on your day off. How is everybody?'

' Fine. Dr Morris was asking for you, and Mick Lanigan, and of course Billy and Brendan. They all miss you.'

' I miss them too,' said Willie, looking down at his hands.

' Is everything going all right?' Halloran swerved to avoid a white hen which ran across the road and plunged into the ditch. ' Dammit!'

' That hen will be killed someday soon, or kill somebody,' said Willie, twisting round and peering through the dusty back window.

' Well, go on, how are you?'

Willie sighed and sucked in his lips.

' I don't know how I am, Peter. It's all very strange coming home after twenty-five years. I think all the people round here that I used to know must be dead. Of course I haven't been out much.' He pointed to a derelict cottage on the side of the road, half of its thatched roof fallen in, the other covered with moss. ' People called Finnerty used to live there. Now look at it. It's like coming back from the dead.'

' It's early days yet, Willie. You've only been home ten days. Did your brother or sister-in-law come to see you?'

' No.'

' The devil mend them anyway for a pair of damned hypocrites!' Halloran shook his pepper-grey head in anger.

' Ah, well, it must be a great shock to them,' said Willie mildly. ' To tell you the truth I didn't expect to see much of Mary, but I thought Michael would come. After all I'm the only brother he has, and didn't he give you ten pounds for me?'

' Yes, he broke his heart.' Halloran's huge body stiffened, and he gave an enormous sneeze which shook the little car.

' God bless you. Are you getting a cold?' Willie held up the frayed cuff of his shabby jacket and wiped his own nose.

76

Halloran took out his handkerchief and blew loud and long into it.

'Here,' he said in a muffled voice when he was finished, and had taken another clean handkerchief out of his breast pocket, 'take this.'

Willie opened it, spread it on his lap, and stroked it gently.

'This is too good of a handkerchief to give me, Peter. And besides I still have the ten pounds. I can easily buy one for myself. I don't think I want a guitar any more now.'

'Have you been into town yet?'

'No.'

Halloran glanced sideways at the little man huddled in his seat, plucking the handkerchief on his lap.

'Scared?' he asked quietly.

'Yes. It's just like it used to be a long time ago. I was never afraid all the time I was in the asylum. Funny, isn't it?' He gathered up the handkerchief and stuffed it into his sleeve. 'When I was young I wasn't afraid of anything. But too many things have happened. I don't suppose anybody cares much now but me, and a few others.' He pressed his back against the seat and straightened his woollen muffler. 'Besides, I haven't got a new outfit yet. That's what I'm keeping the ten pounds for. Do you think I could get any kind of a suit and shirt for that? Things have gone up something awful since I was out.'

Halloran grasped the wheel and lowered his head until his square jutting chin almost touched the top of it.

'The bastards,' he muttered.

'Oh,' said Willie sitting forward suddenly, and peering out on the windscreen. 'I almost forgot we're on the Esker road. This is it. Will you stop here, Peter, please?'

They had been driving downhill and were now passing a high, crumbling stone wall over which a line of beech and chestnut trees were shedding their yellow and scarlet leaves into the ditch. Halloran pulled up and looked around him. Here they were level with the horizon, cloudy and indefinite,

77

with the putty-coloured sky pressing down on the misty bog.

'This is an old place called Esker,' went on Willie, with a note of excitement in his voice as he fumbled with the handle and climbed out of the car. 'It used to belong to people called Dillon. Could we walk here?'

'Come on,' said Halloran, striding off down with his shoulders back at such a rate that he had to slow down to allow Willie to keep up with him. The little man turned up the collar of his jacket about his muffler and buried his hands in his pockets. Halloran took a deep breath and sneezed mightily again.

Willie bent down and picked up one of the spiky green apples scattered under the chestnuts. He put his nail in one of the cracks and took out the smooth mahogany nut.

'Many's the time I used to gather them long ago,' he said. 'Michael and I used to put them on a string, and wallop all the other kids.'

Halloran stopped and looked down with a scowl.

'What's wrong with you, Willie, is that you didn't keep on walloping people. If you did they might have more respect for you.'

'That was only kid stuff,' said Willie sadly, throwing the chestnut away and walking on. 'I was never much of a fighter. All I ever wanted was to be left alone. And there isn't much fight left in me now.'

Halloran clenched his fists and shook his big head.

'I don't mean fighting with your fists. There are other ways of defending yourself. People like you have to be tough, otherwise . . .' he lifted his massive shoulders and threw out his hands. 'Everybody has to pay for their passage. Some with their hands, others with their brains or their bodies, or their tongues. You have to be equipped with something that you can sell.' His deep voice with its bronchial undertones had grown light and bitter, and he ended with a short harsh laugh.

'Oh, I wasn't a bad worker, especially at the beginning. I

always pulled my weight at home. Funny enough I was better on the land than Michael.'

'And yet your mother left the place to him, after all.'

'That was after I took to the drink and began to get a bad name,' protested Willie loyally. 'And even then she said that I was always to have a home there. I never thought they'd put me out.'

'Poor Willie,' said Halloran, laying a hand on his sleeve. 'It's a shocking thing to be as innocent as you are in this world.'

Willie opened his eyes in amazement, and then chuckled.

'Innocent, how are you,' he murmured, with a sly look at Halloran's grim profile.

The wall curved unsteadily round to join a great Palladian gate leaning drunkenly to one side, and opening on to a curving avenue overgrown with moss and weeds. The iron gates, rotten with rust, had been left open so long that they seemed to be growing out of the ground. As they went through, the two men stopped and held up their hands to brush off the cobwebs that slung between the high ornate pillars where the gates should have been.

'God,' said Halloran waving energetically, 'this is like being tied up with strings.'

'Some mornings at this time of year the fields around Summerhill are covered with them, like thread. It's wonderful.'

Halloran brushed his shoulders impatiently, and plucked at the corners of his mouth.

'Well,' he said walking on, 'what about the nephew?'

Willie trotted along beside him already a little out of breath.

'He was very nice to me when I came home first,' he said simply. 'Now I don't know about him so much.'

'Ah. Go on. I was sort of expecting this.'

'It was all right until the girl came out. I think they must have had a row over me, because he isn't the same since.'

'What happened?'

79

Willie told him about Kathleen's visit and the ring. He was so lost in his recital that he did not seem to notice that they were walking through a ghostly net slung from one side of the avenue to the other between the dripping yellow beeches. Halloran kept waving his hand in front of him to clear the way, snorting occasionally to blow the delicate webs out of his nose.

'It's horrible,' he declared fiercely at the end. 'There are times when I'd like to get my hands on an atom bomb, and blow up this stinking, cruel planet. What has ever mattered in the world anyway except force? The only thing that could ever help a person like you to get through it and hold your own would be money . . .'

'No, Peter,' protested Willie, brushing his hand vaguely over the silvery web that clung to his hair. 'I never had much interest in that. I never had any ambition except to live my own life.' His voice faltered and he raised his thin hands in a groping gesture, as if he were making his way through a dark place. He stopped, breathing heavily, and sat down on a fallen tree that lay at the side of the avenue.

Halloran sat down beside him and put his hand on his arm.

'That's the most difficult thing that any man can do in this world,' he said slowly. 'To live his own life. It's not permitted, as you ought to know.'

'I know now,' murmured Willie sadly.

'Did you ever have any friends at all, Willie?' the big man asked with unexpected gentleness.

'I thought I had.' Willie's voice was as dry and tremulous as the rustling of the leaves falling through the branches of the trees above him. 'I suppose that's how it all began in a way. I wanted friends, but somehow they sensed something, and I was never one of them, except for what they wanted, and—and I did it, because . . .' his voice trailed into silence and died away among the rotting leaves.

'You did it because you wanted them too in your own way,' declared Halloran roughly, slapping his knee impatiently. 'Why deny it? Every human being seeks his own kind, and every man has the right to, no matter what society says. But you were afraid, and helpless and innocent—yes, Willie, innocent – and they destroyed you. And now it's starting all over again because they can't explain you, and they can't either buy or sell you. Christ, the hypocrisy of it all.'

Willie straightened up and clutched the collar of his coat.

'Yes,' he said, his weak voice suddenly gathering strength, 'I wanted them all right, but not the way they wanted it, not the way he wanted it . . .' he broke off and covered his mouth with his fist.

'And so the drinking began, and the darkness and the brutality. Yes, I know. You were perfect fair game if you made one false move. And of course you did.'

'I was drunk that day, Peter. I wanted her to like me. I didn't know what else to do. And Michael was all I had left in a way.'

'Was it him?' Halloran turned and looked at Willie sharply.

'In the beginning, yes,' whispered the old man.

'It often is that way.' Halloran's voice was calm and professional, but it rose angrily again as he dug his heel viciously into the soft turf. 'Which is why the bastard never lifted a hand to help you.'

Willie was silent for a few moments. Suddenly he stooped down and picked something up from the ground. It was a small yellow spider with a blurred white cross on its back. He cupped his hands over it and held it in his lap.

'What's that?' Halloran leaned forward and held out his hand.

'A diadem spider. In the old days the women round here used to collect them to put in a box for rheumatism, I suppose because of the cross on its back.' He opened his fingers, and Halloran flicked the spider on to the grass.

'I hate them,' he growled.

'It wasn't Michael's fault,' said Willie, turning with one of his quick supple movements and touching Halloran's cuff lightly with his knuckles.

The other man shrugged and picked up a twig at his feet.

'These things happen.' He snapped the twig in two and dropped the broken pieces on the ground again. 'But there was somebody else, wasn't there? Or am I wrong? Do you want to talk about it?'

'He's dead now.' Willie got to his feet and tightened his muffler. 'Even deader than I am.'

He walked to the middle of the glimmering, overgrown avenue, and beckoned to Halloran.

'Look,' he said, pointing to the big stone house in the hollow below them. Blue smoke drifted lazily from one of its chimneys, and a bed of salvias blazed in a small circular bed in the middle of the avenue before the front door. Two tall clumps of pampas raised their feathery plumes on either side of the broad entrance steps.

'Yes?' said Halloran gruffly as he clumped across to Willie's side.

'That's where he lived. I wanted to see it again.'

'Did he live there alone?' Halloran noticed that the four ground-floor windows were curtained, and all the upper ones shuttered; and that the glass of the conservatory at the side of the house was broken.

'No, he was married, but his wife died. Later his sister came back to live with him. She was a Mrs Whittaker.'

As they watched from the shadow of the trees the door opened, and a woman came out and stood on the steps. A small grey dog waddled after her and plumped down the steps, sniffed the pampas and raised its leg to urinate. The figure stood waiting while the dog wandered about, nose to ground, and then heaved itself up the steps again. The woman stepped back and looked at the open door. The dog shuffled in, and the woman followed him slowly. The plumes of the pampas dipped and swayed in a sudden gust of wind; and the salvias moved a little like a pool of blood.

Halloran looked at Willie. He was staring in front of him with fixed slightly distended eyes. Suddenly he blinked, shook his head, and, as gently as one of the slipping leaves on the trees above him, swayed, crumpled and sank to the ground. Halloran's arms shot out and encircled his shoulders. He lifted him up and carried him over to the log, propped him up with one hand and felt for his pulse with the other. Willie groaned and clutched his throat, his chest. Sweat poured from his green-white face.

' All right, all right,' muttered Halloran, ' don't stir. I'll carry you.'

' No,' whispered Willie, closing his eyes, and opening his mouth in an effort to breathe.

Halloran looked over his shoulder at the grey house below them. Then he lifted the old man into his arms and began to carry him towards the open door, the thin thread of smoke, and the ghostly funeral plumes of the pampas grass.

THE BIG ROOM smelt of wood smoke: beech logs burned in the grate of the marble fireplace. Two great windows looking out on to the avenue framed the darkening landscape: the cloaked trees, the black line of bogland on the horizon, the dull gleam of the river, the leaden arc of sky that seemed to press every object in the great plain back into the purple soil.

Five miles away, through a gap in the demesne wall, the roofs and steeples of the town could be glimpsed, smudged against the sky like inkstains on a sheet of blotting-paper.

Halloran sat facing the windows in one of the two armchairs on either side of the fireplace. He was holding a large glass of brandy, and looking at Mrs Whittaker who was sitting opposite him, crouched forward with one hand ruffling the shaggy neck of the old Cairn terrier asleep at her feet.

'Well,' she said for the third time that afternoon, 'just imagine, Willie Ryan. What an extraordinary thing! We used to know him very well years ago.'

Halloran nodded and looked down at his glass. It was fine brandy and he was warming it.

'Are you quite sure he's all right?' she enquired, looking up anxiously.

'For the moment, yes. He's had these black-outs before, his heart is not good. I don't think it's a heart attack, although of course when he gets the thing he always thinks it is.' Halloran moved in his chair, supporting himself against the sagging springs by pressing his elbows into the chintz-covered arms. The Cairn raised his head, yapped feebly and dozed off again. 'But I don't think it would be wise to move him at the moment,' he went on slowly, meeting Mrs Whittaker's gaze and holding her enquiring glance for a moment.

'No, no, of course not. I hope he's comfortable.' She looked towards the door. At the end of the hall in what used to be the study, Willie was lying on a sofa, hot water-bottles by his feet and side. Mrs Whittaker's gardener, Gallagher, a hale old man of eighty, was sitting with him, while his nephew Patch, who came in daily to milk the cows, had been dispatched on his auto-cycle for the doctor.

'Oh, I don't mind having him in the house,' she went on quickly, clasping her gnarled hands on her knees, and smiling. 'We'll make up a bed for him here in the drawing-room. Gallagher sleeps in the room behind the kitchen, and I moved downstairs these last few years because of my rheumatism. We'll keep an eye on him.'

'You're very kind, ma'am,' said Halloran, moistening his lips with the tip of his tongue, 'but don't you know . . .'

'Yes, of course I know he's been away,' cut in the old woman energetically. 'And I think it's an absolute disgrace. Willie was always a bit different, of course, by local standards, and he certainly drank too much, but I don't believe for a moment that he was ever insane, do you?'

Halloran shook his head in agreement and told her who he was. Mrs Whittaker listened carefully, her head to one side, her sunken blue eyes glazed with age, fixed on the big man's ruddy face.

'There,' she exclaimed when he had finished, 'I always suspected it. They got rid of him because of the place. Everybody said so at the time, including my brother who knew Willie better than anybody. The asylums are full of people that nobody wants.' She bent and stroked the Cairn's ear. 'Sam here is thirteen, which makes him equal to ninety-one.' She chuckled. 'But there's life in the old dog yet. Isn't that right, Sammy?'

Sam wagged his tail and grunted.

'By the way,' went on Mrs Whittaker, looking up with her

sharp, candid glance, 'how is he getting on with his people?'

'So-so,' replied Halloran, waving his hand in a see-saw movement.

'I gathered that. I get the news of the place from Patch who's in town every night since he got his auto-cycle. I'm told that his brother and sister-in-law haven't been to see him, and that Chris's girl has left him over it. Is that true?'

'I'm afraid so. Willie said something about it this afternoon.' Halloran sniffed his brandy.

'Chris is a fine fellow. I hear he insisted on keeping Willie when he came home. That was generous of him, but of course . . .' Mrs Whittaker shrugged and shook her head. Suddenly she chuckled again, and looked at Halloran with a twinkle. 'D'you know it might be a very good thing if Dr Wilson says that he shouldn't be moved for a bit. Do you follow me?'

'Yes, I think I do, ma'am.'

Mrs Whittaker heaved herself painfully out of her chair and went to the table where she had left the bottle of brandy.

'It's just occurred to me that I never offered a glass to Gallagher, and the smell of it in the house will drive him mad.' She took up the bottle and hugged it against her bosom. 'I'll have a tiny drop myself when I get back to keep you company. I'm strictly forbidden it, of course, on account of my rheumatism, which makes it all the nicer when I do have an excuse.'

Halloran stood up and the old lady left the room. Sam struggled to his feet and followed her out, sniffing the worn carpet in the trail of her footsteps. It was only then that Halloran realised that he was blind.

He remained standing alone in the room, his glass clutched against his ribs. The high carved ceiling seemed dim and far away in the fading light. The mottled damp stains, part of the scheme of things in every house in the district, merged into the shadows in the corners. The big chintz-covered sofa was pushed against the wall facing the windows. The occasional tables of satinwood and ebony were heaped with framed photographs, silverware and a collection of porcelain snuff-boxes. A huge gilt mirror loomed over the mantelpiece, which was covered with sea-shells. At one end of it a ball of red knitting wool was wedged between a glass paperweight and a silver candlestick. Two needlework pictures hung on either side of the fireplace, McDonogh's Christmas calendar tacked on the wall under one of them.

Halloran sipped his brandy, and then, forgetting what he had been told about fine cognac, took a long swig of it. He puffed out his lips and shook his head, scratching his chest lazily as he continued the examination of the room. Most of the space in the centre facing the fire was taken up by a huge concert grand piano. It was closed, covered with green baize, and on the middle of it stood a white plaster-cast of a hand pointing towards the covered keyboard. The fingers were bent and raised a little like those of a pianist about to begin playing. In the darkening room the alabaster was bone white, and the fingers seemed almost to move as the firelight flickered over them. Halloran held his glass against his stomach and stared at it.

'Hullo there.'

Mrs Whittaker had come back into the room holding a paraffin lamp. She held it away from her and followed Halloran's gaze.

'That's a cast of my brother's hand,' she explained. 'An artist friend of his in London did it long ago. It's a wonderful likeness too, he had marvellous hands.' She placed the lamp on the end of the mantelpiece beside the ball of wool. In the pale yellow light the hand seemed even whiter than before. Carrying the bottle, which she had been holding in her other hand, the old woman went over to a table behind the piano and took a glass from a silver tray. She poured herself a finger of brandy and came back to her chair.

'Cheers,' she said to Halloran, her blue eyes twinkling merrily. 'Let's drink to our little plan. I hope it succeeds.'

'So do I, ma'am,' replied Halloran, lowering himself carefully into his low chair, and planting his big feet wide apart on the hearth-rug, as if to steady himself. 'Is Willie all right?'

'Quite comfortable now, dozing a bit, and he hasn't been sick.' She held her glass under her nose and stared into the fire. 'It's only now I'm beginning to recognise him. You know it's a strange thing but I saw him the day he came back, outside Summerhill. I must have sensed who it was, but I didn't know him. I suppose it's the white hair. Otherwise his face has changed amazingly little when you really look at him.'

'I often wondered where he learned all those French songs,' said Halloran, waving his glass at the piano.

'That's right,' said Mrs Whittaker, pointing with her own glass, 'at that piano. My brother taught him.'

'He took an interest in Willie?' asked Halloran lightly, looking at Sam as the old dog scratched feebly at the rug before he lay down at his mistress's feet.

'Yes, they were great friends.' Mrs Whittaker's blue eyes were round, which gave her handsome wrinkled face an expression of perpetual wonder. 'He sort of adopted Willie.' She smiled at Halloran. 'We were all very gay then, Willie was such fun, full of life. Did you ever hear about the concert he sang at for Father Mannix's new church? In those days Father Mannix was curate here in Esker, which is our parish, although Summerhill is in the town parish. Anyhow, Willie learned a very naughty French song and sang it slowly as if it were a hymn. Everybody was terribly impressed. Not one of them knew a word of French. My brother, Roger, laughed and laughed.' She sipped her brandy and chuckled. 'I'm afraid it was he taught Willie the song.' She put down her glass and looked around the room. 'Do you know I think I have an old photograph of them together. I remember quite well taking it on the front steps.'

She got up and went to one of the tables at the end of the room. Halloran looked at the white hand poised over the piano. He eased forward in his chair and drew his knees together.

The old woman came back and handed him a photograph. It

was an enlarged snapshot of two men standing before an open door. One was tall, fair-haired, heavily built, with a long face, hooded eyes and a wide curved mouth. He was smiling, looking straight into the camera with an expression at once sleepy and watchful. One long pointed hand was holding a cigarette in front of his chest; the other was thrown about the shoulders of the young man at his side. It was unmistakably Willie, his slanted eyes screwed up, his face tilted away from the camera as if he had heard a sudden sound. His figure was the same, slim with sloping shoulders; but a mop of black curling hair fell over his forehead. His hands were clasped behind his back, and he was dressed in a pair of belted flannels and an open-necked shirt, with the sleeves rolled up above his elbows.

Halloran handed back the snapshot in silence to Mrs Whittaker, who put it down on the piano. She looked at Halloran's glass and picked up the bottle of brandy.

'Here,' she said smilingly, 'have another spot of this.'

'I don't think I ought to, ma'am. I have to drive, you know.' Halloran covered the top of the glass with his hand.

'Nonsense,' said Mrs Whittaker uncorking the bottle, 'you don't look like the kind of man to be knocked sideways by two glasses of brandy. Hold up that.'

Halloran smiled with one side of his mouth and did as he was told. Then he remembered his manners, and slowly rose to his feet, lifting the bottle in the old woman's hand with the rim of his glass as he did so. Mrs Whittaker chuckled as she looked up at the burly man towering over her and went back to her chair at the foot of which the sightless dog was pointing his grey muzzle at her.

'It's sad to see Willie so old and ill,' she said when they were seated again. 'One never gets used to it.'

'Is your brother long dead?' asked Halloran gently.

'Twenty years. I miss him a great deal even now. Especially now. Although I used often to feel that both our lives here were wasted. Certainly his was. All the same I never really regretted coming back.'

'Coming back?' A log collapsed in a cloud of feathery ash. Mrs Whittaker leaned forward and took another block from the box beside her. Halloran got up and took it from her.

'Let me do that, please.'

'Oh, thank you so much.'

He raked the fire and settled the log in its place. Back in his chair he looked at the old woman with raised eyebrows, his large hands planted firmly on his knees, his brandy glass on the floor beside him. She was staring at the crackling wood, her round eyes screwed up, her lips pursed reflectively.

'You see,' she began, 'my brother's wife died young and very suddenly in childbirth. The baby was lost with her. It was a terrible tragedy for Roger – my brother – especially since our mother was still living, and quite helpless from a stroke.' She paused, straightened her shoulder-blades with a slight grimace of pain, and went on: 'I had married some years before and gone to live in London.' She paused, and then said simply: 'My husband left me. Went off with somebody. I never heard from him again. I don't even know if he's still living. So I took a secretarial job in Harrods, and was rather enjoying making a new life for myself when Roger's wife died, and he asked me to come back.' She squared her shoulders again with a frown and finished her brandy. 'This thing goes to my head. Well, anyway, I never really intended to stay, just put him over a bad period and then go back. But what with one thing and another, time passed, and well, here I am.' She shrugged and smiled again, stroking Sam's back with her shoe. 'Perhaps it's better than living in a bed-sitter in London.'

Sam raised his head and wheezed. It was almost dark outside. The white hand on the piano stood out in sharp relief against the shadows gathering behind it.

'Poor Roger was so helpless,' she went on musingly. 'He was never very much interested in farming, although he tried very hard. He was an only son, and of course my parents wanted him to have the place, which was prosperous in those days.

Then he fell in love and married, and after that there was my mother to be considered. She survived Roger by a year. In a sense I suppose he was trapped.'

'Yes,' said Halloran quietly, picking up his glass, 'trapped.'

'I thought at first that when he got over the grief and shock that he'd marry again, and I could go back to London. But he never did, although there were a lot of girls interested in him. One in particular.' She grasped the arm of her chair and moved her stiff body, slowly from side to side, holding her empty glass carefully. 'Do you know who it was?'

Halloran shook his head.

'Willie's sister-in-law. The present Mrs Ryan. She was Mary McDonogh then.'

'What!' Halloran jerked up his massive head and opened his mouth in astonishment.

'Yes, indeed. I think she was very keen on Roger, and I think he did consider it for a while. But nothing came of it. I often thought it was rather a pity in a way. I never liked her much. But she'd have managed the place, and then she had that business and everything, although that came afterwards. She was quite poor in those days, but she had great vitality.'

'I see.' Halloran stroked his forehead with his blunt finger-tips.

'So Roger and I stayed on here. Oh, he was never made for farming, but by then it was too late for him to cut loose. He was forty, and even if he sold the place he'd have got nothing for it, it was during the economic war. Besides he'd been brought up to be a gentleman farmer. He should have been a doctor or something in Dublin or London, where he could go to concerts, and meet people he could talk to and make his own life.' She sighed and left down her empty glass. 'However, he didn't complain, and we used to have a lot of fun, especially with Willie, whom we both were devoted to. He used to sing, and make fun, and was a wonderful mimic. And there were other friends too, young men that Willie knew, and used to bring along with him. As he grew older Roger liked the company of young people.' She chuckled and raised a finger at Halloran. ' I suppose we all do. Which no doubt is why I am boring you with all this talk.'

Halloran shook his grizzled red head and smiled ruefully.

' I'm not young, ma'am, and you're not boring me at all.'

Mrs Whittaker twisted round stiffly and peered at the window. Headlamps flared across the room and gravel crunched outside.

' Well, I won't bore you any longer,' she said, struggling to her feet. ' That's the doctor. I suppose we'd better go and meet him.' She stopped and looked at Halloran, who had risen and was staring at the white hand. ' D'you know, I think we ought to insist on Willie's staying. Doc Wilson is rather an old dear as well as being an old fool, and I can usually get around him.'

Halloran nodded, and finished off his glass quickly. He followed the old woman and the blind dog out of the haunted room, rubbing his hands nervously together.

MISS WHITE slid through the open door and took up her post. Outside the November sky was crystal blue with the promise of frost; and the sun was going down behind the black horizon in a crimson glow that would have done credit to one of Mrs O'Neill's watercolours. That large, impassive lady was seated as ever in her basket chair, knitting a bright blue scarf. Click-click went her purple needles. Her task was nearing completion, and the long length of knitted wool coiled and twisted on her lap like a live thing as she worked.

'How is himself?' asked Miss White, slipping a pencil from behind her ear, and hiding it in the pocket of her mannish grey costume.

'Better,' replied her neighbour placidly without lifting her eyes.

'I'm so glad to hear it. Glory be to God, what a cough! I could hear him last night through the wall when I was in bed. The poor man!'

Mrs O'Neill dropped a stitch and bit her lip with annoyance. Kathleen, who was frying eggs and bacon for her sick father, did not turn from the range. She flipped the egg round with a knife. Danny O'Neill liked it hard. Miss White's nostrils quivered as she inhaled the smoky acrid smell of the small untidy kitchen.

'It's going to freeze though,' went on the visitor. Her shoulder was more than usually itchy, for instead of rubbing it against the doorpost, she coiled back one of her serpentine arms and scratched it delicately, her eyes raised to heaven, her lips pursed with refinement. 'That ought to kill the germs.'

'He got it in the church,' said Mrs O'Neill, needling steadily

93

on. ' Nothing but cough, cough, cough and the sermons never-ending. People have no consideration in the house of God. Not a scrap of self-control. You can hardly hear a word the priest says.'

' You don't have to,' replied Miss White tartly. ' More money needed.' She cupped her hand behind her ear and leaned the upper part of her body sideways through the door. After listening intently for a few moments she slithered back again, and crossed her arms across her bosom. ' I thought it was the bell, but it's the telephone in Hannigans.'

' God bless your hearing,' said Mrs O'Neill, raising her big eyes for the first time, and smiling her sweet smile. Kathleen put the bacon and eggs on a plate and slid them into the oven.

' I agree with you about the coughing in the church,' went on Miss White. ' I never heard anything like it on All Souls' Day when I was doing my visits.' She scratched her shoulder again and looked at the blackened ceiling. ' How many did you do?'

' I did one for every deceased member of my family,' said Mrs O'Neill in a slow, far-away voice. ' And lit candles for the few that's still living and in need of them. Not all relations either.' She turned her massive head and looked at her daughter's back. Kathleen was pouring warm water into the teapot to rinse it. ' I'll have scrambled eggs, alannah.' Her voice became sharp and distinct.

' Aren't you blessed that you have so few Holy Souls to pray for,' sighed Miss White. ' My family was perfectly enormous. Seventy-eight first cousins alone, and thirty-nine of them dead. First of all, of course, poor dear mother and father, I do six visits for them alone, and then my sister Helen who married Mr Justice Evan's nephew-in-law, and then my brother Tom who was in the motor business in America, and then . . .'

' Mrs Hannigan, whose telephone you heard ringing just now, did one hundred and fifty-three visits,' cut in Mrs

O'Neill, clicking away as the blue scarf snaked down her lap and over her knees.

'She did not,' snapped Miss White, grasping the doorpost for support. 'She was in the church the same time as me, and she did three visits less. I detest all that holier-than-thou nonsense that she carries on with. It's so common.'

'There are three churches in the town,' went on Mrs O'Neill implacably. 'She spread them out.' She took up the scarf and spread that out between her outstretched hands, her swarthy face softening with a sense of achievement. Then she glanced up with a quickened voice. 'Kathleen, surely the tea is ready.'

Kathleen took the plate out of the oven and put it on the tray which she had prepared on the table beside her mother's wool, paints and bric-à-brac. She was about to pick it up when Mrs O'Neill spoke sharply again.

'You're forgetting the tea, alannah.'

Kathleen turned round, and stared dully out on the door as if Miss White were not there. She wiped her sweating forehead with her bare arm and sighed. Her eyes were puffy and tiny beads of perspiration glistened on her upper lip. A ring of sweat stained the armpits of her faded print frock. It was too tight for her and Miss White's thin lips curled with disapproval as she inspected the girl's high taut breasts, the nipples of which were clearly outlined under the thin cotton. She was bare-legged and her feet were thrust into carpet-slippers.

She put the teapot on the tray and walked to the door, moving with a sort of lazy insolence. Her unawareness of her firm, heavy-thighed body emphasised that animal vitality of which she herself, apathetic and preoccupied, did not seem to be conscious. She was like a half-naked woman walking in her sleep.

Miss White's lean, sinuous body twitched as she listened to the slip-slop of Kathleen's slippers on the linoleum-covered stairs.

'A sensible girl,' she hissed softly, ' to throw his diamonds back into his face.' She lingered on the final sibilant, her body

95

poised as if to strike, her small lizard head moving from side to side as her shoulders twitched like two small trapped animals inside her tweed costume.

'The O'Neills were always high-spirited,' said the other woman, her heavy eyelids closed, as she worked on automatically, her gypsy face the colour of melted butter.

'And so well they might. A family as old in the town as my own. It was about time she realised that fellow was no class for her. I admire a girl of spirit.' She stiffened, cocked her ear again by the open door, then relaxed, and turned to Mrs O'Neill with a little smile. 'Of course, it's a pity that people are saying that he turned her down.'

'They always say that.' Mrs O'Neill gave a sudden silvery laugh, which topped her slow deep voice like icing on a rich Christmas cake. 'They said the same thing about you when that British officer you were engaged to was transferred in nineteen-nineteen.' She lifted her lazy eyelids to look at Miss White, rigid now as she clawed the doorpost behind her. 'Remember? It wasn't true then, was it?'

'No.'

'And it isn't true now. Kathleen is a proud girl, as well she might be. I'd like to see the man that'd get away with jilting her.' The purple needles stopped clicking, as she laid down the scarf and gazed dreamily in front of her. 'It's a long time since the O'Neills were kings in Ulster, but we don't forget.'

'Well, I for one am glad that she's not going to marry into that set of jumped-up nobodies.'

Mrs O'Neill did not reply. She started to knit again. Miss White stared at her neighbour's smooth impassive face, and waited.

'Of course lovers have those quarrels from time to time,' Kathleen's mother went on, opening her needles and counting her stitches with narrowed eyes. 'The course of true love never did run smooth. I've known many happy marriages where the engagement was broken off half-a-dozen times. If they make it up I won't stand in their way. After all, times are changed.

The old families are dying out, and I must say I always liked Chris myself. A very respectable boy.' She sighed luxuriously, her vast bosom heaving beneath her thick yellow cardigan.

'What's the good of that when there's insanity in the family?' snapped back Miss White.

'I hear,' purred the fat woman, 'that the uncle is failing.'

Miss White laughed, a corncrake sound very different from her neighbour's tinkling merriment.

'That was a nice upset for the royal family, that was,' she crowed. 'Imagine that lunatic walking up Mrs Whittaker's avenue with his keeper – his keeper, mark you, and falling in a fit on the doorstep. And then laid up for three days in a stranger's house. A right laughing stock, I must say.'

'I heard it. Wasn't Mrs Whittaker a brave woman to look after him?'

Miss White drew herself up and raised her sharp nose.

'Mrs Whittaker is a lady,' she declared shrilly. 'Blood will out.'

'A good old family,' murmured Mrs O'Neill, 'although of course they came from Mayo originally. They're only a hundred years out there.'

'Well, anyway, Mayo or no Mayo, she raised the Ryans rightly. Such comings and goings! Chris racing out to Esker in his car, and the father calling twice a day, and a special ambulance to take him back to Summerhill, where I hear they're attending on him hand and foot.' She paused for breath. 'Even the Queen Mother herself. Nobody is going to beat her when it comes to the corporal works of mercy. If Mrs Whittaker is prepared to nurse him, so is she. And how!' She let slip the vulgarism in her excitement.

'Strange that they didn't put him in the County Home,' said Mrs O'Neill, smothering a yawn with the back of her plump, beringed hand.

'Oh no, oh no,' Miss White's shoulders heaved and shuddered like two cats in a bag. 'That would be showing them up rightly. It was all right to have him on the country – paid for by you and me – in the asylum. After all lunatics have to be looked after somewhere. But the County Home, or even the hospital wouldn't be good enough for that clan, now that he's home and everybody knows that he's dying on his feet. Look at how Mrs Whittaker nursed that crippled mother of hers, and then her poor brother during that awful illness . . .'

'What did he die of?' Mrs O'Neill blinked at her knitting.

'Cancer.' Miss White covered her breasts with her crossed hands and looked up to the ceiling. 'The poor fellow, in the prime of life, and a real gentleman.' She sighed and pressed her hands tighter against her breasts. 'And then look at the way Lady Fitzharold looked after her old father for years and years and years. Oh no, the best people don't send their sick to hospital, and naturally the Ryans copy everything they see in that line. All the more since everybody is saying that they treated him so badly that he had to be nursed for three nights in a strange house.'

'Bad for business too,' murmured Mrs O'Neill with a click.

Miss White took a step forward, a daring adventure for her since it meant she could only keep the doorpost in touch with her fingertips extended behind her, like a bird about to take wing. She looked at Mrs O'Neill's scarf snaking over her lap. The needles clicked busily for a few minutes; then their tempo changed, the sleepy eyes were slowly unhooded, and the massive head rose to confront the other woman.

'And that isn't all that's changed up in the hall either,' confided Miss White breathlessly. 'Every cloud has a silver lining, as they say, for someone.' She paused to allow her neighbour's curiosity to fester. But Mrs O'Neill continued to look at her benignly, a sweet smile on her soft pink lips.

Suddenly Miss White stepped back to her post as swiftly and tautly as if she had been leaning forward at the end of a piece of elastic.

'Mrs Carroll has been up to tea,' she went on, never once taking her eyes from Mrs O'Neill's face during her agile manoeuvre. The old gypsy remained smiling sweetly. 'And Susan.'

Miss White looked significantly at the door through which Kathleen had gone with her father's tea. 'It looks to me as if a little match-making is taking place. If Kathleen won't have Christopher with a lunatic in the house, there are others – ' She broke off and slid around the door, her nose high, her ear cocked. 'The bell in the shop,' she whispered, fishing in her pocket for her pencils and disappearing.

Mrs O'Neill knitted on placidly for a few minutes, watching her needles with half-closed eyes. Presently, with a little dreamy sigh she rolled up the scarf, put it on the table beside her, and heaved herself out of her chair. She sniffed, relishing the smell of fried bacon that still hung about the kitchen, as she waddled to the door.

'Kathleen,' she called plaintively in her deep voice. 'Come down a minute, I want you.'

⪻⪻⪻ 4 ⪼⪼⪼

THE TALL, STATELY WOMAN in the Persian lamb coat and the purple toque moved forward to greet her hostess with both hands outstretched. One held a weighty volume and a dangling chamois glove; and the other was grasped by Mary Ryan and warmly pressed.

'How lovely to see you, Kitty. Do come in.'

Mrs Carroll put the book on the hall table and peeled off her other glove. She patted her blue curls on which the toque was set at a daringly rakish angle.

'I brought you back your book, Mary,' she smiled. 'I just loved it. Most interesting. What a splendid woman! I always admired her tremendously.' She untied her grey silk scarf, and glanced at her handsome reflection complacently in the mirror.

Mary looked at the book, its dust-jacket carefully covered in brown paper. She blinked and smiled gently, smoothing her black silk cocktail dress over her angular hips.

'Queen Mary,' she murmured affectionately. 'A wonderful biography.'

They went into the drawing room. The central heating had been turned up, and a huge fire burned in the grate. A desert blast of hot air gave the room the atmosphere of a conservatory. Its porcelain vases, silver bowls and heavily waxed wood surfaces might have been strange exotic blooms; the deep bulky sofa and armchairs great lumps of forced fungi.

'What a glorious coat,' said Mary, helping her friend out of it, and laying it tenderly across a striped Regency chair. 'I adore Persian lamb.' She stroked the soft silky curls sensuously.

'Ted had a cousin in the wholesale drapery in Dublin,'

explained Kitty Carroll, holding her scarf by the tips and rubbing it gently against the back of her neck. 'I got it cheap. I don't see why I should pay fifty per cent more in a shop for a fur coat anyway.'

'I love your dress,' said Mary, reaching out and touching one of Kitty's plump arms encased in stiff blue poplin.

'I got it in London actually, coming back from the Holy Land last Easter.' She giggled naughtily. 'I wore it over that red silk thing I had for the bridge tournament in Dun Laoghaire last year. I must have looked enormous coming through the customs.'

She lowered herself on to the sofa, tucking her legs in tightly against the pleated cover. Unlike Mary she had bad legs, thick and shapeless. Otherwise the two women, so dissimilar in size and figure, had a certain quality in common. They were both hothouse plants: products of years of rich foods, over-heated houses, soft beds, fine linen, and financial security, privileges which had branded them more particularly because they were intensely aware of them. Scented, over-dressed, over-jewelled, they might both have been expensive blooms forced for the same market. The one, slim, sinuous, waxy – a black orchid; the other, fleshly rounded, florid – a prize begonia.

'I love your Crown Derby,' said Kitty looking at the lace-covered table set in front of her, with its silver kettle sitting swan-like on its paraffin nest. 'I think it gives tea a flavour that you miss with ordinary china.' She reached out and touched the handle of the nearest cup. 'The Avondale auction, wasn't it, Mary?'

'Yes, indeed. I thought I was robbed at the time, but when I see the price Crown Derby is making now . . .' she threw up her hands and turned down her mouth.

'The Americans, dear. You can't get into an auction now for the dealers from Dublin. Thank God we were both in on the ground floor.' Kitty tugged at her scarf again, settling it carefully so as to expose the diamond brooch pinned on her queenly bosom.

'Isn't that new, Kitty?' Mary leaned forward and peered at the brooch.

Kitty twisted her head sideways and looked at it smilingly.

'Last week,' she said tenderly. 'A present from Ted. Our twenty-fifth anniversary.'

'Oh, how wonderful, Kitty! It's gorgeous.'

Kitty unpinned it graciously and handed it to her friend, who cupped it in her hands, cradling it to and fro so that the stones flashed in the firelight. Presently she stood up before the mirror and held it against her breast, shaking her head in admiration.

'I'm green with envy, Kitty,' she said as she handed it back with religious gentleness.

'Oh, it's nothing, Mary. It's the thought that matters.' She replaced it on its poplin cushion and patted it. 'If he had given me a box of chocolates I'd have thought as much of it.' Her large brown eyes suddenly glistened with tears, and she bit her lip. 'I know you don't believe that,' she went on, reaching out and laying her small white hand on Mrs Ryan's wrist. 'But it's true. You see I didn't think he'd remember.' She ran a forefinger under her damp eyelids. 'And not only that, but Susan gave me a bottle of scent. "Joy". Here, smell.' She leaned her ample shoulder in Mary's direction. The other woman closed her eyes as she sniffed the famous perfume with its jasmine foundation with which Kitty had so liberally sprayed herself.

'And not only that, dear, but she bought Ned a lovely leather dressing-case. We didn't even know she knew the date. So we opened a bottle of champagne, and I went upstairs to have a good old weep, and Ned went out and got drunk.' She sniffed and sucked in her lower lip. 'Ah, sure it was a lovely anniversary altogether, thanks be to God and his Blessed Mother.'

'Amen,' said Mrs Ryan fervently, taking out her handkerchief which was sprayed with Balenciaga's "Granada". She sniffed it delicately, while above the fine cambric her hollow eyes flickered restlessly as Kitty gazed sentimentally into the fire.

'And how is Susan, Kitty?' she asked after a decent interval.

Kitty scrabbled in her handbag and brought out her compact.

'Oh, yes, I forgot to tell you, Mary,' she said busily repairing her flushed face. 'This is Loretta's day off and Susan stayed at home to get Ned's tea. The way she fusses over that man! But she'll be along presently. Ned has a meeting at half-four, with these dreadful Union men.'

'Aren't you blessed with Susan,' said Mary wistfully.

'The best daughter,' declared Kitty, snapping her gold compact shut, 'that any mother ever had. I mean to say, you wouldn't think that a girl with her education would be content helping about the house, and fussing over her old parents the way she does. When I see the way other girls of her age are carrying on, I thank God every hour of the day.'

'Ah, but look at the way Susan was brought up . . .'

'That doesn't mean a thing nowadays, so far as I can see, dear. And let's face it, Ned and I are dull company for a girl like Susan. We're just lucky, that's all.'

'Oh, come now, Kitty.'

'Well, it's true, dear. Susan isn't like us at all. Ned and I are just two ordinary people with ordinary interests. But Susan . . .?' She stopped and bent her head to smell her raised shoulder. 'All we want is for her to be happy,' she went on in a small voice.

Mary got up and drew the curtains with a soft swish. She plucked the ends together jerkily and cleared her throat.

'I suppose we'd better wait until Susan arrives, Kitty,' she said.

'Well, if you don't mind, Mary.'

'I don't know if Chris will be here this afternoon, Kitty. He said he would, but it all depends on how his uncle is.'

Mary lingered in front of the curtains, her head held high,

her hands pressed against her thighs like an actress taking an unsure call before a risky audience.

Kitty grasped the arm of the sofa and levered her regal torso round to face her hostess.

' How is he?' she asked kindly. ' Willie, I mean.'

' Oh, he's much improved.' Mary picked up a box of matches from a table and shook it. Going back to her place on the sofa she put the matches on the tray beside the kettle. ' He's up and about again. Of course he's a bit weak and shaky, and for a day or two we were all very worried. Dr Wilson says his heart is bad, which was a great shock to us all. Quite unexpected.' She pressed her lips together and breathed deeply through her nose. ' He may live for some years, and . . .' she broke off and shrugged her shoulders.

Kitty covered the place where she imagined her heart was with her hand.

' I had an aunt who was like that according to the doctors. She lived to be eighty-eight.'

' I'm afraid poor Willie won't make that age. It's really touching the way Chris looks after him. Naturally Michael and I wanted to get a nurse, but he wouldn't hear of it. Besides, Dr Wilson says there's no necessity for him to stay in bed. He isn't really any trouble at all.' Having delivered herself of this ambiguous statement, she tugged at the neck of her low-cut frock and twisted her head. Her goitre thrust itself brazenly forward, adding a touch of the grotesque to her exaggerated features. ' I think all he wants is affection really.'

' Oh yes,' exclaimed Kitty, clutching her waist as she drew herself up inside her rubber corset. ' That's what everybody wants when they get old. That's what I mean about Susan.' She released herself, and breathed out slowly and carefully, her majestic bosom settling comfortably on its pneumatic column. ' I mean to say, there's no point in denying that Ned can be difficult at times, especially when he's had one over the eight. And yet Susan never gets irritable with him, as I do, to tell the truth. She seems to be one of those people who really like their elders.' She coughed delicately into a clenched fist. 'Like Chris.'

For a few minutes the two women sat silently staring into the fire.

Rousing themselves from their tactful contemplation they turned and smiled at each other, a smile of perfect understanding. But the moment of truth did not last long. The clock struck half-four. Kitty looked at it and consulted her own jewelled wristwatch, which she held up on an arched wrist half an inch from her round pug nose, as if the time were difficult of belief and in need of corroboration.

'That's funny,' she said, tapping the glass with sensibly short but brilliantly painted nails. 'She said she'd be here by twenty-past at the latest, and Ned has his meeting, I wonder . . .'

'Would you like to ring up, Kitty dear?' Mary consulted her own watch.

'I think I would, if you don't mind. It's odd, because Susan is never late, she's a most punctual child.' She rose with the airy lightness of a woman whose fat is part of her personality, indulged, approved, and carried blithely upon bones evolved by nature for that very purpose.

'You know where the phone is, don't you, Kitty?'

'Of course, dear.'

Mary rustled to her feet in sympathy, while Kitty sailed quickly out of the room and closed the door gently but firmly behind her.

Mrs Ryan waited, staring at her reflection in the mirror. She twisted round and peered down to inspect the seams of her nylons. Keeping an eye on the door, she picked her nose with her little finger and popped it into her mouth. She had just finished and was about to turn her back to the fire when Kitty came back, stroking her nose and looking thoughtful.

'No reply from the house,' she said, 'so I rang up the office and got on to Ned. He says he dropped her at the gate a quarter of an hour ago – as you know I have the second car today. I can't understand it.'

'Perhaps she met somebody at the gate?' suggested Mary hopefully. 'You know how one always runs into somebody when one has an appointment.'

'Mmm.' Kitty sounded doubtful. 'We'll wait another few minutes anyway. You know what Susan is like. She'll listen to some old jackass telling a tale of woe for ages, because she's simply too kind-hearted to shake them off.'

'That's one thing,' said Mary firmly, 'she'll have to learn.'

Instinctively the two women stopped and eyed each other, running their eyes slowly with a sort of shameless gluttony over hair, skin, clothes, jewels, and shoes. Silently with fixed stares and mouths parted hungrily, they moved closer together.

'Now, Kitty,' said Mrs Ryan, touching the material of her friend's dress, 'you must tell me the name of that shop in London.'

'I will if you tell me where you got those shoes. I noticed them the minute I got in. They're not Irish.'

Rings were flashed and examined; hair was patted, and the skills of various Dublin coiffeurs commented upon. Kitty kneaded her jawline with stumpy fingers and gave the name of a new cream; Mary responded with the address of a corset-maker in Curzon Street. Side by side they moved about the stifling room, fingering silver, stroking satin and velvet, and praising pieces of auction china. Kitty guessed high: Mary admitted to half the price. They inhaled again and again the incense of each other's expensive scent; they lingered with caressing hands beside the smooth surfaces of tables loaded with the loot of crumbling mansion houses. They put their heads together comparing consecrated possessions in low tremulous voices. With arms entwined they stood for some minutes in silent communion before a riotous whirl of colour by Jack B. Yeats, bought for a song fifteen years before, framed in gold leaf, and now representing a profit of two hundred per cent. They drew apart, their restless eyes strained with religious fervour, and admired again their own rich vestments: symbols of an ancient faith, whose abundant graces were made manifest to all in their persons and in their homes. Like pilgrims, humbly proud and grateful at a shrine loaded with images that glorified and proclaimed their own pursuit of revelation, they retraced their steps and drew comfort once again in the contemplation of things that do not wilt or die or fall away with the apostate years. At last, drooping a little, but refreshed in spirit, they turned their eyes towards the silver vessels laid upon the snowy table.

'I think,' said Mary, taking up the matches and preparing to light the lamp, 'we might as well have that tea.'

⤜⤜⤜ 5 ⤛⤛⤛

'HELLO, THERE.'

Chris leaned over from the driver's seat and called through the open window of the station wagon. The blonde girl in the leather coat looking into the drapery window turned round and looked about her with a mildly inquisitive glance. She was clutching her lamb-lined collar with both hands against the wind.

'Over here.' Chris opened the door. The girl crossed the path and leaned over the top of the open door.

'I thought you were at home,' she said, raising one eyebrow slightly. 'Having tea.' Her voice was light, clear, impersonal.

'I thought you were assisting at the ceremony too.' He crooked an elbow on the wheel, and stretched his other arm along the top of the seat. 'Was it called off, or something?'

'No.' The wind blew her golden hair across her eyes, and she pushed it back with one gloved finger.

'You'll catch cold, Susan.'

Susan Carroll laughed, and straightened up. She was about to push the door to when Chris grasped the handle and held it open.

'Come on, get in,' he said, picking up a couple of old newspapers from the seat and throwing them into the back of the wagon. Susan hesitated for a moment, looking at Chris's hand patting the leather beside him. Then she got in and the car drove off down the street.

'Going home?' she pointed in front of her.

Chris shook his head.

At this hour the main street of the town was busy. Shop

windows blazed, and the neon signs were going on: over McDonoghs, over Carroll's two pubs, outside the grocers, drapers, and supermarkets in the upper part of the street, the most competitive half-mile in the Midlands. It was a prosperous town, old and sleepy, and only newly aware of the garish. From one of the new supermarkets a loudspeaker announced amazing bargains at thirty second intervals. Cars moved at a snail's pace through the narrow thoroughfare, and lined the intersecting lanes leading down to the river.

It flowed in a great arc about the town, and at this hour was already almost invisible. Only the swaying reflections of the lights on the strand, bobbing like trawling flares on the waters, indicated its silent, menacing presence. And beyond, the frosty sunset sliced the dark horizon of the plain like a bloody knife.

Chris turned round in a filling station and faced back up the street again.

'I told them I might go,' he said, his voice instinctively adjusting itself to the slow tempo of the line of cars. It made him sound as if he was weighing every word. 'But I didn't intend to, not really. And then at the last moment I hopped in and made off. I thought you might be there.'

'I couldn't face it. Daddy dropped me at the gate, so I waited inside for a while and then came into town.'

'They'll be disappointed.'

'I expect so.' Susan took off one glove and laid it on her knee. She glanced at the massive stone front of Carroll's Imperial Hotel, well situated for parking near the church, where the street widened into a crescent. Chris turned off sharply on to the Summerhill road.

'But not if they could see us now,' he said, his voice lighter as he picked up speed. He switched on the headlamps. Trim semi-detached front gardens flashed by, ghostly and colourless like television stills. 'I'm going back to Summerhill, do you mind?'

'Of course not.'

Chris swerved to avoid a cow lumbering out from the grass margin. They had gained the open road.

'It's pretty awful, isn't it?' he went on in a staccato, forty mph voice. 'The match-making, I mean.'

'Oh God, yes.' Susan ran a bare hand through her hair and opened the top of her jacket. 'To give Daddy his due he offered to cut this meeting and fake a headache or something so that I could stay at home. But that'd only mean one up for him instead of Mummy.'

'It's a good thing I ran into you. If I had turned up . . .'

'Well, it'd have been pretty ghastly for you. I can just hear all those heavy hints, with Mummy getting all weepy about the best daughter that any woman ever had.'

'There would also be some mention of the best son in the world.' Chris gripped the wheel, his voice tense and rapid as he touched fifty.

'I wonder if they really believe it all?'

'I think they do. They believe what they want to believe.'

'It's horrible.' The clear voice was bitter. Chris glanced sideways, but Susan was looking away.

'How are things at home?' He slipped into third as they began to mount the hill above the town.

'Much the same. I could make quite a thing out of it if I wanted to. Sometimes I feel like one of those neutral states who go in for playing off East against West.'

'But you don't do it, do you?'

'The thing is that I do, sometimes,' she clutched her lamb-lined collar and opened it wide. 'Daddy bought me this jacket last week, and I took it because I wanted it. So then Mummy went into the sulks until she came up with these pearls.' She lifted the necklace from under her scarf and rubbed it under her chin.

'You're quite a valuable property.'

'Yes, quite. Property is the word.'

'Why don't you cut loose?'

'I wish it were as simple as that, Chris. It seems a horrid

smug thing to say, but I'm the only thing they have. And then, you see, I happen to be fond of them.' She broke off and drew her breath sharply. 'Oh God, now I'm condescending. But if only they'd learn to live together instead of fastening on me. Do you know, the only thing they ever talk to each other about is business. When that's finished they just gape, and look at me. And now I'm being disloyal as well as everything else.'

'And yet your mother is all agog just now to get rid of you.' Chris slowed down as they neared the Summerhill gate.

'That's business. Besides, she's calling the tune. That makes up for a lot, even apparently for the prospect of living alone with Daddy for the rest of her life.'

The station wagon bumped along the uneven avenue, its headlamps turning the big beech to silver. The façade of the long ivied farmhouse was washed flat in the glare.

'Was it always like that, Susan?' asked Chris, turning the car into the stable-yard.

'As long as I can remember. Apparently this thing with the woman in Dublin had been going on since I was about ten. She never forgave him, and he never forgave her for finding out. It's all stupid, really, because when they had their silver jubilee recently I got Daddy to give her a brooch, and she broke down. He didn't want to give it, but I bullied him into it, to tell you the truth. Since then things haven't been so bad.'

Chris stopped the car and switched off the lights; but neither of them made an effort to get out. A square of light from the kitchen window glimmered on the bonnet.

'And you?' Susan pressed her back against the door and faced the shadowy figure beside her.

'So-so.' He said sulkily.

'How is your uncle?'

'Oh, he's all right. I wouldn't be surprised if he hadn't staged that fainting fit out at Mrs Whittaker's.'

'Oh no, Chris.'

Chris rubbed his forehead and shook his head in the darkness.

'I don't suppose you can blame him in a way. He's had a rotten deal all his life, and he doesn't trust anybody.'

'Not you?'

'I don't think so. And it irritates me. I admit I went for him a couple of times before he got sick, because it got on my nerves the way he acted, as if he were a servant or something. And I hated myself for it. But I did my best, although you can't wipe out twenty-five years just like that.'

'No,' said Susan slowly, 'that's something I've learned too.'

'Now I have them all about my ears like a swarm of bees, telling me to do this, that and the other. It's worse than it ever was. The latest is that he must be got to go to confession. Apparently he hasn't been to Mass for years, even before he went away. So I expect a call from the Reverend Mannix any day now.'

They were silent for a few minutes, neither daring to move in the intimate darkness. Presently Chris stretched his arm along the top of the seat and leaned towards the girl. She did not turn aside; and he kissed her on the lips, cupping the back of her neck in his hand, and stroking her leather-covered arm lightly. When he took his mouth gently away, he did not draw back, but took her chin and held it between his thumb and forefinger.

'Do I make a good substitute?' she said softly.

'No. You make a good beginning.'

He kissed her again, lightly and lingeringly. Her body relaxed, but she put her hand on his crouching shoulder and gently pushed him away.

'I'd like to meet Willie,' she said.

Chris opened the door for her, and then got out himself. They went inside the house through the back door.

Willie was sitting in the armchair in the kitchen with Toby at his feet. He looked up as they came in and the bitch barked and struggled to get to her feet. The old man caught her by the neck and held her fast as he watched the strange girl coming towards him with a smile on her face. Susan Carroll was one of those exquisite golden creatures that are sometimes produced by the most unlikely parents. The eyes which smiled at Willie were periwinkle blue, their expression good-humoured and slightly remote – she was short-sighted. A short, delicately sculptured nose, a wide mobile mouth, and a small firm chin gave character to a face at once vibrant, and slightly detached because of its beauty.

Willie rose slowly to his feet, and the blankets that covered his knees fell to the ground. Toby, liking the stranger, wagged her tail.

'This is Susan Carroll, Uncle Willie,' said Chris in a gruff, nervous voice.

'Hullo,' said Susan, holding out her hand.

Willie took it and bowed his head. Chris pulled out a chair from the wall and the girl sat down facing the old man. He stood looking down at her wonderingly. Susan laughed and looked around for Chris. But he had left the room. She stood up, picked up the blanket from the floor, and threw it over her arm.

'Do sit down,' she said, touching Willie's hand gently. He did so, and she placed the rug over his knees again.

'What age are you?' he asked suddenly with a smile.

'Twenty-three.' Susan unbuttoned her coat and took off her scarf before she sat down again.

'I'm sixty,' said Willie, running his fingers through his white hair. 'But I look eighty.'

'No, you don't. You look younger than your brother,' Susan put her gloves on her lap and crossed her long slender legs.

'I always looked younger than Michael,' Willie lifted his chin and ran his knuckles along his jaw-line, 'although I'm two years older. I got a shock when I saw him, he's fallen into flesh a great deal. I'd hate to get fat.' He paused and looked around the kitchen. 'Have you known Chris long?' he asked in a lower voice.

' All my life. We're neighbours. Perhaps you know my father, Ned Carroll. My mother was Kitty O'Connell before she married.'

Willie thought for a few moments and then shook his head.

' I don't remember them.' He shifted in his chair and plucked at the blanket. ' That's a nice coat you have on. You know how to dress.'

' My father bought it for me.'

' I suppose he's always buying you things, is he?'

' As a matter of fact he is,' replied Susan slowly. One of her gloves slipped from her lap to the ground. She bent to pick it up, but Willie was too quick for her. He threw the blanket aside and snatched the glove from the floor swiftly and lithely. Susan raised her eyebrows in surprise and smiled as Willie slipped his hand into the glove and held it out admiringly. It was a perfect fit.

' I always had small hands,' he said flexing his fingers. ' I never could get a man's glove to fit me.' He took it off slowly and handed it back. ' Have you many brothers and sisters?' he asked, picking up the blanket and throwing it over the back of his chair before sitting down again.

' No, I'm an only child.'

' Like Chris.' Willie chuckled and looked at the door. ' I expect he's giving us time to break the ice. You must come again.'

' I will if you like.' Susan put her elbows on her knee and cupped her chin in her hand. They smiled at each other.

' You like music,' said Willie with no question in his voice.

' Yes.'

' And you read.'

' Yes.'

' But you don't dance much, do you?'

Susan raised an eyebrow and looked at him quizzically.

' How on earth did you know that? Has Chris . . .'

' No, he never mentioned you. He doesn't talk about women much, I've noticed.'

114

' But why do you say . . .'

' Because I think you don't like crowds much, and you don't like being handled by strangers.'

Susan leaned back in her chair, and crooked one arm over the top.

' Yes,' she said thoughtfully, ' I think you're right.'

Willie nodded and smiled. With another quick look at the door he fumbled in his pocket, and brought out a five pound note.

' Will you do something for me?' he said in a low voice.

' Of course.'

' Would you mind buying me a pair of gloves like yours? I always loved good gloves. You don't mind, do you?'

Susan shook her head and slipped the note into her pocket.

' I wouldn't ask you if I thought you did. Michael gave me the money to buy a guitar, but I don't want that any more.'

Chris came back into the room, his face shining and smelling strongly of talcum powder. He clapped his hands heartily and smiled at Susan.

' Did you know that Uncle Willie is a great man for a song?' he said, putting his hands in his pockets and planting his legs wide apart. ' You two should have a lot in common.'

' I read somewhere that the Latin people sing when they're happy,' replied the girl quietly. ' But all our songs are sad.'

Willie looked at her and smiled.

' Oh, but Uncle Willie sings in French, don't you?' said Chris.

' Yes,' said his uncle enigmatically, ' but Susan knows French.'

The girl slipped her hand into a glove and laughed.

' Susan,' she said, ' is hand-in-glove.'

' What's that?' asked Chris, puzzled. ' What's that?'

⋘ 6 ⋙

WINTER SET IN. Holly berries blazed; and late roses shrivelled. Frosty mists blurred the edge of the world; and the river ran black in the short November afternoons. Beech leaves purpled like decaying flesh; and grey skeletal trunks raised their bony arms to the still sky. Smoke rose from chimneys straight and unwavering like stretched silk. Sounds sharpened and tingled through the naked land: trains that passed unnoticed through the murmurous autumn night now seemed to roar through shuttered rooms. The old slept longer.

Life took on a certain stiff formality on that chessboard landscape. Across the striped plain figures moved slowly and deliberately, at the will of forces they did not altogether understand.

At Summerhill, in the Ryans' town house, in the Carrolls' equally sumptuous villa nearby, and in Mrs O'Neill's stuffy little kitchen, the game, its pieces intricately locked, awaited the next move. A single pawn cannot give mate, but wins if it can be promoted. Willie, not unhappy, and unaware of the kings, queens, rooks, knights and bishops by whom he was surrounded, stood still in his little square, pleased, as pawns are, with small mercies. His new chamois gloves fitted him perfectly. He wore them often and inhaled their warm leathery smell luxuriously.

He was now quite a valuable pawn. Mrs Ryan and Kitty Carroll, after their adjournment over the tea things, were not altogether pleased when they discovered that the two young people had played their own game admirably, and without any prompting from behind the shoulder. But as the days passed and Chris and Susan continued to make exactly the right sort of moves, the mothers found themselves congratulating each other with growing conviction on their own prescience.

Willie was cherished as never before. Chris, his nerves soothed by the presence of a beautiful girl, found it easy to be kind and affectionate to his uncle again. Susan, suddenly thrust into the centre of the combat, looked forward in a straight line. There were elements of tenderness and understanding in her relationship with Willie Ryan which conceal from mortals the terrible inevitability of the pattern they help to form and to complete. For Susan too was a pawn. Although the clocks had been stopped for an interval, and the next move written down and sealed, the game was not at an end.

Mary and Kitty encouraged by the scent of victory now saw their opportunity to conquer with one final classic manoeuvre. That accomplished, checkmate would follow; and the fates would applaud the victors.

They could not stay still, these two women who, themselves defeated in their time by forces which seemed to them blind and lacking in skill, itched to rearrange with their jewelled fingers the positions of others.

'Wonderful, isn't it?' Kitty remarked one day, 'the way Willie has taken to Susan?'

'A spot of cream, Kitty?' Mary picked up the silver jug. Kitty nodded and stirred her tea slowly, a dreamy smile playing over her soft Renoir face.

'Well, I always said poor Willie was all right, if one knew how to handle him,' went on Mary, picking up the tongs and helping herself to a lump of sugar. 'Of course some people are primitive about cases like that. The law of the jungle is all they understand. But civilised people know how to manage these things. I knew Susan would like poor Willie when she met him.'

'So did I. Didn't I tell you how good Susan was with old people?'

The ormolu clock struck five; but they did not give it a glance. Today time was of no importance. Chris had called for Susan before Kitty set out on her call. Both of them felt thoroughly relaxed in their scented hothouse. They had been fed; their roots stirred in rich predictable soil – they swelled and bloomed.

'Of course, Kitty, Susan mustn't allow herself to get too attached to Willie, because . . .' Mary paused and looked down at the shoes which had incited her friend's curiosity.

'Because what?' Kitty's spoon tinkled in her saucer as she twisted round to inspect the other woman's face. Her voice was perfectly attuned to the sharp little chime.

'Well, for one thing he's a very sick man, you know. I'm afraid Susan won't have him long.' She sighed. 'None of us will. After all it's in the nature of things, isn't it? The young take over. But I hope it won't be too much of a break for her.'

Kitty relaxed and smiled gently. She raised her cup and stirred her tea placidly.

'Susan is a very practical girl, Mary. When the time comes – which God forbid – she'll cope, you'll see. She's a really wonderful manager.'

Mary twisted her shoe and admired its slender, pointed, deadly heel.

'I know, Kitty, but I wouldn't like to think of Susan wearing herself out with the care of an invalid.' She paused again. 'Especially if . . .' she let the implication float like a falling petal on the hothouse air.

Kitty left down her cup on the tray and turned round impulsively. Her eyes were shining, her begonia skin was radiant.

'Oh, I know what you mean, Mary dear,' she blurted out. 'But one mustn't talk about it. I never, never believe in interfering with young people. Let nature and true love and affection take their course, is my motto.'

'Of course, of course, Kitty.' Mary clasped her friend's hand while balancing her cup expertly on her lap. 'All the same, you know it's my dearest wish that Chris and . . .'

Kitty squeezed her hand.

'And mine too, dear. I'm praying night and day. Storming heaven, as poor mother – Lord be good to her – used to say.'

'Amen. But all the same, if our prayers are answered, I don't want Susan burdened, especially in those difficult first years.'

Kitty took her hand lingeringly away, wiped a tear from her eye, and reached for her cup again.

'The poor mites,' she sighed. 'How wonderful and terrible it all is.' She sipped her tea. 'Prayer, Mary, prayer is the only thing.'

Mary Ryan set down her tea half-finished and drew up her angular body. She blinked and pulled in the corners of her mouth.

'Willie might very well become a complete invalid, you know,' she said in a cold, clear voice. 'It might be too much for the poor girl.'

Kitty finished her tea with a neat little flick of the wrist.

'Ah, the nuns, the nuns, Mary! In Our Lady of Refuge they're so kind. How many have I seen them ease out of this life with the pure power of prayer.' She belched delicately into her fist. 'And very reasonable too. The Reverend Mother is a cousin of mine. Do you know, I think I'll have another cup of that delicious tea. Greedy me, I'm a hog.'

'But at the moment, of course . . .' Mary tilted the silver kettle.

'God forbid, dear. Only in the case of dire necessity.'

'Later on,' murmured Mary, closing the lid of the teapot. She left it to brew for a few minutes, and idled among the sugar lumps with the tongs, lifting and dropping, selecting and discarding the small cubes with great attention. 'And then there's one other thing.'

'What's that?' Kitty, who had been eyeing the sugar with a fond, sentimental gaze, turned with one of her swift pneumatically light movements and confronted the other woman. She thumped the cushion behind her with a sudden vicious little jab of her plump white hand.

'Well, you see,' began Mary, letting a cube fall and picking it up again, 'I'm afraid poor Willie doesn't go to his duties.

It was your mention of Our Lady of Refuge that brought it to my mind. By the way, you know that I had a cousin a nun there myself?'

Kitty expelled a long sighing breath, her bosom deflating like a punctured tyre. She closed her eyes and clasped her rosy cheeks in her two hands.

' Oh, the poor, poor man. May the Lord deliver us from all evil. How long, Mary dear?'

' Well, I really don't know, Kitty.' Mary knitted her jet-black brows as she concentrated on the ceremony of pouring tea. ' You know how some men are about these things. Two, isn't it?'

' Yes dear, thanks. Oh, God in heaven, what a terrible thing to have on one's conscience! The poor man. And in that state of health.'

' Is the tea all right?'

' Delicious, Mary, absolutely super.' She sipped and licked her lips.

' Did Susan say anything about it?' asked Mary, pouring out a cup for herself.

' Oh, no! I don't suppose it ever entered the child's mind.'

' Well,' said Mary firmly, ' something will have to be done about it. And soon.'

' I'll have a Mass said. No, I'll have two.'

' Naturally. So will I. But I'm afraid Willie is such a helpless person that somebody will have to make the first move for him. We simply can't take the risk of letting things drift. Now, if it were cancer or something, one would have time, but with a heart . . .' She stared over the rim of her cup with a worried expression.

' Father Mannix?' suggested Kitty, helping herself to another crumpet. ' I hear he's a great man with the old lags,' she coughed lightly. ' I mean with difficult cases.'

' I must say I don't like him much.'

' Nor me.' Kitty swallowed a bite of crumpet too fast, and choked. Mary took the cup from her friend's heaving lap while she coughed breathlessly, her rosy face turning a dark shade of scarlet.

'God bless you, Kitty.'

'Oh Lord,' panted Kitty, clutching her bosom. They were silent while she heaved and swayed and thumped her breast like a penitent in an agony of remorse. At last a semblance of decorum was restored, although Kitty's eyes were ruined with tears, and she lay back weakly against the satin cushions.

'Take a sip of tea,' said Mary, handing her her cup. Kitty complied with great care, and closed her eyes thankfully as she felt her windpipe clearing.

'Well, anyway,' she said presently, returning to the argument with renewed zeal. 'Will you put it up to Mannix?'

'It's my duty. And his too. After all he's the parish priest. It's his duty to call on the old sick people of the parish.'

'Instead of playing golf and driving round in that big yoke of a car he has. That's where all our money goes. Robbed we are. Nothing but one collection after another, and of course it's the same people who have to fork out each time.' She nibbled carefully at the crumpet and washed it down liberally with tea.

'Isn't it terrible! But what can we do? Business is business.'

'Well, it's the least he can do for you after all you've given him. I'd get on to him at once if I were you, Mary dear. What I'm surprised at is that he hasn't called out to Summerhill before now. Too busy golfing, I suppose.'

'I'll get Michael to call on him tomorrow.'

'Good. Although I suppose if Mannix pulls off the hat-trick you'll have to hand him out another wad of money.'

'I suppose so,' sighed Mary, looking at the tea-leaves inside her cup with narrowed eyes. 'All the same, what doth it profit a man if he gain the whole world . . .'

Kitty leaned forward eagerly, and held out her own cup.

'Are you reading the tea-leaves, Mary?' she exclaimed excitedly. 'Oh, how wonderful that you're in the mood today! Here, read mine. I can't wait.'

⁅⁅⁅ 7 ⁆⁆⁆

'ARE YOU QUITE SURE this man wants to see me?'

Father Mannix let the lace curtain fall back into place and turned from the window.

Michael wriggled his plump body on the shiny horsehair chair and clasped his hands on the mahogany table. It was a long table with twelve chairs arranged in close formation about it, for the parish priest's front parlour was always used for diocesan conferences. A great fumed-oak bookcase filled the wall-space facing the window; an oleograph of the Blessed Virgin hung over the green marble mantelpiece; and a large black-framed photograph of the reigning bishop decorated the opposite wall, together with an architect's plan of the new church which Father Mannix hoped to complete as his life's work. The floor was covered with dark brown linoleum, and a large Chinese vase filled with dyed pampas grass stood in front of the empty fireplace. The room was freezing, and smelt curiously of starch from the lace curtains which had just been laundered.

'Well yes, Father. I mentioned it to him in a nice sort of way, and then he asked me to come and see you.'

The priest grunted and transfixed Michael with his glittering blue eyes. Bereft of his breviary he clutched one of the chairs, and tapped his fingers impatiently along the back of it.

'There's no point in my descending on this poor fellow if he doesn't want me to. I hope you understand that. It often only makes things worse.' He swung the chair backwards and held it against his stomach. 'Are you quite sure that he agreed with your wife to see me?'

Michael hunched his shoulders inside his overcoat and stared fixedly at the oleograph of the Blessed Virgin.

'Well, that's what she told me, anyway, Father. I was very relieved when I heard it. I can tell you. We've all been very worried. After all his health is not good, and . . .' his voice trailed away.

'All right then,' said the priest, thrusting the chair back into its place and clasping his hands behind his back. 'I'll go out this evening.'

'Oh, thank you very much, Father,' Michael scrambled to his feet and fumbled in his inside pocket for his wallet. He took out a five-pound note and laid it on the polished table. 'Will you say a Mass or two for a special intention, Father?'

The parish priest stepped back and nodded his head curtly. Michael picked up his hat and gloves and began to move towards the door. Father Mannix opened it for him, and stepped aside to let him into the tiled hall. At the front door they shook hands and complained about the weather. When Michael had driven off the priest went back into the parlour and looked down at the note, his heavy underlip thrust out. The phone rang, and Father Mannix, sighing and shaking his head, picked up the money and stuffed it into his trouser pocket.

It was past eight when he reached Summerhill. Chris's station-wagon was parked at the gable-end, and the light was on in the hall. When he got out of his car the priest stood looking down on the plain below. There was a frosty ring round the moon, and the river glittered like an oiled blade. Tiny specks of light from cottage windows dotted the plain like will-o'-the-wisps; and the sleeping back of the bog was dead, flat and sharp against the crystal sky.

Father Mannix gave two loud raps on the door-knocker and turned his back, as was his custom. When the door opened, throwing his shadow before him on the gravel outside, he swung round and confronted Chris. The young man, wearing a tweed overcoat, looked at him in surprise.

'Good night, Father,' he said in a high, hearty voice: the voice one uses when greeting an acquaintance long unseen and quite unexpected.

'Good night, Chris. Weren't you expecting me?' The priest frowned and glanced sharply into the young man's eyes.

'Well no, Father, not exactly, but come in, come in, you're always welcome.'

Father Mannix stepped into the hall and lowered his voice.

'Is your uncle expecting me?' he asked.

'I don't think so, Father. At any rate he didn't say anything to me about it.'

'I thought so,' said the priest grimly, thrusting out his lower lip and looking at the ground. When he lifted his head he stared past Chris's shoulder with a fixed, piercing expression in his small bright eyes. Chris looked round. Willie had come out of the kitchen and was standing at the end of the passage. He was wearing a new blue suit, a soft white shirt, and a yellow tie. Freshly shaved, his white hair oiled yellow and neatly brushed, he looked ambiguously young, slender and lithe. A faint smile flickered over his pale face.

'This is Father Mannix, Uncle Willie,' said Chris in an uncertain voice.

The priest hesitated. Then, with a sudden brusque movement he took off his hat and went heavily to meet the young-old man with the yellow-white hair. Chris, turning away to close the door, did not see his uncle step back with a slight inclination of the head to allow the priest to pass into the kitchen. Nor did he see the ironic, faintly mocking smile with which Willie regarded the hand so tentatively held out to him. The two men had gone from the hall when Chris turned from the door. They had not shaken hands.

'You've done a fine job here, Chris,' said Father Mannix, throwing his gloves on the table and looking round him. 'The last time I was here you looked as if you were camping out.'

Chris laughed and pulled forward a high-backed, carved

wooden chair for the priest to sit on. Willie leaned against the table, his arms folded across his chest, and looked at the low wooden box in the corner where Toby was nursing her six puppies: tiny, thrusting, blind, black-and-white harlequins.

'Are you going out?' asked Father Mannix, sitting down and looking up at Chris.

'Well, yes, Father, I was going into town, but it doesn't matter.'

'In that case, go ahead.'

'But you'll want a cup of tea, Father,' protested Chris earnestly.

'I will not,' declared Father Mannix fiercely, slapping his knee. 'I'm fed up with tea. Go on now about your business. I'm all right.'

Chris hesitated for a moment and looked at his uncle. But Willie was rubbing his eyes with his hand. The young man went out on the back door. He started the car and drove off. Willie went over to the puppies, and squatted down on his hunkers to pat the bitch's head. Toby licked his hand and then turned away to attend to her litter. He stood up and turned round. Father Mannix's shoulders were hunched as he leaned forward holding out his hands to the fire.

'You're looking well, Willie,' he said slowly, without turning his head. Willie moistened his lips and straightened his tie, but made no reply.

'Well, for heaven's sake, come and sit down,' said Father Mannix gruffly, peering over his shoulder with a frown. 'I'm not going to eat you.'

'You don't look like a man who's been sick,' went on the priest, when Willie was seated opposite him in the armchair.

'I've got a new suit,' replied Willie mildly. 'Susan bought it for me.' He shot out the cuffs of his white shirt. 'It makes a difference.'

'And you haven't changed a great deal, except for your hair.' Father Mannix lowered his massive head and looked at the neat little man from under his bushy eyebrows.

'You have.' Willie rested his chin on his fist and looked at the priest with a blank detached stare. 'You've got very old looking.'

'Priest's don't wear well. Besides, it's been a long time.'

'Yes, Father, a long time.'

Silence fell. Father Mannix seemed uneasy. He shifted in his chair and crossed his legs. He drummed his fingertips together, and cleared his throat noisily. He began to unbutton his coat; stopped and buttoned it up again. He took out his handkerchief and blew his nose.

Willie looked at him and a slight smile again crossed his pale smooth face. He ran his fingers along the inside of his collar and stared into the fire as if he were alone in the kitchen. The electric bulb, now covered with a yellow shade, no longer threw harsh shadows on the wall. Willie in his well-cut suit and clean linen seemed to have changed subtly. There was now no suggestion of fear in his bearing; no hint of the grotesque; no eagerness to play the clown. His slim body was relaxed; his long white hands calm and controlled; his expression detached and even ironic.

It was he who broke the silence, rather in the manner of a tactful host putting an embarrassed guest at ease.

'Michael was out this afternoon,' he said softly. 'He told me he was going to ask you to call.'

'Did he, did he?' asked Father Mannix eagerly, rousing himself and shaking his head almost as if he had been dozing. 'So you were expecting me?'

'Yes.' Willie nodded and smiled. 'But I didn't tell Chris. I knew he was going to meet Susan this evening, and if he knew you were coming . . .'

'Quite, quite.'

'I think they're all anxious about me,' went on Willie with a smile. 'Especially Mary.'

'Yes,' said the priest shortly, studying his nails with a frown. 'How are you getting on with them?'

'All right, I think. At first, of course, there was some trouble.

Then when I got sick they came out to see me. And since then they've been very friendly. I don't see Mary much though, mostly Michael.'

'I'm very glad.' Father Mannix smiled, and looked at Willie enquiringly. 'You didn't, er, object when they mentioned me, did you?'

Willie shook his head and looked into the priest's eyes.

'I'm always there, you know, any time you want me.' Father Mannix's voice was gentle.

'It's nice to see you again, Father, after all these years,' said Willie affably.

'It's all such a long time ago, I've . . .' the priest paused and rubbed his forehead. 'I've almost forgotten.'

'I haven't,' said Willie gently.

Father Mannix took out his handkerchief again and mopped his brow. He wiped his lips nervously before putting the handkerchief back in his sleeve.

'Well,' he said, 'I suppose when we get older we begin to look at things differently. I often wondered . . .' his deep voice faltered.

Willie leaned forward with a smile. The priest's ruddy face was pale and mottled, and his forehead was glistening with perspiration.

'What have you often wondered, Father, all these years?' Willie's voice was soft and mocking.

Father Mannix did not reply. He looked at the other man for a few moments with a hard stare.

'If you didn't want to see me you could have said so,' he said roughly. 'There are other priests.'

'But I don't want any other priests.'

'Are you mocking me?' Father Mannix half-rose in his chair and thrust his leonine head forward aggressively. Colour rushed back into his face, which became purple with anger. Willie regarded him with an amused expression, one eyebrow raised, a finger crooked over his smiling mouth.

'I can see that you haven't changed.' The priest stood up

and pushed back his chair. He lowered his voice as he attempted to bring his anger under control.

'People don't change, Father,' said Willie, smoothing his hair with his palm.

'No,' snapped the priest, 'they die as they live.'

'In that case why bother to call?' replied Willie with a chuckle.

Father Mannix turned away and strode across the kitchen. Toby raised her head over her litter and growled; but the priest did not hear her. In his agitation his foot kicked against the box. Immediately Toby's head flashed out, and she snapped at the black-clothed leg that threatened her brood. Father Mannix grunted and stopped dead, looking down in amazement at the furious bitch. Willie got up and hurried to his side. He knelt down, took Toby's head in his hands and gently disengaged her teeth from the priest's trousers. Father Mannix stepped back hastily and bent down to examine his leg.

'A close shave that,' he said straightening up with a rueful grin. 'She might have had her pound of flesh.'

'Oh, but your trousers are ruined,' exclaimed Willie, shaking his head sorrowfully.

'Nothing that a few stitches won't cure. Anyway it was my own fault.' He turned away and sat down on his chair again, sighing and passing his hand wearily across his brow. 'Sit down, Willie,' he said in a tired voice. 'We're too old to go on fighting.' He waited until the other man had sat down again. Then he looked at him with a shy smile. 'Thanks for rescuing me.'

Willie shook his head and leaned back in his chair. His pale face tilted towards the light was like a plaster-cast.

'Are you all right?' said Father Mannix anxiously.

'Quite all right, Father.'

The priest bent down and fingered his torn trousers.

'I want to help you, you know,' he muttered.

'I know you do, Father.'

'I didn't really want to come out here. I tried to avoid it.

Now it doesn't seem as if I can. It's all very difficult.'

'Especially if you die as you live,' murmured Willie.

The priest jerked up his head with something of his former aggressiveness.

'Are you still a complete pagan, or are you just sunk in apathy? Are you not afraid at all, now that . . .' he stopped and bit his lip.

'Now that I haven't much longer to live,' Willie completed the sentence with a slight smile. 'No, I'm not afraid at all.'

'Despair is a terrible thing,' insisted the priest, leaning forward and stabbing his knee with his forefinger. 'There's nothing worse.'

'No, Father, nothing worse.'

'It's death in life, it's awful.' Father Mannix's voice rose and cracked with emotion.

'I've been dead for twenty-five years, Father. Also I'm supposed to be mad.'

'No, Willie, you're not mad. I thought at one time that you were. But I don't think so now. But you are sick, and I don't mean physically.'

Willie was silent for a few moments. Politely he roused himself and stood up.

'Would you like a cup of tea?' he asked, looking at the dresser, now filled with gleaming new china.

'No, I would not. I'm poisoned with tea in every house I go into. I don't want anything. Sit down and don't worry. I'll stay here until Chris comes back.'

'He may be late.'

'I'll stay here,' repeated Father Mannix grimly, rubbing his hands and holding them out in front of the fire. Willie looked down at him thoughtfully.

'Do you still play chess, Father?' he asked suddenly.

The priest looked up in surprise.

'Yes, I do, sometimes.'

Willie smiled and held up one finger. Silently he left the room. The priest sat, his head cocked sideways, listening to the light step on the stairs, and the patter of feet overhead. Toby growled ominously, and Father Mannix looked at her anxiously over his shoulder. In a few minutes Willie came back holding a small red leather box. He put it down on the table, opened it and disclosed a chessboard, and a set of ivory figures. The priest drew his chair to the table and looked at them admiringly.

' Are these belonging to Chris?' he asked.

' No,' said Willie, sitting down and arranging the chessmen in place. ' It's mine. I had forgotten about it, but when Chris and Susan were tidying up the house they found it in an old chest upstairs.'

Father Mannix took up a king and examined the small exquisitely carved figure.

' Nice,' he remarked, stroking it with his thumb.

' Yes,' said Willie, nodding agreement. ' Roger gave it to me years ago.'

The priest put down the piece and drew back from the table. Willie looked at him with a smile.

' Aren't you going to play me, Father?' he said softly. ' For my soul.'

Father Mannix was silent. His heavy mouth was set in an embattled line. Then he too smiled and shook his head.

' No, Willie, not for your soul. But I'll play you.' He ran his fingers gently over the ivory pieces. ' And I'll win.'

8

SUSAN KNELT on Willie's armchair and looked out the window. Chris came behind her and put his arms about her waist. He kissed the nape of her neck, and clasped his hands over her stomach.

'Stop it, Chris,' she said in a low voice, 'they'll see us.'

'No, they won't, they're walking the other way.' He hid his face in her soft blonde hair, and drew his knees together, pining her ankles between his legs. Susan's body relaxed as she felt his chest against her shoulders and his hands reaching up to cover her breasts. Her elbows imprisoned by his pressed against the bones of her hips, and her hands made limp and powerless loosened their grip on the back of the chair as he drew her closer. Her face was flushed and her eyes were closed as she leaned back in his embrace and rested her head on his shoulder. She could feel his growing hardness against her buttocks and shivered. His grip eased and he turned her round, huddled in the big chair as he leaned over her. His mouth closed over hers, sucking her lips between his. Slowly, with a sort of lingering care, as if he were drawing apart the flesh of one body, he took his mouth away from hers and drew back. He was pale and frowning.

'I'm sorry,' he muttered.

'Don't be,' she said, allowing him to slip his hands under her armpits as he half lifted her from the edge of the chair and propped her up like an invalid against the back of it. She leaned her head against the chair and looked up at him. Her lips were swollen, and trembled a little as she smiled.

'I didn't mean . . .' he began, confused, as he looked down and saw himself still half-kneeling, straddling her slim thighs.

He stood up abruptly and turned away, burying his hands in his pockets. He had been painting upstairs when she came in, and was still in his shirt-sleeves with his cuffs rolled back above his elbows. The old flannel slacks he was wearing were flecked with paint stains. He smelled faintly of turpentine.

'Don't be silly, Chris,' laughed Susan, holding back a lock of hair that had fallen over her eyes. 'This isn't eighteen fifty, and I know all about the facts of life.'

'It's not that,' he mumbled, sitting down on the high-backed chair Father Mannix had used the night before, and crossing his legs. 'You're not that sort of girl. I don't know what came over me.'

'But I am that sort of girl, Chris. Most girls are. I like it when you make love to me.'

He looked at her with a frown.

'You don't have to say that just to save my face,' he said severely.

'Oh, Chris.' Susan got up and went over to him. She put her arm about his shoulder and rubbed her chin on the top of his head. He sat stiffly upright, staring in front of him with a set face. She stroked his cheek with the tips of her fingers. He took her hand roughly in his and held it tightly as he turned and looked up at her.

'You mustn't do that, Susan. I may forget myself now and again, I'm sorry about that. I can't help it sometimes when I look at you, but . . .' he stammered and turned away, clutching her hand against his chest.

Susan leaned against him, feeling the warm flesh inside his shirt and the rapid beating of his heart against the pulse in her wrist.

'Don't make a plaster saint of me, Chris,' she said softly. 'I'd hate that.'

'You're lovely,' he said, pressing his thumb over her wrist.

'Am I?' she said with a touch of coquetry, pulling down the corners of her mouth and raising her eyebrows.

'You know damned well you are.'

'You're lovely too,' she laughed, ruffling the thick hair only a little less fair than her own.

'Oh, for God's sake!' he exclaimed, his face scarlet with annoyance as he thrust her hand away from him.

'I don't see why women shouldn't compliment men if they want to,' said Susan, stroking her wrist tenderly.

'Men aren't like women,' replied Chris in a stiff voice.

Susan laughed again and flicked his cheek with her nail.

'If you only knew how pompous you look when you say that.'

'Listen Susan, I'm sorry,' Chris rounded on her fiercely. 'How often do I have to say that?'

The girl bent down swiftly, took his head in her hands and kissed him on the lips. For a moment he sat rigid under her caress, his eyes staring fixedly up into hers. Suddenly he grasped her waist and pushed her to her knees at his side. When he let her go, he sat back with darkened eyes and tightened lips from the corner of which a little spittle oozed. Susan got to her feet slowly and went back to her chair.

'Are they still out there?' Chris asked.

She twisted round and peered through the window. Willie and Halloran were still walking on the avenue.

'Yes,' Susan patted her hair and smoothed her grey woollen frock.

'A nice thing,' went on Chris sulkily. 'They might have walked in and found us.'

Susan laughed and fingered her rope of pearls.

'I don't think it would shock either of them very much,' she said lightly. 'Why should it?'

Chris began to unroll his sleeves and button his cuffs.

'Father Mannix was out here with Willie last night,' he said.

'Yes, so you told me.'

'But he was still here when I got back.' Chris wrinkled his forehead and crossed his arms over his chest. 'I was very surprised, I can tell you. There they were playing chess, as great as pick-pockets.'

'Who won?'

'I don't know.' He looked at her in astonishment. 'I didn't ask.'

'If you ask me it would take Father Mannix all his time to beat Willie.' She held down her head and slipped her necklace over her chin. 'Why on earth was he ever sent to an asylum?'

'Drink mostly, I think, from what I can pick up. He used to go berserk when he had too much of it.'

'I wonder why he took too much?'

'What's that?'

'Oh, nothing. Anyway I'm glad he's seeing the priest.'

'Are you?' Chris's face softened. 'Are you, Susan?'

'Yes, of course. For one thing it'd make things so much easier for him.'

'Will you put in a good word?' asked Chris, leaning forward eagerly, his eyes flickering over the girl's face and breasts. 'It's horrible to think of anybody dying without making their peace with the Church. I mean, after all, no matter what we say.'

Susan lay back in her chair and looked at him through lowered eyelids. His face was hard, and mask-like: staring humourless and white.

'Of course,' she said softly. 'I want Willie to be happy.'

He rose slowly with tensed thighs and looked down at her, bending forward a little like a man carrying a sack.

'I gave Father Mannix a pound last night to say a Mass for him,' he said in a low husky voice.

'Why don't you have Mass said in the house?' said Susan lazily as he moved towards her, his fingers uncurling from his damp palms.

'A Mass, here?' he said as he bent over her chair, resting his hands on the arms. 'Oh, Susan, that would be wonderful! Do you really want that?'

134

'Yes, I think it would be a very good thing.' She touched his arm lightly.

'I don't know why I never thought of it before.' His legs quivered as they pressed against hers. 'I wouldn't have thought about it except for you.'

'Ask Father Mannix,' she murmured drowsily.

His glazed eyes were very close to hers and she could smell the sweat through the clean sharp tang of turpentine.

'I will, I will.' His body arched over her, crushing her thighs in his. Susan's face, its fine, delicate beauty a little blurred and softened by acceptance and longing, quickened. Her eyes opened wide and she smiled as she reached up her arms and encircled his neck.

'Yes, Chris, yes.'

'I'll ask the priest,' he repeated stupidly. 'I'll ask Father Mannix.'

'No, don't talk about that now. Later. Now there's only us. No, not like that. Here, here, now.'

Suddenly he tore himself away from her and stood up, turning his back and sucking in his lips as if he had received a blow.

'Chris,' she called softly, leaning forward and holding out her hands.

He strode across the kitchen towards the hall.

'I've got this painting to do,' he muttered as he went out.

Susan sank back in her chair with closed eyes. Presently she picked up her bag from the floor by her side, opened it and began to repair her face. On the floor above she could hear his heavy tread. She twisted round and peered through the window. Willie and Halloran were still walking on the avenue. She turned back and went on painting her mouth.

9

THE FROST OF THE DAY BEFORE had given way to
soft moist skies. They pressed down, obscuring the horizon,
draining the plain of its dark winter colours. Everything was
grey, misty, blurred: land watched over by a myopic God.

The two men walked slowly towards the house. Halloran,
who prided himself on never wearing an overcoat summer or
winter, was walking slowly like a grenadier at a funeral to keep
pace with Willie, who was wrapped in a heavy tweed overcoat, a
little too large for him since it had belonged to Michael. He
was wearing his chamois gloves and a blue silk scarf.

'I was wondering when it would come,' Halloran was saying. 'I must say they've been very clever about it. Nothing
hurried. Just a casual call from an old friend after you've been
laid up. They take advantage of everything.'

'Oh, I know that,' agreed Willie. 'All the same, I think
they more or less tricked Father Mannix into it by telling him
that I wanted to see him. I knew it by the way both he and
Michael acted.'

'Poor fellow, he can't have much of a life with that bitch of
a wife,' said Halloran viciously.

'She makes up his mind for him. Michael was always afraid
of everything.' He clapped his gloved hands together. 'Besides,
I didn't object to seeing Mannix. I was curious. I didn't think
I'd ever see him again.'

'I suppose not, but they never give up. I bet he's in on this
just as much as they are. They can't bear to have anybody
around who doesn't toe the line, publicly at any rate. If you
had died in the asylum without a priest it would have been
put down to madness, and everybody's conscience would have

been clear. But that won't work any more. God! the whole thing maddens me.' He clenched his fist and punched his hip angrily.

'Oh, I know all about what's done in darkness not being done at all,' replied Willie thoughtfully. 'I know that's the way the rest of them, except Susan, think. But I don't think Mannix feels like that.' He stopped and kicked a stone along the avenue with his small, highly polished shoe. 'I think he wants to prove something to himself.'

'Yes, he wants to prove that there isn't anything they haven't an answer for. I know a lot of things they have no answer for.'

'Well, maybe he feels like that too.' Willie stooped and picked up the stone he had kicked, a small gleaming cube of granite. He tossed it up in his gloved hand and looked at it thoughtfully. Halloran reached out his big raw hand and took it from him.

'Would you like to see how far I can throw this stone?' he asked grimly.

'Yes,' said Willie, turning back and pointing to the big beech inside the front gate. 'Over that tree.'

Halloran pointed the toe of his left boot and bent his knee. He swung his right hand back and threw the stone with a powerful thrust from his hip. It arched up like an arrowhead and sailed over the bare top of the huge tree.

'Good man,' said Willie admiringly.

'When I was young I used to take it out on the world in handball and Gaelic,' said Halloran with a sideways smile. 'Now I'm reduced to shooting stones at the sky.' He rubbed his nose with his finger and shook his head. 'They don't ever seem to hit it.' He turned round and they continued walking towards the house. 'Go on about this Mannix. I'm interested.'

'Well,' said Willie tightening his scarf. 'It was he who found out about Roger and me. And all the others too.'

'Christ,' swore Halloran softly. 'Go on.'

Willie did not speak until they had reached the white railings at the end of the avenue and had turned their backs on the house. The little man began to walk more quickly, so that Halloran loosened his stride as he marched along by his side. High above them, beyond the thick blanket of cloud that sagged over the plain, an aeroplane headed south with a faint pulsing throb.

'You know,' began Willie slowly, 'there was hardly anything like that between Roger and me, until the very end. Then everything broke down. I don't suppose you believe that.'

'I believe it.' Halloran looked up at the lowering sky, over which a pilot and a group of people were riding high against the blue heavens, free of the sodden earth, yet no less trapped in their glittering machine than the specks of humanity they had left so far below them.

'You see, at the beginning Roger was more or less like a father to me. I never had anybody like that. I suppose that was what I was looking for. No music, no books, no one to talk to – you have no idea of what it was like in those days. He changed all that. I used to work here all day – and I was a good worker no matter what Mary and Michael may say now, they only remember what came after – because I knew I would be going over to Dillon's in the evening. It was like escaping into another world, a world I had only dreamed about.'

'But surely you must have known why a man like that, so much older than you, would take such an interest.'

'Well, yes, of course I suppose you always know, and very few people in country places are all that innocent. I knew there was more to it than just the music and the talk. But I didn't want Roger like that. I suppose I built him up into a sort of God, the way you do with somebody you love.' He paused and looked up at the sky; but the throbbing had died away.

'How long did this last?' asked Halloran, clasping his hands behind his back and pressing them tightly against the base of his spine.

'About five years. I was lucky, wasn't I? Five years is a long time to be happy.'

138

'And then?'

Willie looked back across his shoulder at the house with its long golden roof on which the sky seemed to rest, tired and heavy and full of rain.

'And then Roger began to . . .' Willie faltered, his pace slowing, his hands reaching out on either side as if he were trying to preserve the balance of a body which had lost its equilibrium.

'He made love to you,' said Halloran harshly.

'Yes.' Willie's voice was almost inaudible. 'Just like Michael.'

'Ah,' said Halloran with a sigh, 'I see.'

'I wasn't such a fool,' went on Willie, speaking slowly and deliberately as if he were talking a foreign language. 'I knew for a long time that it could have happened. But' – he raised his voice – 'I didn't want it to.'

'And then?' Halloran picked up another stone and threw it over the bare chestnut tree.

'I just couldn't think of him in that way. But I did what he wanted because, well, I would have done anything for him, and I didn't want to lose him. But he knew. And then I began to drink heavily and go into bars in the town some nights instead of going over to Dillon's. And that was another kind of life, and I had to have somebody to talk to. Michael had got married and it wasn't any easier with Mary in the house.'

'After the ivory tower, the jungle,' said Halloran bending down with a grunt to pick up a few pebbles.

'And so I began to bring my new friends along with me to Roger's, because I thought I hated him, and because I didn't know then that no matter how we fought or tortured each other I would always go back.' He took a deep breath. 'And then he started with the others. Oh God, it was horrible.'

Halloran pressed the pebbles into his palm with his thumb as if he were moulding tobacco.

'Strange how people always try to destroy one another,' he said, 'when they love too much.'

Willie held his gloved hand under his nose and sniffed. Halloran glanced at him briefly. A tear was running down his waxen cheek. Far away over their heads the pulsing drone began again, faintly at first, then with growing intensity. Halloran looked up at the leaden sky. Willie wiped his face with the back of his glove and turned his head away.

'I suppose it was all my fault,' he said presently in a dry voice. 'If I had lived with him as he wanted to, maybe it would have been different. I don't know. All I know is that I couldn't break away, even when I found out what was going on with those others. I began to drink more and more. I suppose I really was mad for a while.'

Halloran lowered his massive head from the skies and looked down at his brown boots.

'It was a bad day for you when you met that man,' he said gruffly.

'Oh no, Peter, you mustn't say that. He was the only friend I ever had. And he loved me too, even to the end. I know that. Everything that happened happened because of that. I couldn't forgive him for being like Michael, like myself, and he couldn't forget that he had destroyed something, and he wanted to destroy more and more. It was almost as if we had passed beyond ordinary love, or vice or whatever you like to call it, and wanted to – to kill.'

Halloran was silent as they approached the gate. A car passed on the road outside, and a white blurred face looked for an instant at the two men taking a peaceful walk on a country avenue before the rain came.

'And where did the Reverend Mannix come into all this?' went on Halloran, turning smartly and facing for the house again. The plane throbbed over their heads. 'That can't be the same one again. They must be diverting them to Shannon today.'

'What's that?' said Willie looking at his companion.

'A plane.' Halloran threw away the pebbles and pointed at the sky. 'Go on.'

'Well, one of those young fellows told his mother who ran to Father Mannix. It's curious, but he was by far the most obvious and the most shameless of all of them. I think it was jealousy. You see none of them were innocent. They knew a lot more about what way the lands lie than I did.'

'And what happened then?'

'Mannix went to see Roger. There was an awful scene, but there was nothing Roger could do. His mother was still alive, and his sister was living with him. That's Mrs Whittaker. She was always very nice to me.'

'Did she know anything?'

'Oh no,' said Willie in a shocked voice. 'There were never any orgies or anything like that. They were introduced as my friends, and most of the time she was with us anyway.'

'And Mannix?'

'Roger denied it, of course. I don't know whether Mannix believed it or not, but it made no difference anyway because he forced him to promise never to see me again. In fact Roger got off easier than I did, because he had always gone to Mass and paid his dues and all that sort of thing. And after Mannix's visit he was frightened. He began to go to the church more often and to communion too. And the curious thing about it is that Mannix became very friendly with him. He used to call on him a lot. He even said Mass in Dillon's, and that of course more or less made Roger respectable again. Not that he was ever anything else so far as the people were concerned. The so-called friends I made said nothing – they didn't want to be involved, and the fellow who started it all went off to England.'

'And you?'

Willie tightened his scarf again. His face was chalk-white, and his forehead damp with perspiration.

'I stopped going to Mass long before I knew Roger, when I was about twenty-one. I used to go for a walk on Sunday morning, but people knew, although my mother never said anything. So I think in a way Mannix blamed me more than Roger.' He flapped his hands over his shoulder in the direction of the road. 'I met him once walking along the road. Curiously enough he was quite nice. He asked me to come to see him. But I hated him for what he had done and I refused. I told him exactly what I was and that I could never be any other way. Then he told me that I must never see Roger again and I really lost my temper. We were both young – about the same age – and we very nearly came to blows. I told him that in his heart he didn't care what went on so long as nobody knew about it, and that his religion was nothing but a fraud and a humbug. Well, that was the way he talked. There wasn't much sense in it. It would have been better if we had taken off our coats and fought it out. Maybe then we might have come to some sort of terms. But we didn't.'

Halloran stopped in the middle of the avenue and held out his hand. The first drops of rain were falling.

' So you never saw him again?'

' Oh, I saw him all right, but I never spoke to him, and give him his due he never complained to Michael or Mary about me. I don't think anybody knew what passed between us.'

' And Dillon?'

Willie smiled faintly and lifted his head.

' What Father Mannix didn't know was that Roger never gave up seeing me. I never went to the house again, but we used to meet here, there and everywhere. At night. It got more and more desperate, and we quarrelled most of the time, because I couldn't stand that sort of thing. Roger going to Mass and communion on Sundays, and making love to me in the dark, and I hated him and myself for it, and I began to go wild. I did no work at all, and I was drunk most of the day, and Mary disliked me more and more. I suppose you could hardly blame her, I was asking for it.'

' Did you know that she wanted to marry Dillon at one time?' said Halloran quietly.

' Yes, but I didn't know then that women sense a lot of

things that they don't understand. And I think I must have realised what I was heading for, because I tried to make it up with her. I had to go on living at home if I was to go on seeing Roger. So one day when I was sober I went up to her and told her I was sorry for everything and would she forgive me? She wouldn't answer, so I put my arm about her shoulder and kissed her on the cheek. I don't know why I did it, except that I really did want to make friends with her. But she got hysterical and accused me of trying to rape her. Of course it was ridiculous, but she kept it up, and I went sort of wild with fright, so they called the police and the doctor and got me committed. You know how easy it is to do that.'

'I do indeed,' said Halloran grimly, pursing his lips and spitting on the gravel.

'I suppose the police knew something about me in the town. But they didn't want a public scandal because of the Church. So this was a golden opportunity. Michael and Mary both swore that I had been dangerously unbalanced for a long time, and that was that.' They had reached the railings, and Willie slumped against them and closed his eyes.

'Are you all right?' said Halloran anxiously.

'Yes, yes,' said Willie weakly, taking a pill out of his pocket and swallowing it.

'But surely your brother should have known that you wouldn't have tried to rape a woman.' Halloran lowered his voice because they were close to the house, and spoke rapidly because it was beginning to drizzle and he did not want to keep Willie out in the rain.

'Oh, Michael was never any kind of a man. He did what he was told. And he was glad to get rid of me, not only because it meant getting the place without me being there to embarrass them, but also because he was afraid of me.' He turned up the collar of his coat, and shivered. 'But Mannix could have helped. He also knew that I would never have tried a thing like that. But he never lifted a finger. I didn't fit into the scheme of things, and so I was got rid of.'

'And now?' said Halloran, taking Willie's arm and leading him towards the house, where Chris was painting upstairs and Susan was unhappily making up her face. The grey world ended at the gable; below the plain was hidden under the leaning sky.

'And now,' said Willie, opening the door, 'he wants to prove that I do.'

THREE

THE SLOW, MEASURED FOOTSTEPS sounded above
their heads. They were all – Michael and Mary, Chris,
Susan and Father Mannix – sitting in the Summerhill parlour,
in a thick haze of wood smoke. A large front room across the
hall from the kitchen, it had not been used since the Ryans
went to live in the town.

But now the old house was coming to life again, room after
room emerging from the dust and shadows of years to take on a
new character as Chris painted, papered and cleaned, and
Susan polished and arranged the new carpets, curtains and
furniture. Neither of them would listen to their parents' anxious
suggestions to have a maid to help them, or a paperhanger to
do the heavy work.

For the parlour Susan had selected a sensible grey-blue
carpet, chintz curtains, a comfortable modern sofa and armchairs, and some pieces that she had picked up in the auction
rooms: a small mahogany bookcase, a Sheraton glass cabinet,
and some solid, handmade occasional chairs. The pictures on
the walls were eighteenth century etchings of the town as it
had been then: a wretched collection of thatched hovels by the
river's edge, dominated by the great walls of the British garri-
son and the square tower of the Protestant church. It was a
bright, unpretentious room, and would have been comfortable
if the chimney had not smoked.

So they sat listening to Dr Wilson's heavy footsteps and
looking at the smoke billowing out of the fireplace.

' Dr Wilson is a great man for walking,' said Father Mannix,
looking at the ceiling through the shifting pall of smoke. ' I
remember when I was sick a few years ago, he nearly drove me

out of my mind walking round the bed.' He slapped his breviary on the arm of his chair. ' Round and round and round. I was dizzy.'

Susan, sitting in the armchair opposite the priest, looked at Chris slumped on the grey pouffe, his legs spread wide, his hands clasped between them, as he gazed with furrowed brows at the fire. Another puff of smoke caused him to close his eyes in despair.

' I'm sorry to hear Willie is laid up again,' went on Father Mannix, his white head surrounded by a whirling halo of smoke.

Michael, whose eyes were beginning to water, leaned forward on the sofa and rubbed his hands nervously together.

' It was a chill he got one day last week walking outside in the rain,' he said, looking at the tea things on the low table in front of the sofa where he and Mary were enthroned. They had all finished their third cup of tea.

' Heart cases are very susceptible to colds,' said Mary. ' The least thing and it flares up into pneumonia. And then . . .' she sighed and looked at Susan. But the girl was staring unhappily into the fire.

' What does Wilson say?' asked Father Mannix, rubbing his eyelids with his fingertips.

' Yesterday he said he should be able to get up tomorrow,' said Chris. ' He's giving him penicillin, or whatever they're using instead of it now. He's all right, just a little weak.'

' Still, you never know, God help us,' said Mary, pressing her hand to her bosom and clearing her dry throat.

' They have a new drug every week now,' said Father Mannix, taking up his breviary and slapping his knee. ' Still, in the heel of the hunt it's the old body heals itself.'

Suddenly Chris stood up, took the poker and gave the blazing fire a vicious poke. The logs crackled and flared, and another puff of smoke billowed out. Father Mannix choked and covered his mouth with his hand.

' Very windy weather,' said Michael politely.

'You wouldn't know where you are,' said Mary, pulling her skirts down discreetly as she crossed her legs. 'One day fine, the next bad. Frost one minute and storms the next.'

'November,' said Michael gloomily.

'I love your room,' went on Mary, squinting at the furniture through the drifting blue haze. 'But you must get a nice piano. No drawing-room is complete without a piano.' She had already expressed this opinion three times that afternoon.

'Chris did all the work,' said Susan mildly. Her eyes too were watering, and she had been wiping them surreptitiously with the back of her hand.

'You have the place transformed,' said Father Mannix, smiling at both of them.

'Well,' replied Susan, 'we have to have it nice for the Mass.'

'Oh yes,' exclaimed Mary, clasping her hands, 'the Mass! It's wonderful to be having Mass in this old house again. In the old days we used to have the stations here. It's very good of you to arrange a private Mass, Father.'

'Very good of you,' repeated Michael, patting his plump belly with his soft white hand. 'It'll bring a blessing on the place.'

'Does Willie know about it?' asked Father Mannix suddenly.

A fit of coughing seized the other four. Chris took up the poker again and brought it down with a bang on the topmost log, which collapsed in a shower of sparks. Another puff of smoke blew into his face. He stepped back coughing and glaring at the fireplace, the poker held in his hand like a sabre.

'Don't worry about the fire, Chris dear,' said his mother, panting a little as she struggled to recover her breath. 'It's quite cosy in here. I love the smell of beech-logs.'

Susan looked at Father Mannix with smarting eyes.

'I told Willie, Father,' she said.

'I suppose he'll be well enough,' replied the priest, holding his fist at the ready in front of his mouth while he spoke. Then he coughed.

Chris went back and sat on the pouffe, grasping the poker and pointing it angrily at the smoking, spluttering fire which spat back at him like a wild animal at bay.

'Yes,' went on Susan, closing her eyes tightly, 'he's not really very bad. Dr Wilson is just taking precautions.'

'Very wise too,' said Mary with a significant look at the priest, a look completely lost in the general fog. 'You never know.'

'There he is now,' exclaimed Chris, jumping up and putting the poker back on the fender. The heavy footsteps could be heard stumping down the stairs. Chris went out into the hall and closed the door firmly behind him. It would not have done for Dr Wilson to see the bright new room shrouded in smoke. Inside the atmosphere grew denser.

'Is that an hour-glass you have there?' said Father Mannix, leaning forward and pointing at the mantelpiece.

'Yes,' replied Susan, 'I have a passion for them.'

'That reminds me of a story one of my curates told me once,' said the priest, standing up and turning the glass upside down. Another gust of smoke forced him to retreat hastily to his chair, which he edged back slowly and carefully with his heels as he told his story. 'He was in the habit of visiting an old lady in London when he was on the English mission. She was the landlord of a hall the parish was renting as a youth centre. A non-Catholic by the way, so she was – indeed I doubt if she was anything. Anyhow, be that as it may, every time he went he was treated to a slap-up high tea, but every couple of minutes she got up to turn an hour-glass she had on the mantelpiece. Now naturally this performance made him curious – priests are full of curiosity you know – and one day he asked her why she kept turning it before the sands had run out. "Well," says she, "that's my husband's ashes in there. That man never did a damned stroke of work in his life, but by Jove

I'm making sure he's doing it now." Which is one way of spending eternity. Isn't that good?'

'Oh, very good, very good,' said Michael and Mary, staring fixedly through the smoke.

Susan choked and bent double in her chair, coughing with the smoke and gurgling with laughter. When she straightened up her eyes were streaming.

Suddenly they were all seized with another and more violent fit of coughing. Father Mannix pressed his clenched fist to his mouth, the Ryans covered their noses with their handkerchiefs, while Susan hid her face in her hands. When they had all recovered a little she stood up and looked at the untameable fire despairingly.

'I'm terribly sorry about the smoke,' she said breathlessly.

Father Mannix waved a hand in front of him in deprecation, and also to clear the air.

'Not at all, not at all, Susan,' he said. 'Sure, it's nothing at all.'

Mary took the handkerchief carefully from her nose.

'It's a pity,' she said, 'that the wind is blowing a little in the wrong direction today.'

'Nothing like a fire of logs,' said Michael huskily, wiping his eyes.

They all instinctively drew themselves up with inflexible Irish politeness, and began to talk about the weather, while smoke billowed about their heads like a London fog. The front door banged, and Chris came back into the room, leaving the door wide open behind him.

'What does the doctor say?' asked Mary eagerly.

Chris glared at the fire and took a deep breath, which nearly strangled him. They all waited silently for him to recover.

'The same,' he croaked at length. 'He's to get up tomorrow, and stay indoors for a few more days. Dr Wilson says he won't be responsible if he gets another chill.'

'Do you think I could go up and see him?' Father Mannix rose eagerly from his chair and made for the door.

' Of course, Father, I told him you were here.' Chris stepped back to allow the priest to escape into the hall and followed him out.

Michael, who had stood up respectfully with the priest, patted Susan's arm gently.

' You know,' he said soothingly, ' that fireplace always smoked, I remember it well.'

' It did no such thing,' snapped his wife, fitting the cups into one another, and gathering up the plates and knives. ' Something has gone wrong with it. You'll have to get a man to inspect it, Susan.'

' It'll ruin the furniture,' said Susan miserably, looking at her brightly polished new pieces with dismay.

Mary picked up the tray and looked at her husband with a frown.

' Open the window, Michael,' she commanded.

Susan got up and turned the hour-glass the other way.

' That was one of the best stories I ever heard,' she remarked, watching the falling sand intently.

Mary turned in the doorway and blinked at the girl through the smoke, which was now coiling into the hall and blowing back and forwards through the open window like a shadowy blue curtain.

' I'm surprised at Father Mannix to tell a story like that,' she said sharply. ' About cremation, the Lord save us!'

' Disgusting, if you ask me,' said Michael, coming back from the window.

' Absolutely,' said Mary, sweeping from the room with a clatter of cups and cutlery.

Michael and Susan waited motionless until she had disappeared into the kitchen.

' You know,' began Susan in a hesitant voice, ' I'm worried about this Mass. It was just a suggestion I made. I didn't really think Chris would get so enthusiastic about it. I don't want Willie to think, well, that we're forcing anything on him.'

She stopped, confused and worried, and waved her hand in front of her face.

'Don't worry about it, girl,' said Michael Ryan with sudden heartiness. 'It'll be the saving of him. Just you wait and see.'

⸸ ⸸ ⸸ 2 ⸸ ⸸ ⸸

FATHER MANNIX paused on the landing and looked through the back window. The high wind had come with mountainous clouds: high, towering peaks and cones that soared aloft, range after range over the flat land. The plain was transformed into a valley, at the end of which snow-capped pinnacles reared above the horizon, shrinking the great river into a placid meandering stream and turning the savage black bogland into a small waste, sheltering in the shadow of the foothills. But the plainsman's mountains were mountains of dreams: tomorrow or the day after they would dissolve, and the river would swell again, and the bog would crouch and arch its back against the horizon.

'You certainly have done a job on the house, Chris,' said the priest, looking at the glistening green walls of the landing.

'We have only two of the rooms up here finished yet, Father. There's two other bedrooms to be done yet, and the fifth we are turning into a bathroom.'

'Good, good,' nodded Father Mannix approvingly. 'That's what I like to see – young people building up the country instead of running off to England. You have a septic tank, of course?'

'Oh yes, Father,' Chris knocked at the door at the top of the stairs, and stood back to let the priest enter.

'Well Willie, how are you?' Father Mannix strode forward with long steps as if he expected the room to be a big one. Actually it was quite small, and he had to pull himself up abruptly half-way across the carpet.

'Still alive,' replied Willie, getting up from the armchair in front of the fire. He was wearing a camel-hair dressing-gown over blue striped pyjamas. Father Mannix turned round the wooden chair at the end of the bed and sat down on the other side of the fireplace.

'This chimney is not smoking,' said Chris suddenly.

'Oh no,' said Willie, sitting down and arranging his dressing-gown neatly over his knees. 'It's a lovely fire.'

'Well, the one in the parlour isn't. The smoke is just coming straight down the chimney. I'd better go and see what I can do with it.' Chris closed the door gently and left the two men alone.

'It always smoked,' said Willie stroking his nose thoughtfully, 'when there was a strong wind from the north.'

'Ah, it's not much,' said Father Mannix politely, 'just a few puffs. Susan and Chris have the room lovely. And this one too.' He looked about him with an expression of strained interest.

The bedroom was simply but comfortably furnished. Like all the upper rooms in Summerhill it had a low sloping ceiling which curved down over the bed in the corner like a canopy. The walls were painted grey, and the windows hung with red bawneen curtains. An old-fashioned, white, tasselled quilt covered the small brass bed.

'That's a nice wardrobe and dressing-table you have, Willie. I like satinwood. We used to have a lot of it at home in my mother's time.'

'Susan has gone to a great deal of trouble. A lot less would have done me.'

A few books were piled on the mantelpiece. Father Mannix cocked his head sideways and narrowed his eyes to read the titles. *Madame Bovary, Dead Souls, Great Expectations, The Brothers Karamazov, South Wind, The Ambassadors*, a volume of seventeenth century English verse.

'Susan got them for me,' said Willie, standing up and taking down *Madame Bovary*, which was on the top of the pile. 'I've read them all before, years ago. Roger lent them to me. But I'm enjoying reading them again.' He opened the cover of the novel and looked at the fly-leaf. 'She got this in a secondhand bookshop in the town. It's a curious coincidence, but it's Roger's, the same book I first read. Mrs Whittaker must have sold some of his books after he died. Look, here's his name.' He held out the open book before the priest's face. Father Mannix looked at it blankly, before rising from his chair and walking to the window with his hands clasped behind his back.

The room overlooked the stableyard over which the great cloud-cones towered, giving the long low buildings the cosy, pastoral look of cowhouses in an Alpine valley. Gone today under the soaring sky was that stark, gibbet-like appearance taken on by even the meanest shed on the great plain, outlined as they usually were against the rim of the world.

'I suppose you know about this Mass,' said Father Mannix, leaning forward so that his breath clouded the glass.

'Yes, Susan told me.' Willie sat down, holding the book on his lap.

'They hope to have it at the beginning of December.'

'Yes, I know,' Willie flicked the pages with his thumb. 'She and Chris are working very hard to have the house ready.'

'And you?' The priest turned round quickly, and grasped the brass knob of the bed for support.

'Me, Father?' Willie looked up in surprise. His chair faced the window, and as the priest moved away from it the light fell full upon him. His face was as white as a clown's mask, and his dark slanting eyes were so blank that they might have been painted on with charcoal.

Father Mannix cleared his throat, and stroked the brass knob with a heavy hand, like a clumsy old man patting the head of a strange child.

'You'll be here, I mean?' he said hesitatingly.

'I don't expect to die in the next three weeks,' replied Willie with a smile. 'No, not in three weeks.'

Father Mannix sniffed the air, and looked at the swab of

cotton wool lying in the fender. There was a strong sweetish smell in the room after the injection which the doctor had given Willie.

'It's just a private Mass, you know. Not the stations. So there won't be anybody here except yourselves.'

'I suppose you want to know if I'm going to attend,' said Willie picking up the cotton wool and throwing it on the fire. 'I expect I will.'

Father Mannix freed himself from the knob and sat down heavily on his chair.

'It was Susan's idea, you know, in the first place,' he said slowly.

'Yes. I wonder why?'

'Young people who are planning to get married, as I suppose they are, like to have their future home blessed,' replied the priest sharply.

'They're not married yet.' Willie rested a slippered foot on the fender. 'And Chris is only playing at being a farmer. He may live here for a time after getting married, certainly. But when he settles down he'll go back to the business, you'll see.' He looked at the priest with a faint smile. 'Mary knows that. And so did Kathleen O'Neill. They're very alike in some ways. But Susan is different. I hope things work out all right for her. She's been very kind to me.'

Father Mannix slipped his elbow over the back of the chair.

'Well, it's none of my business,' he said, flapping his hand. 'I like Susan. She's a nice girl.'

'A very honest girl,' said Willie firmly. 'It's a pity Chris isn't in love with her.'

Father Mannix frowned and looked at Willie from under his bushy eyebrows.

'What did the doctor say to you?' he asked abruptly.

'He told me I could get up tomorrow and that I must avoid catching cold.'

'Do you feel well?' the priest went on in a gentle voice,

somewhat at odds with his glittering eyes and set mouth.

'Fairly well.' Willie opened his book and looked at the fly-leaf again.

'Don't you feel anything at all, well, about this Mass?' The voice was still soft and oddly appealing.

'I'm happy for Susan,' Willie shrugged. 'Otherwise, it's none of my business. I gather Mary and Michael are enthusiastic. Well, naturally.'

'I don't like it,' burst out the priest in a strong, gruff voice. 'I don't like it at all. They're taking far too much for granted.'

'They always did. Susan made the suggestion in all honesty, I'm sure, and they seized on it.'

Father Mannix stood up and strode to the window again. On the ledge outside a robin ruffled its orange breast, chirruped its spring song and fluttered away.

'There were always stations in this house. They've been due for years. I couldn't very well refuse. All I did was arrange to have it said privately. I shouldn't have done it.' His voice was hoarse and angry.

'You haven't changed, Father, have you?' said Willie quietly.

Father Mannix spun round and grasped the brass knob again.

'I have not changed,' he spluttered, slapping the knob so violently that the small bed shook. 'I know what the truth is. I was trained to know my duty. I knew what it was then, and I know what it is now.' He wiped spittle from his lips with the back of his hand.

'I wouldn't worry too much about it, Father,' said Willie, leaning back and crossing his legs. 'It doesn't matter. It doesn't matter at all.' He took the book from his lap and held it against his ribs.

Father Mannix sat down on the bed and clasped his hands between his knees. The springs creaked under his weight.

'I see,' he said coldly. 'It would have been better if you had objected.'

'It would have meant a postponement, that's all. And I didn't want to upset Susan.'

'Is that the way you think of it?' The priest's voice rose angrily. 'Something to be passed off because you don't want to hurt a young girl's feelings. Something of no importance whatever. The Mass!'

'I'm sure it's of importance to all of them,' said Willie mildly. 'I haven't been to Mass for many years.'

'Is your conscience completely dead then?'

'Would you want me to be a hypocrite? I could so easily have been.'

The priest thrust out his lower lip and looked down at his clasped hands thoughtfully.

'Will you attend?' he asked, after a moment's silence.

'If I'm well enough, yes. After all I've been given a home here' – he smiled crookedly – 'in my own house. I don't want to embarrass anybody. All I want now is to be left alone to die in peace.'

'Are you not afraid?' asked Father Mannix, wringing his hands.

'No.'

'In fact you don't care?'

'You could put it like that.'

'I pray for you every day, you know.'

'Did you pray for me while I was away?'

The priest hesitated.

'At the beginning, yes, often.'

'And then of course one forgets. And after all appearances had been preserved.' There was no bitterness in Willie's voice. He might have been talking about the weather.

'Priests are human, Willie.'

'Yes, very.'

Father Mannix reached forward, grasped the back of his chair and pulled it to him, as if he felt in need of some sort of barricade.

'You said the last time I was talking to you that you had

not forgotten, well, all that happened long ago. I mean . . .

'I have not forgotten.' Willie stood up and put the book back on the mantelpiece.

'Then we're back with the same problem we had then?' Father Mannix tilted the chair against his knees, and rocked it gently from side to side.

'Not quite. I was young then, and prepared to fight. I still had hope.' Willie leaned his shoulder against the mantelpiece and held his dressing-gown tightly against his legs away from the fire.

'Hope.' The priest lifted his hands from the chair which fell forward noiselessly on the carpet. 'There is always hope— and mercy and forgiveness, and love.'

'Love,' repeated Willie, looking down at the white head bowed beneath him. 'Can it be divided?'

'Love is one thing,' answered the priest doggedly, 'vice is another.'

'So the Church says. The official version. I know all that.'

'Would you condone adultery, the seduction of the young, murder, sacrilege, incest? They're mortal sins too. And mortal sin is death no matter what form it takes. There is an equality of guilt.'

Willie sat down and rubbed his white face wearily.

'The old answer.'

'These are old questions,' said Father Mannix quickly and with a hint of impatience.

Willie sniffed and looked over his shoulder. The smoke from the parlour had drifted up the stairs like a wraith and was coiling in under the door: a ghostly thread that weaved feebly over the wine-coloured carpet. Turning back, his eyes met the priest's, who had also glanced at the door. Willie smiled, and Father Mannix blinked and looked away.

'You aren't prepared to forgive,' he said in a muffled voice.

'Oh yes, Father, it's easy to forgive.' Willie smiled again. 'In fact it is one of the great pleasures of life.' He passed his fingertips lightly over his lips. ' It's not so easy to forget.'

Father Mannix's body stiffened; when he spoke his voice was equally rigid.

' Even if I admitted that I was wrong – which in conscience I cannot do – you would still not admit that there was anything wrong in your attitude, or in the life you led?'

A wisp of smoke coiled across the room and rose like the shadow of a serpent in front of the window.

' You would not have to admit any such thing.' For the first time Willie's voice rose and hardened. ' There was much that was wrong.'

The priest leaned forward quickly, a little too eagerly; and then abruptly pulled himself back with flushed cheeks and closed eyes.

' In that case . . .' he muttered.

' It's not quite as simple as that,' said Willie, lowering his voice.

' Then in heaven's name,' burst out the priest irritably, ' what is on your mind?'

Willie rested his chin on his hand and sighed.

' I think,' he said wearily, ' that we're not talking the same language.'

Father Mannix stood up and buttoned his frock coat.

' Your friend Roger Dillon once said the same thing to me. It didn't mean anything then, and it doesn't mean anything now.' He looked down at Willie. Two spots of colour blotched his white cheeks: like his eyes they might have been painted on a mask.

' It's one of those things that people say when they're consumed with pride,' the harsh voice went on. ' We both speak the same language and you know it. You know also that no Catholic ever gives up his religion except for personal reasons. And lack of communication is never one of them.' He walked to the door and grasped the handle. ' Roger Dillon realised that in the end.'

' He hadn't much choice, had he?' The high, husky voice

seemed dim and far away, as if the white mask of the face were smothering it.

'Is that what you think?' Father Mannix released the handle and turned round. 'Well, you're wrong. I knew him for five years after you went away.'

'I doubt if you ever knew him, Father,' Willie laughed weakly, making a sound like old wood trampled underfoot.

'I think so,' replied the priest earnestly, wrinkling his brows and looking down at the ground.

Willie laughed again, but did not reply.

'Do you mind if I call again?' said Father Mannix quietly. 'I've tired you. But I think we're not finished with each other yet.'

Willie got to his feet slowly.

'No, Father,' he said, 'I have not finished with you.'

⫸ 3 ⫷

SUSAN HELD UP the small ebony figurine, a copy of the Venus de Milo. 'Look,' she exclaimed excitedly, 'it's not worth anything, I know, but I love it.'

Willie put back the puppy which he had been holding in its box, where it collapsed on its hindquarters and looked up at him with sleepy eyes.

'Chris won't like it,' he said gravely.

'Do you think so?' Her smile faded and she looked at the figurine uncertainly. 'No, I suppose he won't.' She smiled again and held out the black Venus. 'Here, you take it. Do you like it?'

Willie stroked the smooth figure with his fingers and nodded.

'I love it. It's just the sort of cock-eyed thing I'd buy myself.'

Susan laughed and began to take off her fur coat.

'That's just it, cock-eyed. Keep it, Willie, will you? You'll appreciate it, a little black folly.' She threw the coat over a chair, and ran her fingers through her hair. She was wearing the old black cocktail frock she had taken to wearing since she began to help Chris with the house. It was stained with paint and made her look like an elegant young widow who had seen better days.

'You're always giving me things,' said Willie, holding up the figurine to admire it. 'I'm ashamed.'

'I'm selfish,' said Susan gaily. 'I like giving things to people. They say it's a sure sign of egotism. Besides it's an occasion for a present. Your first day down after your cold.'

Willie slipped the Venus into his pocket and smiled.

'Where's Chris?'

'Upstairs. I heard him hammering away a few minutes ago.'

'Everybody's getting into a frenzy about this Mass. They're working themselves . . .' She stopped and impulsively touched Willie's arm. 'Look, I'm sorry about the whole thing. I just suggested it on an impulse. More selfishness, I suppose, although I do like the idea. But you can always get a parliamentary cold. I'll prepare the ground for you if you tell me.'

Willie patted the pocket into which he had slipped the figurine.

'I'll let you know, Susan,' he said gravely.

'Good.' The girl looked up at the ceiling. 'Now I must go and join my lord and master.' She turned at the door. 'Can I get anything for you, Willie?'

He shook his head and smiled. Susan ran up the stairs, and went into the big front room which was not yet completely papered. It was empty. She hurried back across the landing and was just about to burst into Chris's room when she stopped herself, and knocked at the door.

'Come in.'

He was sitting on his bed holding up his hand which he had gripped by the wrist. His forefinger was wrapped in a blood-stained handkerchief.

'I cut my finger in the front room,' he said irritably.

'Oh, but your handkerchief is soaked.' Susan reached for his hand, but he snatched it away, holding it up higher and squeezing his wrist tighter.

'It's nothing.'

'But Chris, you should wash it and bandage it properly.'

'I have washed it.'

'Does it hurt?' she touched his arm.

'No.'

'Chris.'

She leaned forward and kissed his cheek lightly.

'Don't do that,' he said harshly, standing up and walking across the room. It was very like Willie's: the same grey wall-paint, the satinwood furniture, the red curtains; but a large crucifix hung over the mantelpiece, and a reproduction of Titian's Frari Assumption hung on the opposite wall.

'Why not?' she said lightly. 'I love you.'

'Don't say that,' he said, pressing his shoulder against the jamb of the door and holding his hand above his head. 'You don't know me.'

'Well, for heaven's sake, Chris, let's get to know each other. I've been coming out here every day for . . .'

'You don't understand,' he said shortly, closing his eyes and shaking his head as if he had a violent headache.

'But I want to understand,' she pleaded, holding out her hands to him. 'What's the use of two people living together in the same house and not trying to get to know . . .'

'We are not living in the same house,' he broke in roughly, and brushed past her to stand with his back to the mantelpiece. A tiny trickle of blood ran down his finger and on to the back of his hand from under the handkerchief.

'Oh, let me,' she cried impulsively, looking at his uplifted arm.

'It's nothing, I tell you. It happens every day of the week when you're hammering and nailing.'

Suddenly she giggled, and then began to laugh outright. He looked at her in amazement, with open mouth and baffled eyes.

'What on God's earth!' he exclaimed. 'Stop it, will you?'

But a sort of hysteria had now gripped Susan and she stumbled to the bed and slumped down on it, burying her head in the pillow. He licked the blood from his hand and looked at her angrily. He waited for the muffled sounds on the pillow to cease, and when they did not he walked to the bed and looked down at her shivering body in bewilderment.

She twisted round and lay looking at him, her body coiled sideways with legs dangling over the edge of the bed. He stared at her shoulder where his hand had stained the black cloth with blood when she had kissed him.

'Don't you want me at all?' she whispered, sitting up and grasping his arm.

'Don't talk like that,' he muttered. 'You know damn well I do.'

He looked down at her hands clasped about his elbow, and made an effort to break free, dragging her forward on the bed as he drew back. With a swift predatory movement she released her hold on his arm, and snatching his bandaged hand drew it to her and held it against her breast. It turned and twisted like a trapped animal in her grasp, and he put one knee on the bed in an effort to steady himself. For a few moments they grappled silently, while his blood oozed on to the silk covering her breasts. When at last he broke free he stood staring at her with a dazed expression.

'I've ruined your frock,' he said abruptly, twisting the handkerchief tighter about his finger.

She pressed her hand against her breast and took it away when she felt the hot sticky blood on her palm. She smiled, and slowly and deliberately began to lick it, like a cat nursing a wounded paw.

His hand shot out and grasped hers with brutal clumsiness. She whimpered with pain, but did not shrink from him.

'Is that the kind you are?' he whispered hoarsely, leaning over her threateningly, holding his bandaged hand stiffly behind him. 'You!'

She looked up at him searchingly: taut, composed, cold-eyed.

'I love you and I want you,' she said in a clear distinct voice.

'Christ!' he swore savagely, digging his fingers into her flesh.

She looked at her imprisoned wrist and smiled again. Slowly he released her, making no resistance when she stood up and unwrapped the handkerchief about his finger.

'Here, tear it into strips,' she said calmly.

He tore the blood-stained square of linen as he was bid,

slowly and automatically with his teeth and his free hand.

'That's better,' she said, binding up the finger swiftly and expertly, and finishing it off with a neat little bow. 'There.'

'Thanks,' he mumbled.

Susan put her hands on his shoulders and kissed him on the mouth. For a moment he stood rigid under her caress, before his arms went about her waist and he pressed her to him and covered her face and neck with kisses. She twisted her head from side to side and cupped the back of his head in her palms.

'Say it, Chris, say that you love me. Say.'

His hands ran down her body and he silenced her mouth with his. She began to beat his shoulders with her fists, softly at first, but with increasing urgency and violence. His hard body softened under the blows and he buried his head in the crook of her neck. Gently she pulled him forward, pressing on his shoulders until he was sitting awkwardly on the edge of the bed. She took his head in her hands and kissed him, forcing him backwards until he was lying crossways on the bed and she was kneeling over him, stroking his face and hair. He lay abject and supine beneath her; submitting with closed eyes as she opened his shirt, and brushed her lips on the soft golden hairs on his chest. He moaned and shivered as her teeth touched his nipples and her fingers explored and caressed his belly. Sighing, he opened his legs, stretched his arms above his head and folded them together on the pillow. She slipped her body over his and was about to cover him when she found herself grasped by the arms and pulled down. He began to fumble with her frock, but she released herself with a whispered word, stood up and threw off her clothes, before exposing with careful delicate fingers the throbbing excitement of his naked loins. She stifled a cry of pain as she lowered her white body over his; and with rising arrogance used him for her pleasure, as he lay passive and hard beneath her.

When it was over he thrust her from him and turned on his side, drawing up his knees and pulling the quilt over his loins. The pillow was bloodstained. Susan stood up and began to dress, quickly, lightly, with a hint of impatience. She was opening the door when she heard his voice, sleepy and languorous and muffled by the rumpled bedclothes.

' You'll be here next Thursday, won't you?' he said.

' Yes, Chris, I'll be here.'

' It's important that you should,' he murmured, turning over on his face.

' Very,' she said crisply as she went out.

Downstairs in the kitchen Willie was sitting in his chair admiring the ebony figurine.

' Is everything all right?' he asked anxiously, looking at the bloodstains on her dress and hands.

' Yes, or no, whatever way you look at it,' she said taking up her fur coat and slipping into it. ' I'm afraid it's no go, Willie. In a way I always thought it wouldn't be.'

' I know,' he replied sadly, stroking the small black figure. ' Will I be seeing you again?'

' Oh, yes I'll be here until the Mass next Thursday. Nothing will be said.' She went to him and kissed him lightly on the forehead. He took her hand and held it for a moment, letting the little black Venus fall into his lap.

' I'll miss you.'

' I know," she said, clutching the coat about her neck and shivering as she gazed into the blazing range. ' I feel awful about that.'

' Oh, it won't be so bad now that I have Father Mannix calling. That'll please them.'

' God, is there any religion in this country at all?' she murmured, pushing her yellow hair back from her forehead.

' Very little, I'm afraid.' He took up the ebony figurine again and stroked it gently. ' What happened?'

' I didn't play the game as it ought to be played,' she said. ' I never do. He'll not forgive me. But of course he'll never talk about it.'

' No, they never do. Did he make love to you?'

Susan laughed, and looked at her bloody fingers before putting on her gloves.

'I made love to him.'

'Ah.' Willie was silent for a few moments as he flicked the head of the black Venus with his fingernail. 'What he wants is a woman who makes him feel superior, and who'll not let him touch her until it's sanctified by bell, book and candle. Then she can take over. A girl who knows the rules, and can mould her man without yielding an inch.'

'Like Kathleen O'Neill?'

'And Mary.'

She kissed him again and hurried out of the house to start up the chic little Mini-Minor her father had recently given her as a guilt offering, because he too had broken the rules.

<ff< 4 >ff>

RITUAL TOOK OVER, and kept them from thinking.

Linen had to be sorted out and sent to the laundry: Mary brought her best tablecloths to Summerhill to be fitted for size. The kitchen table which was to be used as an altar had to be draped to the ground in thick, expensive white. Many lace-edged teacloths had to be examined and commented upon before the best was chosen for the small side-table which was to hold the cruets and the holy water. There were napkins to be prepared for the taking of communion and the heaviest silver candlesticks to be selected and polished for the altar. The second-best dinner cloth was ear-marked for the breakfast table, with more napkins in antique silver rings. There were cutlery, china, vases, glasses, flowers and food to be selected. The redecoration of the house must be completed inside and outside; the avenue raked and the gate painted; every surface polished and every window made to gleam for the greatest occasion that any Catholic can hope to witness in his own home: the entry of the living body of Christ under his roof.

For the first time since his return Willie found his brother and sister-in-law more or less at ease with him. They allowed him to do small jobs, talked, joked, bickered and moved about him with a new, and to him, entirely unnatural spontaneity. Although he had gained strength he spent more and more time in his room, reading and waiting for the few minutes that Susan could spare with him in the afternoon when she brought him up his tea.

'I'm perfectly able to go down for tea,' he said, taking the tray from her and putting it down on the dressing-table.

She sat on the bed, tucked a leg under her and lit a cigarette, quickly, with cupped hands and hunched shoulders: an ungraceful, almost furtive gesture that she would not have allowed herself to make before anybody else. It gave her beauty a sudden desperate quality, as if unhappiness had forced upon her the ugly, fugitive physical movement that betrays the outcast and the unwanted.

'I know,' she replied, blowing smoke through her nostrils, 'but you don't really want to sit around talking to Mr and Mrs Ryan about Father Mannix's tastes in soups, do you?'

'No, I do not.' Willie poured out the tea and handed it to her.

'That's for you,' she protested. 'I brought only one cup.'

'Take it. You need it.'

'What about you? It's your tea.'

'I'll use that cup when you're finished,' he said, going back to the fire and sitting down. 'I'm not at all refined in that way. A friend of mine long ago used to say I was a handsome animal.' He chuckled, flexing his fingers on his thighs like a cat. 'The animal isn't quite dead yet.'

Susan sipped her tea too quickly and a drop ran down her chin which she wiped away impatiently with the back of her hand. It was awkward for her, balancing her tea, holding a cigarette and sitting on the bed with one leg doubled under her. The golden girl with the grimy hands and the soiled frock crouched over her cup like an old woman twisted with age and made furtive with hunger. She glanced at the door every few moments as if she expected to be called away from her stolen treat.

'I envy them,' said Willie, flicking his wrist towards the door. 'Things are so certain for them, or seem to be. Do you really think they believe this Mass will solve everything?'

Susan shook her head and made a grimace which twisted her beautifully moulded lips.

'No, not really. In a sense they don't believe anything at all. It's just that it puts the seal of respectability on things.'

She gulped her tea down, and stood up, almost losing her balance as she straightened her leg under her.

'And when it's over and you're gone?'

She shrugged and walked over to the dressing-table to put her cup down. It rattled like a bone as she replaced it on the tray.

'Kathleen will come back, I suppose. It'll be a different line-out, but things will go on.' She leaned her knuckles on the table and stared into the looking-glass, resting her weight on one hip. From behind it was an ungraceful pose: shoulders rounded, torso twisted, buttocks protruding, one slim leg buckled under her weight.

'I don't look forward to that,' said Willie anxiously.

Susan frowned at herself in the mirror and pulled down the corners of her mouth. She seemed to be interested in distorting her beauty. Then she turned round and crossed her arms mannishly over her breast.

'It won't be quite the same, Willie. For one thing she will accept the symbol of the Mass. For another it must be clear to all of them now that you are as sane as they are. A lot saner in some ways, I think. Then there is Father Mannix. He will continue to call, I suppose, and that will go down with her.'

Willie stood up with one of those sudden lithe movements that even now surprised people. But there was nothing graceful in the emotion which distorted his body. His face, so watchful, mask-like and composed, was flushed; the features blurred like a reflection glimpsed in running water; his eyes smudged with tears, his mouth twitching and his chin wrinkled up and thrust out. He stood with legs and hands splayed out in an attitude from which all self-consciousness had disappeared.

'Oh, God,' he burst out in a crackling voice, 'it's the same old pattern all over again. Toe the line and play the hypocrite! If I had done that twenty-five years ago I wouldn't have been sent away.' He raised his clenched fists and dug his knuckles into his eyes.

Susan, surprised by pity and jolted out of her own unhappiness by the nakedness of his emotion, regained something of her old composure. She waited, only her sagging shoulders betraying her own private humiliation, until the stifled cries, like the far-off moaning of an animal, died away, and Willie took his fists from his eyes and looked at her with no hint of embarrassment on his ravaged features. He put a finger in his ear and shook his head.

'You mean you were never . . .' she began haltingly.

'No, Susan, I was never insane at any time, except that once I went berserk with drink and fear,' he said in a weak dry voice. 'If I had covered my tracks by pretending to believe in something I didn't believe in I might have gone on living here. But I wouldn't serve.' His voice rose and cracked. 'I didn't even bother to deny something which they would never admit existed, although in their hearts everyone of them knows all about it.'

'But that's horrible, Willie,' cried Susan, her body poised and upright now in its old graceful lines as she completely forgot her own defeat in a wave of sympathy that smoothed her nerves like the stroke of a loved hand. 'When you were a month or two in the – the asylum couldn't you have bolted as you did last month?'

'I had no place to go, I had no money and no clothes to go anywhere else.' He dropped his hands by his sides limply and swayed a little. 'And I didn't very much care by that time. If my mother had been alive I might have broken out sooner. I don't think she'd have sent me back, but she died two years before I was sent away. You can be broken you know. I only came home now because I didn't want to die in that place,'

'And now?' Susan touched Willie's wrist gently. He was trembling. Sweat gleamed on his forehead and on his upper lip. The girl put her hand under his elbow and helped him to his chair. He looked up at her with a weak smile.

'You're very kind. I hope you'll be happy again.'

She shook her head and stroked his cheek. Suddenly they

both drew back like guilty lovers and looked at the door. It swung open and Chris burst into the room.

' Susan, for God's sake, what have you been doing? Mammy and Daddy have been driving me crazy down there about that chimney in the parlour. If it's not fixed before the Mass they'll go berserk.'

❦❦❦ 5 ❧❧❧

RITUAL WHICH ORDAINS the outward gesture cannot always prevent accidents or bickering.

Two days before the Mass was due to take place Chris fell from a ladder and broke his wrist and was driven in to see the doctor by Susan. The two men who had been brought out from the town to fix the chimney argued interminably about the ways and means of doing it. Ladders were put up, tools were unpacked, cement was mixed, and nothing was done; while Mary, coming round from the yard, found one of them making water in the most public fashion up against the gable of the house.

She returned in a fury to the kitchen where, too refined to describe what she had seen, she attacked her husband for hiring two such inefficient fools. Terrified to tell her that it was Chris who had engaged them, Michael rushed out determined to get something done, and spoke so sharply to the man who had not been exhibiting himself that he downed tools and left. Confronted with his surly mate, Michael went to the other extreme in an effort to placate him, and was met with such a welter of arguments as to the impossibility of doing anything without an assistant that he turned on his heel, slipped on the damp ground and came down on his face, cutting both hands and one of his knees. He returned to the kitchen pouring with blood to find his wife weeping because she had dropped and broken a Sèvres vase, which she had brought out to decorate the parlour mantelpiece for the breakfast.

Chris, returning from the doctor with his wrist in a plaster, found his parents squabbling about a small amount which had not been collected from the shop.

'It was you who told them to give her credit,' Mary was shouting furiously.

'All right, all right,' mumbled Michael, trying to bind a towel round his bleeding knee, with hands clumsily tied up with handkerchiefs.

'For God's sake, Daddy, what has happened to you?' demanded Chris.

'Are you all right, child?' asked his mother, calming down and touching her son's plaster wrist with trembling fingers.

'I'm OK.' Chris turned away and looked anxiously at his father.

'Your father slipped and cut himself outside, talking to those two blackguards he got to fix the chimney,' said Mary touching her hair and making an attempt to smile at Susan who had just come in from the car.

'You'll have to go into the chemist and get them properly dressed,' insisted Chris, plucking at his father's bloodstained handkerchiefs with his free hand.

'No, I won't,' said Michael, looking slyly at his wife, and pouting.

'Yes, you will,' snapped Mary, rounding on him. 'Didn't I tell you you'd have to go into town the moment the car got back? You know perfectly well you can't drive with your hands in that state.' She turned to Susan and threw out her hands helplessly. 'I haven't driven in twenty years and even then only to a funeral.'

Susan, who had sat down to light a cigarette, stood up again with a strained smile.

'I'll drive him in,' she said.

'Come on,' commanded Chris, putting his hand on his father's shoulder.

Michael got to his feet. His trousers stuck to the towel about his knee, and Mary swooped down and tugged it into position, causing him to cry out with pain. Susan opened the back door to throw out her newly lighted cigarette. The workman who had remained was passing by buttoning up his fly.

'Oh,' cried Mary, who had turned round just in time to see him. 'Oh, that blackguard, Billy Graham! I thought you told me he was gone.' She glared at her husband accusingly. He was standing uneasily balanced on one foot.

'It's not Billy Graham that's gone, it's Tom Murphy,' he said weakly.

'Come on now,' said Chris, putting his hand under his father's elbow.

'Oh, my God,' moaned Mary looking distractedly at the ceiling. 'Murphy was the only one of them that was any good. That Graham is an absolute good-for-nothing, a proper tinker. I told you . . .'

Susan picked up her gloves and went out into the hall.

'He is not,' snapped Chris. 'He's far the better man of the two. I only took on Murphy to help him. Now who's going to fix the chimney?'

'Not Graham,' said his mother furiously.

'All right then, let the damn thing smoke to blazes,' shouted Chris.

With her quick, tight stride Mary swept round in front of them and planted her hands on her hips.

'Murphy must be got back,' she insisted in a voice shaking with fury. 'That chimney must be fixed before Thursday, before the Blessed Lord comes into this house.'

'Oh, oh,' moaned Michael, starting and staring down at his feet. The towel had become unstuck, and was hanging down about his shoe. 'Oh, my knee.'

'It's all your own fault,' shouted his wife, getting down on her knees and wrenching up his trouser leg. Blood was seeping down his plump white calf. She dabbed it with the towel and then tied it so tightly about his wound that he groaned in agony. 'If you hadn't rushed out and attacked them the way you did they'd both still be here. If Graham hasn't that fool Murphy to help him we'll be smoked out of the parlour, priest and all.' She got to her feet and rubbed her hands frantically together.

'All right, all right,' said Chris impatiently, 'I'll see Graham before he goes and fix it up with him. Now, come on, Daddy. Susan is waiting for you.'

Michael moved painfully to the door, walking awkwardly on the heel of his injured leg.

' How am I going to get home?' called out Mary suddenly, darting into the hall after them.

' Oh, for heaven's sake, Mammy, I'll be here, and Susan will be back again. You'll get home somehow.' Chris was helping his father into his coat.

' But our car, I can't drive it, you can't drive it, your father can't with his hands in that condition.'

' You can send one of the drivers from the yard out for it in the morning. Susan will leave you home.' He stopped and turned heavily towards his mother, his plaster hand bone white in the fading afternoon light. ' I wish to God I never mentioned this Mass. What in the name of God are we having it for anyway! '

His mother started back and clasped her hand to her cheek as if he had struck her. Michael snatched his elbow away from his son's hand and exchanged a quick glance with his wife.

' May God forgive you, Chris,' said Mary quietly, all passion fled. ' You're upset. I know you don't mean what you say. Sure, it'll be the happiest day in all our lives.'

AND THEN IT BEGAN to rain: the slow, heavy, blinding rain of the great midland flats. The sky moved down; the world shrank; all colour was drained from the land. Houses, farms, and, in the town, two sides of the same street were cut off from one another by the wall of rain which blurred every visible thing. It was a grey world under an iron sky. Only the earth moved, sodden and shifting and damp. It was cold, but no smoke could be seen rising from the chimneys of the beleagured houses. The torrent had banished smoke; people piling on more fuel on their fires shivered and were silent. Households, isolated behind the swaying curtains of rain, were also silently divided among themselves. It was almost impossible, with vision reduced to a few yards, to feel part of humanity. Everybody was patiently and silently alone, waiting for the world to light up again.

Father Mannix remarked on this as he stood at Willie's bedroom window, watching the cobbles in the yard below ripple under the streaming water like a pool in a high wind.

'Yes,' said Willie, poking the fire, 'I've often noticed that. Nobody talks much when it rains like this. I suppose if people lived in a world as colourless as this all the time they'd have to invent new things to talk about, and what a job that would be.'

'Nonsense,' retorted the priest, drumming the window-pane with his fingers, 'the blind talk just as much as we do. It's only that everybody feels drained in all this damp. No energy.'

Willie sat back and crossed his hands over his stomach, stifling a yawn. The room was very close and humid.

'The house is very nice,' went on Father Mannix. 'You've all done a wonderful job.'

'Yes. Pity about Chris and Michael plastered and bandaged like war casualties.'

'It's a shame. But people get fussed about a Mass in a house. I've often noticed it.'

'Fussed.' Willie nodded and smiled faintly. 'Yes, indeed.'

'But it'll be all right in the morning once the Mass is over.' The priest turned round and looked at Willie. 'You'll be there?'

'Yes, I'll be there.' Willie clamped his jaws together to stifle another yawn.

'I'm glad to hear that.' Father Mannix held out his large red hand and studied it, as if it were something of new and unusual interest to him. He cleared his throat and looked at the books on the mantelpiece. 'There isn't anything that you want me to talk about?'

'No.' Willie crossed his legs and clasped his knees with his joined hands.

The priest cleared his throat again, and rubbed his hands.

'Are you sure?'

Willie looked up and smiled at him.

'Quite sure.'

Father Mannix sighed and sat down on the wooden chair. He rubbed his curiously white forehead, and then covered his mouth with his hand to fight the yawn to which he too was prone in the damp days.

'I'm not trying to force myself on you,' he said in a weary voice. 'As I told you before there are other priests. But this is different. I'd like to do something if I could.'

'It's different, all right,' said Willie with a sudden unexpected giggle.

The priest made an impatient gesture with his hand and frowned.

'I don't mean it in that way,' he said raising his voice lazily, like a man who had just wakened. 'As far as the Church is concerned that's an old, old story.' He pressed his thick lips together and closed his eyes. When he opened them he found Willie looking at him with a mildly interested expression. The priest leaned his hands on his knees and stared into the fire with heavy eyes. 'It's just that as I was mixed up in your life at the beginning of all this, I'd like . . .'

'To be in at the end,' interrupted Willie.

Father Mannix ignored him and went on quietly.

'After all I attended Roger Dillon.'

'Yes, you were in at the end there, too.'

'It's my duty, Willie. He asked for me. Roger died a holy death, thanks be to God.' He covered his mouth closely again and gritted his teeth.

'Did he speak to you about me? I mean, generally, in your conversation. I'm not asking you to break the seal of confession.'

'As a matter of fact, he didn't,' replied Father Mannix, holding his forefinger thoughtfully against his nose.

'I thought not.' Willie rested his head against the back of the chair and gazed up at the ceiling.

'Why so?' Father Mannix took his finger from his nose and held it up in front of his shoulder in an incongruously beckoning gesture.

'Because, Father, you know very little indeed about Roger or me.'

The priest let his hand fall heavily on his lap, shifted his weight in the chair and put one of his mud-stained feet on the fender. An inch of his thick grey socks showed above the top of his old fashioned boots.

'That may be so,' he conceded, blinking sleepily.

'Then you weren't his confessor?' Willie lowered his head until his chin rested on his chest, and he was looking at the other man from under his long black lashes.

'Why do you ask that?' Father Mannix stifled another yawn as he took his boot off the fender and tucked it in under his chair. 'I told you I attended him when he was dying.'

' Yes, but in the five years previously, the years immediately after I was sent away, were you his confessor then?' Willie's voice sharpened a little as his insistence grew.

Father Mannix raised his heavy head and looked at him narrowly for a few moments before he replied.

' What are you suggesting? I warn you . . .'

' Were you, Father?' Willie leaned forward and returned the priest's stare.

' No,' said Father Mannix looking away. ' I was not. But I can tell you that he died a holy death, and was completely reconciled.' A yawn caught him unawares and he yielded to it, not even bothering to raise his hand to his mouth.

' I have been told that cancer is a death-wish disease?' said Willie in a low voice.

' Don't talk nonsense,' replied the priest with lazy irritability. ' God's ways are not our ways. Roger did his best to pull his life together during his last years. I was his friend and I know.'

Willie, trapped by another rising yawn, paused and tightened his jaws before replying.

' And I suppose it made it easier according to your lights that I wasn't there. Is one soul saved at the expense of another?'

' No.' The priest's deep voice lingered on the open vowel. He took his handkerchief from his sleeve and blew his nose. The rain drummed outside, and a few drops came down the chimney and made the fire hiss. The two men were silent, avoiding each other's eyes, slumped in their chairs and lazily watchful. Father Mannix twisted his handkerchief slowly into a knot while Willie beat his hands on the arm of his chair in time with the slow, muffled downpour outside. The priest was the first to break the heavy silence.

' The older I grow,' he began in a low voice, almost as if he were talking to himself, ' the more I realise that there's a pattern in everything in life. We don't see all of it, we only catch a glimpse of it here and there, and then only by accident. But nothing is wasted, nothing is meaningless. Sometimes one sees why at the end of a life. Sometimes one never sees it.' He sighed and closed his eyes.

'No, it's not always easy to see it,' said Willie, stretching his legs, and contracting his shoulders. 'Unless you want to. It would make a nice pattern to fix me up now, wouldn't it? First Roger, and then me. All very neat.'

Father Mannix sighed again and stuffed his handkerchief absentmindedly into the pocket of his showerproof overcoat.

'I don't know which is the greater evil, bitterness or pride,' he remarked, aimlessly drawing the toe of his boot over the pattern on the hearthrug. 'Pride, I suppose.'

'So you became Roger's friend,' said Willie, as if he had not heard him. 'What a strange world it is. Did you play chess?'

'As a matter of fact we did.'

'Roger was a very good player. I suppose he won most of the time.'

'In the beginning, yes.'

'And towards the end, you won?'

'What is it you wish to say to me?' said the priest slowly. 'What is it you want to know?'

Willie stood up. He was wearing his new blue suit and looked neat and trim; but his face was chalk-white and his lips were blue. He raised his elbows and stretched his arms with his fists pressed against his chest.

'I don't think I want to know anything else, Father,' he said with an indolent smile. 'Roger did not betray me.'

'There was no question of betrayal,' replied Father Mannix in a droning voice, as if he were repeating the catechism in a schoolroom to a sleepy class. 'It was simply that he realised that there were certain aspects ' – he covered his mouth with his hand – 'certain aspects of his association with you that were criminal in the eyes of God. Remember that he had ceased to see you for nearly a year before you went away.'

'And if I weren't sent away?' Willie leaned a shoulder

against the mantelpiece and stared through the window at the languid veils of rain.

'It wouldn't have made any difference. Roger realised how dangerous it was. He admitted it. I did my best to help him. That's what I'm here for.' He put his hand in his sleeve to search for his handkerchief, and looked about him as if he expected to find it on the floor.

'And me?'

The handkerchief found, the priest held it in his hand and looked at it indifferently.

'You didn't want to be helped, Willie. After what I had been told my duty was clear.' He rolled his handkerchief into a ball and wiped his palms. 'You didn't forgive me for that. Roger did.'

Willie rested his arm along the mantelpiece and looked at the priest with quiet, withdrawn attention; his slanting eyelid drooping, his white hand still as marble beside the pile of books.

'Are you so sure?' he asked with a slow smile.

'Yes, quite sure,' replied Father Mannix, carefully putting his handkerchief back into his sleeve. 'Why do you ask?'

'Because I knew him better than you did.'

Father Mannix sighed; a sigh which with difficulty he prevented from becoming a yawn. He stretched out his legs and crossed his boots.

'I don't deny it,' he said slowly, his chin resting on his chest. 'But he's dead, Willie, dead these twenty years. He has passed beyond you and me, and is, I hope, at peace with the help of God. We're arguing about a ghost.'

Willie's hand slipped over the edge of the mantelpiece and lay dangling from an inert wrist. He looked at the pile of books beside his arm; at Susan's little ebony Venus; and at the hour-glass which she had taken from the parlour and given to him, because he too had a passion for watching time turn into sand.

'He's not dead to me. He's as alive as if he were in this

184

room today. I wonder what he would say if he were. Whose side would he take?'

'There's no question of taking sides,' said the priest quietly. 'What's passed is passed. It's now your turn to avail yourself of God's mercy. And remember it's your own choice, your own free choice. Nobody is trying to force you.'

Willie took up one of the books and slid his thumb along the spine.

'Free,' he murmured. 'I wonder.'

Father Mannix got up heavily and looked around for his hat.

'Yes, quite free,' he said, going over and picking it up from the dressing table. He glanced at his reflection in the mirror before going on: 'There is Mass in the morning, as you know. There will also be confessions beforehand, as is customary.'

Willie opened the book *Madame Bovary*, and flicked through the yellow pages.

'I have never been a hypocrite, Father. It would have been better for me if I had.'

Father Mannix, who had been twirling his hat idly in his hands, raised it and held it against his chest.

'Are you suggesting that Roger Dillon was?' he said, thrusting forward his massive head with leonine impassivity. 'It seems to me that thought is at the back of your mind.'

Willie closed the book and put it back carefully on top of the pile, beside the shifting sand. He turned back to his chair, rested one knee on the cushion, and grasped the arms with his fingers. Half-leaning, half-crouching, he looked at the priest sideways and licked his dry lips.

'You knew him in his last years, didn't you? He was your friend then. You would have known if he was a hypocrite, wouldn't you? You say you helped to save him. Roger was the kindest man I ever knew, and the most honest. You would never have forced him to live a lie, would you?'

Father Mannix took his hat from his chest and twirled it slowly again between his hands.

'How are you for transport?' he said in a tired slack voice. 'Neither Michael nor Chris can drive and Mrs Ryan doesn't. In this rain . . .'

'Oh, Susan carries them in and out. She puts up with a lot. People who are in love do. She's not here now, but I expect she'll be out later.'

The priest moved slowly to the door.

'Well, I'll be back in the morning. I suppose I'll see you.'

'Yes, you will.'

Father Mannix went out, leaving the door ajar behind him. Willie stood up and looked at the hour-glass. The sand had all slipped to the bottom. He turned it up and watched the time fall softly and inexorably as the silent rain outside.

⇇⇇⇇ 7 ⇉⇉⇉

NEXT DAY it was still raining, although the skies had lifted
a little, and sounds were sharper on the ear. But there was no
high wind to encourage the chimney to smoke – a great relief
to everybody. Damp however persisted, and in spite of fires
lighted from early morning it seemed to penetrate the thick
walls of the house. Napkins, freshly laundered and ironed by
the nuns, drooped, and at the last moment had to be folded
instead of standing proudly erect in bishops' hats. The newly
painted walls were streaked with moisture; and the best white
linen cloth hung limply from the altar in the kitchen.

Mary and Susan, with the help of the Ryans' cook specially
imported for the occasion, had been working hard since seven
o'clock, preparing the lavish dinner menu – honeydew melon,
cream of asparagus soup, sole *bonne femme*, roast chicken and
baked ham with peas, carrots and croquette potatoes, trifle
Chantilly, and coffee, which everybody was expected to con-
sume at ten o'clock in the morning, together with Monrachet,
port and brandy. Michael and Chris, plastered and bandaged,
wandered about in their best dark suits, getting in the way.
And Willie kept to his room.

At half-past eight the ladies retired upstairs to repair their
faces and change into the hats which they had brought with
them. They arrived down at five to nine to welcome Kitty
Carroll, the only outsider invited. She was resplendent in a
black satin two-piece, a purple tulle hat, a mink stole, and every
cultured pearl she possessed. She kissed Mary reverently and
pressed her hands.

' This is a great day,' she whispered, rolling her bold handsome eyes with awe. ' A great blessing on the house. May you

have all sorts and conditions of luck. What a lovely costume you're wearing, Mary dear. Is it Sybil Connolly?'

Mary rubbed the sleeve of her bottle-green tweed suit affectionately. 'Oh no, Kitty, just a little dressmaker I know in London. She makes for the Embassies.'

'I'm green with envy, dear,' said Kitty, twitching her mink. 'Is the address a state secret?' She looked about the hall with admiring eyes. 'What a wonderful job you've made of this lovely, lovely, old house. It's almost Tudor, isn't it, on the outside, and every mod con on the inside, I can see.'

Mary held up a finger and stretched out her sallow neck.

'Is that Father Mannix's car I hear?' she said anxiously.

'Oh, Mother of God,' exclaimed Kitty darting lightly into the kitchen, 'I mustn't be in the hall. Are there going to be confessions? I went last night.'

'He's not coming yet,' said Mary, following her and taking in every detail of the black satin and the softly gleaming mink. 'Chris, have you the matches ready and the candle?'

Chris rose from one of the chairs which had been arranged in front of the altar as kneelers, and shook hands with the visitor.

'Oh, your poor wrist, Chris. What an awful thing to happen, and at this time too. But God fits the back for the burden, that's what I always say, and wouldn't it be worse if it was your right wrist.' She turned and beamed at Willie who had risen from another chair. 'And is this your Uncle Willie?'

'This is Mrs Carroll, Uncle Willie.'

'Delighted, delighted,' gurgled Kitty, giving him a plump hand encased in white suede. 'I'm sure you're thrilled about this Mass. We all are.'

Willie bowed, smiled and looked at Susan who was staring at her mother blankly.

'Where are my beads? Oh, where are my beads!' exclaimed Kitty, opening her handbag and scrabbling about. 'Oh, thanks be to God and His Blessed Mother. Wouldn't it be awful if I left them behind in the fuss and rush.'

Michael came downstairs and crept into the kitchen, where Kitty immediately pounced on him.

'Oh Michael, Michael, how are you? I won't shake hands with you because of your poor crucified hands. Isn't it awful the way things happen at a time like this? I remember when we had a private Mass the cook had a fit in the back hall, and I had to send out to the hotel for somebody at the very last moment.'

'Chris, Chris,' warned his mother, 'light the candle, I hear him. Hurry, hurry.'

Chris went into the hall carrying the silver candlestick. Mary struck a match, lighted it, opened the door and hurried back into the kitchen. Father Mannix got out of his car with his acolyte: the priest carrying his Mass-box; the little server with his soutane and surplice rolled up in a paper-bag under his arm. He held up the candle in his right hand as the priest approached, and accompanied him to the kitchen, where they were all kneeling for the reception of the Blessed Sacrament. Michael, Mary and Kitty were already in their places in the front row of chairs, leaving one vacant for Chris as the man of the house. Susan and Willie knelt behind; and presently, Philomena, the Ryans' cook, crept in, a heavy black coat over her white apron, and a purple hat with a daring red rose secured with a pin to the side of her frizzy hair.

Father Mannix dumped his box on the altar and opened it, before he turned round and looked over the heads of the seven people kneeling before him.

'Is there anybody for confession?' he asked. 'If so I'll hear them in the other room.'

There was a negative murmur. Father Mannix took off his coat, handed it to Chris, and began to unpack his box. He took out the altar stone and slid it under the linen cloth. He placed a small wooden stand on the Epistle side of the altar and placed his missal on it. He handed a small bottle of wine to his server, who had opened his parcel behind the door and bundled himself into his soutane and surplice. Chris came back from the hall where he had hung up the priest's coat and handed a box of matches to the little boy to light the candles. Slowly and methodically, Father Mannix took out the Sacred Vessels: the Paten, the Chalice, the Veil, the Burse, the Corporal, the Purificator, the Pall, the Golden Spoon.

Then he began to vest. He threw the white linen Amice over his shoulders, symbol of the cloth with which the Roman soldiers blindfolded Christ, thereby signifying the helm of salvation. He drew his arms through the Alb, the sign of purity of heart, representing also the white robe of mockery with which Herod clothed Jesus. He tied the white girdle, emblem of purity, about his waist. He drew the Maniple on his left arm, as a reminder that it is his duty to fear neither suffering nor labour. He hung the Stole about his neck and crossed it over his breast, the symbol of spiritual power and dignity of the priesthood. And lastly he put on the Chasuble, which, as a compliment to the house and to the occasion, was of cloth of gold. He stood at his altar covered with this last and noblest of sacerdotal vestments, the emblem of the royal virtue of charity, the eternal symbol of the robe in which Jesus was clothed and mocked while He was crowned with thorns. The acolyte took his bell and knelt down. Father Mannix joined his hands and bent his head. The sacrifice of the Mass began.

The immemorial Latin words sounded in the warm crowded kitchen, an antiphon commenced by the priest in his deep rumbling voice and taken up by the clerk in his shrill breaking tones. The Ryans opened their missals and began to riffle through their mortuary cards, recalling friends and relations long dead. Kitty produced a very splendid mother-of-pearl rosary beads blessed by Pope Pius XII, kissed the cross, then signed herself. Chris opened his tiny masculine prayer-book and leaned his elbow on his chair, shading his eyes with his hand. Susan knelt bolt upright and stared in front of her with unblinking eyes, while Philomena – whose patron had to her amazement recently been removed from the calendar of the saints – rattled her beads of coloured glass, blessed by an itinerant Jesuit at the last Mission, and began to mumble her prayers and beat her breast.

Slowly and carefully Willie turned round his chair and sat on it. He had neither beads nor prayer-book, but he followed every motion of the priest closely and intently.

Father Mannix, having completed the Preparatory Prayers, made the sign of the cross and began to read the Introit of the day. The server crossed one foot over the other as he knelt and scratched his heel with his toe.

' *Kyrie eleison*,' chanted the priest.

' *Christe eleison*,' sang out the clerk.

The sacrificial ritual went on from the Collects and the Epistle to the Offertory, while the kitchen resounded with the murmur of prayer as the celebrant went through the hieratic gestures of his holy office.

There are priests who say Mass quickly, gabbling through the sacred words as if they were written in morse code, darting from Book to Chalice with frenzied gesture, and bolting through the last prayers as if they were suffering from a sudden attack of diarrhoea. And there are priests who say Mass so slowly, enunciating every syllable and raising their arms in heavy ponderous gestures, that they produce the same effect upon their congregations as if they were subjected to mass hypnosis. Father Mannix belonged to neither school. His movements were easy and graceful; his Latin clear and distinct; his voice solemn yet natural. In his white linen and cloth of gold, he made a splendid figure, carrying into the homely kitchen with its pots and pans, its gleaming china and crackling range, all the mystery and dignity of his sacred office.

Having washed his fingers in the silver bowl held by the clerk, and recited the great poetic words of the Lavabo, he repeated the Secret Prayers and began the Preface. The bell tinkled and the Canon of the Mass began. Willie turned his chair round and knelt down. Philomena thumped her breast with violent fervour, and Mary and Kitty covered their faces and bent low. The bell tinkled again as the priest held aloft the consecrated Host, and the Chalice containing the Precious Blood. The Communion began. Father Mannix broke the Host and ate the Body and drank the Blood of his Saviour.

There was a stir in the kitchen. Chris stood up and moved his chair aside with his leg, before he knelt down beside his parents and Kitty at the feet of the priest to receive communion. Susan and Philomena, who were not receiving, withdrew to the back of the room. Willie remained in his place. Father Mannix turned round, elevating a particle of the Sacrament.

'*Ecce Agnus Dei, ecce qui tollit peccata mundi.*' They bowed their heads as he intoned the solemn words. 'Behold the Lamb of God, behold Him who taketh away the sins of the world.'

The clerk had taken the white napkin which he would hold under their chins as they received communion. The boy was the first to communicate, and then Father Mannix approached Chris and placed the wafer on his tongue with the immemorial words: *Corpus Domini nostri Jesu Christi custodiat animam tuam in vitam aeternam, Amen.* The Body of Our Lord Jesus Christ preserve thy soul unto life everlasting.

In the hushed silence broken only by the solemn murmur of the priest's words another sound intruded: the scraping of a chair. Willie stood up and knelt down beside his brother at the end of the line of communicants. The clerk held the white napkin under his chin, Father Mannix laid the small wafer on his tongue, and turned back to the altar. Willie went back to his chair, knelt down, clasped his hands on the seat and stared at the priest's gold-embroidered back. Covering their faces with their hands, the others bowed over their chairs to mumble the prayers after Communion, the ritual prayers learned long ago from the nuns. The Gospel of St John was said – In the beginning was the Word, and the Word was with God, and the Word was God – and in a few minutes Mass was over, and Father Mannix began to say the prayers for the health, success and salvation of the house.

They all rose stiffly from their knees. Mary and Kitty looked back and smiled at Willie before hurrying across to the parlour to see that everything was in order. The priest began to take off his vestments, and the little clerk his soutane and surplice. Philomena slipped off her coat, unpinned her hat, and looked anxiously at the range, eager to be at her pots and pans and feed the priest. Michael, Susan and Willie followed the others into the parlour.

' Well, thanks be to God,' said Kitty, clasping her hands and rolling her eyes upwards, ' that was a beautiful Mass. Isn't Father Mannix a real saint? I love the way he says Mass.'

The others looked shyly at Willie, who had suddenly become for them an object of awe. He sat down inside the door, crossed his legs and smiled.

' Did you like the Mass, Uncle Willie?' said Chris with an affectionate smile.

Willie nodded and smiled back. His smooth unlined face, flushed a little now, was more youthful than ever. He looked like a man of forty who was prematurely grey. Michael laid his hand impulsively on his shoulder.

' Good man, Willie,' he whispered. He turned away and dabbed his eyes with a snowy handkerchief liberally sprinkled with eau-de-cologne.

Kitty removed her mink stole and asked if she could be of any help.

' Oh, no, no, Kitty dear,' said Mary, pressing her hand warmly. ' Philomena will see to everything. She's a real treasure.'

' Indeed she is!' declared Kitty excitedly.

Susan stood beside Chris, unsmiling and grave. She took no part in the chatter about the richly-laden table, free on this blessed day from the hateful smoke. Outside the rain fell softly, its veils unflurried by a breath of wind. It was perfect.

Father Mannix came in, beaming and rubbing his hands.

The acolyte, a chubby solemn little boy with thick spectacles followed him, peering round with inquisitive uncertainty. Mary took his hand and led him to his place at the bottom of the table. As a member of a good family in the town and a server of the Holy Sacrifice he was entitled to sit down with the family. They all waited for the priest to break the silence.

'Well now,' he said jovially, 'this is a right royal spread. Sure, you shouldn't have gone to so much trouble. A boiled egg would do me.' He looked at Willie and nodded his head approvingly. They all looked at the small, neat white-haired man with affection; except Susan, who was staring at the rain beyond the window with a blank expression.

'You have the place lovely,' went on Father Mannix. 'I never saw such a transformation, it's a credit to you all.'

'A Mass is a Mass,' said Mary, pulling back the priest's chair and standing behind it humbly.

'I'm afraid I let you all down at the last moment,' said Susan suddenly, jerking her gaze away from the mesmeric rain, falling as slowly and quietly as the sands in her hour-glass. 'I didn't come out at all yesterday, just when you wanted me most.'

'Oh but Susan, you've worked yourself to the bone,' declared Mary, grasping the girl's arm affectionately in a vice-like grip.

'She had a terrible headache,' put in Kitty quietly. 'I made her lie down.'

'None of us were here yesterday,' said Michael, 'except for a bit in the afternoon when I got one of the drivers to leave Mary and me out. All the work was done by then, except for the cooking, and Philomena came out at cock-crow this morning. So don't worry, Susan, you were great. I don't know what we'd have done without you.'

'Chris tells me that you were here after we left, Father,' said Mary with an eye on the table. 'So good of you to call. I'm afraid poor Chris and Willie were marooned all the evening.' She touched her son's injured hand tenderly. 'All my fault, I'm afraid. I took the evening off.'

The priest, who was preparing to say grace, stopped and looked at Willie, who had taken up his place behind his chair opposite Father Mannix. His supple body swayed slightly as he gripped the back of the chair, and he flashed the priest a sudden smile, in which the muscles of the mouth only were involved. His slanting eyes remained inscrutable. Father Mannix looked down at the gleaming table, blessed himself and said grace.

It was a strangely muffled meal, enlivened only by Kitty's chatter, and Willie's expressive hand movements, as he told story after story in a variety of different accents. He seemed happy and excited and gave full rein to his gift of mimicry, which was brilliant. Chris and his parents, still regarding him with affection, would have liked to join in Kitty's uncontrolled laughter, but they were put off by the priest's strange silence. It was Willie's morning, and they were pleased that he was impressing Kitty with his cleverness. As for Father Mannix, it was well known that he was moody.

When it was all over and they had, with the exception of the priest who ate hardly anything, stuffed themselves with food, they rose heavily from the table. They made the ritual protests when Father Mannix left at once, accompanied by the acolyte, flushed and sleepy from his rich breakfast. A reaction from the nervous tension of the past few days set in, and they were all tired. Kitty and Mary chatted half-heartedly for a while as Philomena cleared the table. Nobody knew exactly how to break up the gathering. It was Susan who broke the ice. She went upstairs and came down with her coat on her arm.

'I think we ought to be going, Mummy,' she said briskly.

'Oh no,' said Mary and her husband politely, but without much enthusiasm. Chris turned away and kicked a log on the fire. The Ryans shook hands with Kitty who was looking a bit puzzled, and Susan went over to Chris.

'Goodbye,' she said in a low voice. 'I'm sorry.'

The party was over. It was an occasion they would all remember.

⸨⸨⸨ 8 ⸩⸩⸩

'THE MASS WENT OFF VERY WELL,' said Willie. He was curled up on the sofa in the parlour, one leg tucked under him, plucking at the lace of his shoe with a languid hand. The room, cleared now three days after the Mass of its sumptuous table, seemed bare. The rain had stopped; the chimney was still unfinished; the wind was in the wrong direction; smoke billowed from the fireplace in which a small fire burned.

Father Mannix coughed into his fist and made no reply. His ruddy face had grown paler, and there were purple circles about his china blue eyes. He seemed to have aged quite suddenly; just as Willie seemed to have grown younger. He gesticulated a great deal with his small white hands, pursed out his mouth before he spoke, and shrugged his shoulders in a self-indulgent way. It was as if gestures, attitudes, poses long suppressed had become more exaggerated by what seemed to be a growing self-confidence.

'They're all so pleased with themselves,' he went on, taking out a scented handkerchief and holding it to his nose. 'Quite transformed with happiness and grace. I must say I loved your cloth of gold.'

Father Mannix looked at him with disgust and coughed again.

'I'm terribly sorry about the chimney, Father. But the men haven't turned up for the past couple of days. Some other job I suppose. It's very naughty of them.'

The priest tapped his knee with his breviary and frowned at the fire.

'Susan hasn't been here since either,' continued Willie, suddenly and disconcertingly dropping his frivolous tone. His face clouded and he shook his head. 'I don't think we'll be seeing her again. Poor Susan.'

Father Mannix stood up abruptly, and began to pace up and down the room behind the sofa.

'She wasn't here the last time I was talking to you,' he said accusingly. 'There was nobody here except you and Chris, and Chris can't drive with his hand. How did you get into town for confession in that rain?'

'I'm quite tough you know,' replied Willie lightly. 'I walked all the way home from the asylum in weather just as bad.'

'You walked in then?' The priest stopped and raised his eyebrows.

Willie pursed his lips and fixed his handkerchief carefully in his breast pocket with a little affectionate pat.

'No, Father, I did not walk in.'

'Somebody gave you a lift then?'

'No. After you left I went to bed. I knew it was going to be a strenuous day.'

The priest sat down suddenly in one of Susan's hand-carved chairs and held his hand to his forehead. He was silent for a while; and when he looked up his eyes were damp.

'I see,' he said quietly.

'It's what you wanted,' said Willie peering over the top of the sofa and smiling. 'It's what they all wanted. Everybody is very happy. The prodigal son returned to the fold. It has even helped Mary to get over the shock of Susan.'

Father Mannix avoided the other man's mocking smile. Then, as if with a great effort of will, he turned his head and looked at Willie with a curious expression of appeal in his child-like eyes. The stern mask of authority which the years had fashioned, softened; he looked hurt and vulnerable.

'Why did you do it?' he pleaded.

'I told you,' replied Willie flippantly, waving his hand before his face to clear the smoke.

The priest shook his head and sighed.

'No, you haven't. And the whole thing was unnecessary. It

would have been quite easy for you to go to confession, you know.'

'But I don't want to go to confession, Father. I lost whatever faith I had a long time ago.'

' 'Well, suppose you have, why insult what's sacred? People who have no faith don't do that. No, Willie, there's something else you're not telling me. I wish you would. I pray to God that you would.'

'Perhaps I'm insane,' replied Willie in the same bantering tone. 'After all I spent twenty-five years in an asylum. And you helped to send me there.'

'If you did this out of some perverse desire to get your own back on me,' replied the priest wearily, 'you have, I admit, succeeded. But not entirely.' He raised his voice, and thumped his knee with his book. 'It's God you have insulted. You may mock me – maybe I deserve it – but you won't mock Him.'

'God, God, God,' said Willie, puffing out his lips and blowing at the smoke. 'You all talk about Him, the whole lot of you. I'm tired of hearing about God. He's a convenient excuse for the hypocrites to get their own way.'

'And now you're the biggest hypocrite of them all,' retorted Father Mannix. 'I've noticed that we always accuse other people of our own vices.'

'Hypocrisy seems to pay. Have you noticed that too?' Willie's voice lost its soft frivolous tone and became hard. He stood up, put his back to the smoking fire and faced the priest.

'Why did you do it?' repeated Father Mannix. 'I'm not going to put it down to frivolity, because frivolity brought to that pitch really is insane.'

Willie folded his arms behind his back and stretched his shoulders. He looked at the ceiling thoughtfully for a while before he replied in a calm, detached voice, as if he were speaking of something which had nothing to do with himself.

'It's quite simple, Father. There's only one thing that Mary and Michael, and Chris too, respect in the last resort, and that's conformity. I don't think any of them believe now that

I'm dotty. After all they can persuade themselves that I was successfully treated.' He paused and unlocked his arms. 'And then there's Kathleen. It's only a matter of time until she's back here, and she's the worst of them all, narrow-minded, bigoted, and with an inferiority complex to cap it all.' He stepped forward and leaned towards the priest who was staring at him silently. 'Now I want to go on living here for whatever time is left to me. It'll make it so much easier if I conform, outwardly at any rate. A pious old uncle can always find a place in the corner in this country. From now on I intend to be very pious. And after all religion has nothing to do with it, has it?' He turned and looked at the smoking fire. 'That damned chimney!' he exclaimed. 'Perhaps we'd better go up to my room, or into the kitchen.'

Father Mannix ignored the last remark. The vulnerable expression vanished; and the mask of authority was now more firmly adjusted then before. He curled his mouth with distaste as he looked at his antagonist.

'Do you think that I'm going to put up with a disgusting exhibition like that?' he rasped. 'If you do you had better do some re-thinking.'

'Oh, I don't expect you to encourage me,' replied Willie lightly. 'And of course you won't tell, will you? Unless of course it's your mission in life to stir up scandals.'

The smoke was now so thick that Father Mannix had to narrow his eyes and strain forward to see the other man. When he spoke his voice was trembling.

'There is such a thing as infernal grace. You are filled with it, and it has given you a new lease of life. You are changed, diabolically changed. Every gesture you make proves it. You are disgusting.'

'Apparently you didn't find Roger disgusting,' said Willie, carefully adjusting his tie. 'Perhaps you only recognise what you call "infernal grace" when you're told about it. After all it's easy to preach to the converted, even if they only pretend to be converted.'

'What do you mean?' demanded the priest, starting back as if he had been struck.

'I find myself in the same position as Roger,' said Willie, smoothing his yellow-white hair with the back of his hand. 'He too was forced to compromise.' He stepped forward and pointed his finger at the priest. 'You saw to that.'

Father Mannix sprang from his chair, clouds of smoke swirling away from him like water from a wader.

'Is there nothing that you'll stop at?' he shouted hoarsely. 'I can see the influence you must have had on that man. You're evil, do you hear me!'

'I hear you,' replied Willie calmly. 'You have a very carrying voice.'

'I'm glad now that you were sent away,' the priest went on wildly. 'It wasn't enough for you to deprave your friend, but you had to try and corrupt every young man you met with your filthy vices. And now you want to defame the dead. Have you no shame?'

The smoke filled his lungs as he spoke and he doubled up in a fit of coughing and let his breviary fall on the floor. Willie moved forward to pick it up, but the priest put his foot on it and glared at him.

'Get away from me,' he croaked.

Willie shrugged and turned away, patting the handkerchief in his breast pocket. He sat down in one of the armchairs and crossed his legs.

'I think it's time you knew the truth,' he said, tapping his fingertips together gently. 'It might be good for your soul, besides teaching you that the world is not as simple as you imagine.'

Father Mannix picked up his breviary and dusted it with his handkerchief. He grasped it tightly and stared down at it as he listened to the high, husky face speaking to him through the smoke.

'Roger never gave up what you like to call " vice ". If it's of any interest to you now I never wanted it, not with him anyway. It was he who – how would you put it? – seduced me. Yes, that's how you'd put it. I hated it; but I did it because I loved him.'

The priest fumbled in his pocket, took out his stole, kissed it and held it in his hand over his prayer-book. Willie, staring into space, did not see him.

'You thought you reformed him, didn't you? But you didn't. All that year after you came on the scene, Roger was meeting me every night . . .'

'You're lying . . .' shouted Father Mannix, taking a step forward and holding up his breviary and stole as if he intended to hit the other man with them. But he stopped himself and turned his back, covering his eyes with his hand.

'I don't care whether you believe me or not,' the voice went on behind him. 'Anyhow, the truth is rarely believed – it's not very comfortable. For instance, you wouldn't like to be told that Roger used to laugh at you for being taken in so easily. But the way he was placed there was only one thing to do, and he did it. With your help, and me as the scapegoat.'

Father Mannix turned slowly to face the speaker. He had regained something of his self-control, and his voice, though still trembling, was quiet.

'All right,' he said, 'supposing what you say is true, it was a mortal sin like any other. It can be forgiven. But he lived five years after you went away. And the last thing he did was to send for me. I anointed him and gave him the last sacraments. Whatever sins he committed he atoned for them. Let him rest in peace, please.'

'But you didn't hear his confession, Father. You told me you didn't. Roger hated the Church. He hated it for its hypocrisy, its greed, and for the way it tries to have it both ways so far as people like him are concerned. We used to make up the little venial sins he was going to tell at his next confession. Who did he go to? one of the friars wasn't it?' His voice took on a whispering, intimately reverent tone; and it was the accurately observed voice of a man long dead. 'I cursed three times, Father. I told four lies. I didn't say my morning offering. I – '

'Stop it,' said Father Mannix in a low firm voice. 'In the name of God, stop it.'

'No, Father, I will not stop it.' Willie's voice, no longer impersonating anybody, was harsh and high. 'You've had it all your own way for a very long time. It's about time you knew the price that was paid for your comfort – your spiritual comfort.'

'No one could keep up a monstrous sacrilege like that for so long. It's inhuman,' Father Mannix covered his nose and mouth with his handkerchief. Smoke was coiling about the furniture, slowly and menacingly like the arms of an octopus.

'You can get used to anything. And remember, Roger was not a believer. When you don't believe in hell it's easy to conform to local ritual, if you're forced to.'

'I was with that man when he died,' said Father Mannix, taking the handkerchief away from his mouth and wiping his eyes. 'He believed all right. I've attended at many deathbeds and I know.'

'Do you, Father?' the voice mocked, and again it was the voice of Roger Dillon. 'Do you?'

'Roger Dillon died a Christian death,' went on the priest, giving no sign of being aware of the cruel mimicry. 'There was no need for him to send for me at the end. There was no point in doing that, even if he did hate me. He sent for me because he wanted to make his peace with God.'

'How can you be sure, Father?' asked Willie quietly in his own voice.

'Because it doesn't make sense. Even if what you tell me were true – and I don't believe a word of it – it wouldn't have been necessary to keep it up to the bitter end. There was no more acting to do.'

'How can you be sure, Father?' Willie went on inexorably. 'Roger hated you. You wrecked his life. You made him live a lie. You took from him the only person he loved.' He rose from his chair with a lithe cat-like movement and moved through the smoke towards the priest. Father Mannix recoiled, and Willie stopped a few steps from him. 'I know Roger. I know what he was capable of. Oh, he was gentle, and tender and kind. But human beings are not like that all the time, even the best of them. And in the end he defeated you and your kind of religion. Holy water and pious aspirations! They didn't save you from being mocked at the edge of the grave. You believe what you want to believe about Roger. But you can't be sure now, can you?'

The priest put his breviary under his arm, kissed his stole, rolled it up and put it back in his pocket.

'Can you?' insisted Willie softly. 'Can you be sure?'

'I am sure of the mercy of God, Willie,' replied Father Mannix in a level voice. 'Of that I am quite certain. If I have erred, I am sorry, and I am suffering for it. We are all suffering.'

'I'm glad that you are,' said Willie bitterly, turning away and walking to the window where he pressed his hot cheek against the glass.

'Something will happen that will make sense of all this madness, I know it will. I don't know how, or why, or when, but it will.' The priest took a step forward and peered through the smoke. Willie was staring intently through the window.

'Yes,' he said flippantly, 'something is happening. I see Kathleen O'Neill coming up the avenue, all set for the big reconciliation.' He leaned his forehead against the glass and chuckled. When he turned round and walked back across the room the priest was gone. He could hear his car starting up and driving off as he went up the stairs to his room. A little while later the sound of voices in the kitchen told him that he had seen the end of Susan Carroll. The sands were run out but he did not turn up the hour-glass.

⟨⟨⟨ 9 ⟩⟩⟩

KATHLEEN POINTED A FINGER at the black Venus
on Willie's mantelpiece. Her engagement ring, sparkling in the
firelight, made her hand appear dirtier still.

'That black nigger,' she said severely, drawing her thick
eyebrows together, 'it's a disgrace in a Christian country with
no clothes on, that's what it is. What would Chris say if he saw
it? And Father Mannix, the Lord save us!'

Willie took out his handkerchief, unfolded it with some
ceremony, shook it, and carefully draped it over the ebony
figurine.

'Now,' he said, standing back and cocking his head sideways, 'no one can object to that. The lady is covered.'

Kathleen rubbed her mouth with the back of her hand and
suddenly giggled.

'You're a holy terror,' she said with rough admiration,
'that's what you are. I wonder what Father Mannix has to say
to you at all?'

'Oh, lots of things,' replied Willie airily, smiling at the
girl. 'We're very old friends, you know.'

Kathleen pursed her lips and fumbled with the strings of the
nylon apron she wore over her green frock, which was as usual
a little too tight for her.

'You weren't always such friends, from what I hear,' she
went on with a sly look.

'Well, we had our disagreements. But we made it up.'

'It's great bad luck to fight with the priests,' said Kathleen
earnestly, picking up the duster she had put down on the dressing table, when the ebony figure attracted her attention. She
rubbed the looking glass with slow circular movements and

204

Willie catching her eye in the mirror nodded his head gravely.

'Yes, I know.'

'Honest it is,' went on Kathleen firmly, pressing her duster more firmly against the glass, as if to emphasise her words. 'It's enough to bring a curse on any house, the Lord save us!'

'Well, it's all fixed up now,' said Willie, taking another handkerchief out of his pocket and arranging it in his jacket pocket.

'And not before it's time,' said Kathleen at her reflection in the mirror. 'It was a shocking risk to take.'

She looked around the room to see if there was any work for her to do. But everything was neat and tidy and Willie was adept at making his own bed. It was the first time she had been in the room since her return three days before. Her visit had not been as unexpected as it seemed to Willie at the time. She had met Chris in the street the day after the Mass; she coming out, he going into the chemist. They had spoken; an easier matter than they had imagined. Chris remarked in the most casual fashion that it was a long time since she had been to Summerhill. Kathleen replied that her mother had not been well. He expressed surprise and concern; she explained that the invalid was now much improved. They parted much affected by their meeting.

Next day it became known in the town that Susan Carroll was going abroad. A winter in Italy was spoken of, others said Switzerland, Morocco, Madeira, Greece: it was not really important. The real thing was that it was 'all off' between her and Chris Ryan – that was certain. The affair provided pleasant gossip, but little sensation. It had all been too sudden, too irresponsible. Susan was popular with all in the town and trusted by few. She had never quite fitted in and was judged to be agreeable, but not quite 'safe'. It was sensed that if she settled down at all it would be in Dublin – regarded as a foreign capital – or abroad. Carrolls, in the opinion of the gimlet-eyed unknowns who mould the thinking of a country town, was a property likely to be under the hammer in the next fifteen or twenty years. Kathleen, in the opinion of the curtain-twitchers, was a far more suitable match, in spite of her lack of fortune. For one thing she was entirely predictable.

Mrs O'Neill, acutely attuned to the local idea of the difference between the probable and the inevitable, advised her daughter, in her oblique and murmurous way, to strike while the iron was hot. And the girl, lonely, miserable, longing for Chris and the position his name would give, remembered that it was he who had spoken first at the chemist's door. With no fuss at all, the status quo was regained.

And now, as she contemplated the neat, comfortable little room, her frown was not accompanied by any real harshness of voice or gesture. With her sleeves rolled up to her elbows, her black hair tumbling about her rosy cheeks, and her duster held aloft like a flag of possession, she was a woman at ease in her own surroundings. In the first flush of victory, Willie represented a completed pattern. He was the prodigal returned to the fold, endorsed with bell, book and candle, and the personal interest of the parish priest. She was in the mood to be generous.

'Aren't you coming down for tea?' she said agreeably. Not waiting for an answer she turned and looked out the window. A faint amber glow lingered over the edge of the horizon; the river was one with the purple plain: in half-an-hour there would be no sense of space, only night.

'I suppose the two boys will be in for tea too?' said Willie.

Kathleen nodded. What with rain and another job on hand, Billy Graham and Tommy Murphy were still hammering away at the chimney. Kathleen had taken to giving them a cup of tea after they knocked off with the daylight, in the interests of good staff relations.

In the kitchen the two men were already sitting at the table with their caps hung on their knees. They nodded politely at Kathleen and grinned at Willie. Billy, a short stout man with a face as red as a harvest moon, held up his thumb in greeting; and Tommy, long, gangling, yellow-skinned, and bald as an egg, winked.

206

'God bless the work, boys,' said Willie sedately.

The two men chuckled: Billy deep down in his barrel chest; Tommy shrilly, from some strangulated cavern behind his wobbling Adam's apple. Willie lowered himself with exaggerated care on to a small, three-legged stool at the far side of the range from the armchair in which he had been accustomed to sit. Since her return Kathleen had instinctively claimed that; and Willie was careful to avoid it.

'Which of you put on the kettle?' asked Kathleen with a friendly smile.

'I did,' they both said in unison; stopped; glanced at each other, and then looked at Willie.

'Ah, sure it's a very big kettle,' he remarked innocently.

'Mighty,' said Billy, transferring his cap from one knee to another.

'Well,' said Kathleen, pouring the water into the pot, 'it saves time.'

It was a very formal tea, given and taken with a certain ritualistic light-heartedness. Kathleen was well aware that the two men would be going home to an enormous 'fry'; and they conscious of the need to preserve a good-neighbour policy, allowed her to give them two strong cups, and one slice of bread and jam each.

As they were finishing off Chris came in, blowing his lips out with the cold, and banging the yard door shut with the heel of his Wellington boot.

'Well, well,' he exclaimed jovially, 'this is a right feast. Is there nothing at all for the man of the house?'

Kathleen turned away with a slight frown. It had been Chris's habit to join the men during their tea, but not to take it with them. Kathleen approved of hospitality; but this smacked to her of socialism.

'And how about you?' said Chris, looking down from his towering height at his uncle sitting on the three-legged stool.

Willie looked up at his nephew with a smile, and glanced at the two workmen, with whom he had during the past few days struck up a merry friendship. They were looking at him expectantly. Chris crossed his arms on his chest and looked at his uncle with good-humoured expectation. Willie's lively banter with the workmen had greatly helped to ease the tension in the house. Chris's expression indicated that he was in the mood for a joke.

'Nothing I'd like better.' Kathleen looked around from the range with a frown of disapproval for his especial benefit, for she did not give him his tea either when the men were having theirs, although she liked him to be present. But instead of standing up to sit at the table Willie clutched the stool and stared at Kathleen with a puzzled expression. He drew in his lower lip, shot up his eyebrows, and stirred his body uneasily from side to side. They all looked at him wide-eyed and silent. A shiver ran through his lower limbs, his shoulders twitched and he gripped the stool tightly. He pressed his feet against the floor, and began to wriggle frantically, shaking his bottom and thrusting his head forward with little animal grunts. They watched intently as he relaxed his body, braced himself and still clutching the stool, rose a few inches on his bended knees. The stool rose with him. He kept the crouching position for a few moments and looked about him with a trapped, agonised glance: eyes popping, body rigid again, mouth dropping open. Slowly he lowered himself back into a sitting position, still holding on to the stool.

'God!' said Tommy Murphy, grasping the seat of his own chair instinctively, 'is it stuck you are?'

'Stuck!' exclaimed Kathleen, glancing uncertainly at the workmen and turning back to Willie who was now wriggling like an eel on the stool, his eyes starting from his head and his tongue protruding with the effort. Suddenly he paused in his gyrations, looked at Billy with one eyebrow raised, and continued to struggle with closed eyes until, as the three men leaned forward as if to help him, a slow smile spread over his pale face.

Billy guffawed and thumped his thigh.

'Stuck is right,' he roared delightedly. 'Glued, be God!'

Chris clapped his hands and grinned approval, while Billy and Tommy rose to their feet, chuckling with their high and low versions of merriment. Encouraged by his audience Willie took a few steps forward, bent in two, clutching the stool behind him.

'Is it a hand you want, you poor thing?' said Tommy, rubbing his hands on his overalls to clean them for the job.

Willie rolled his eyes and tottered around the kitchen groaning.

'A hand is right,' boomed Billy, adopting a crouching position as he set out to stalk Willie and the three-legged stool. He made a grasp for one of the legs, missed, growled with artful annoyance, and grabbed again. This time he connected and Willie was stopped dead in his tracks. Billy tugged, puffing and blowing out his lips. Willie moaned and swayed, screwing up his face into a contorted mask of frustration and pain, but he held on to the stool with unexpected strength.

'Hold on, Billy,' piped Tommy.

'What else can I do, ya eeejit,' he roared, looking back at his mate and sticking out his tongue, 'amn't I stuck too?'

Kathleen chuckled while Chris held up his plaster hand and roared with laughter. Suddenly there was a sharp wrenching sound; and Billy landed on his back with his knees in the air and the leg of the stool clutched against his stomach.

'Oh, oh, I'm destroyed,' he moaned, keeping his pose with his legs up, but winking at Tommy who had started forward to help him.

'Yaul bugger,' piped Tommy, prodding him affectionately in the ribs with his boot.

Willie propelled forward violently as the leg gave way, saved himself by dropping the stool and broke his fall by clutching the wall with his outspread hands. He turned round slowly, panting and sweating. But for the moment the centre of the stage was held by Billy who sat up, hugging the leg of the stool against his chest, and glaring at Tommy, as if he expected

209

him to take it away from him. Happily sure of his audience, he grinned foolishly as he raised the wooden leg to his mouth and began to nibble it.

'Mmmmmm,' he purred contentedly, pointing at Willie, 'it's no wonder ya stuck to it. Sure it isn't wood at all.' He paused for effect and wriggled his boots. 'It's Galway Rock, that's what it is. Gorjus!' He nibbled again and looked round him happily, his moon face beaming with delight.

Chris stamped his foot on the floor in appreciation. Kathleen chuckled and shook her head, while Tommy cackled his approval of the performance.

Willie, not to be outdone, sidled along the wall towards the door, reached up for the towel hanging on the nail, and stealthily wrapped it about his middle. He opened the door and looked into the hall.

'Hey, there, where ya going?' shouted Billy after him.

Willie's mobile face was a study of affronted dignity, as he gathered the towel closer about him.

'I'm going upstairs to change,' he said loftily. 'I've lost the seat of my pants.'

The men went home in high good spirits. Willie came down again in ten minutes to have his tea with Chris and Kathleen. After which they all knelt down to say the rosary.

10

WILLIE WOKE UP a few days afterwards with a pain in his chest. The symptoms were familiar to him. Pincers seemed to be crushing his heart, and a sharp hot pain ran down his left arm. He struggled for breath and eased himself up inch by inch into a sitting position, and lay back against the pillows clutching his chest with his fist. He had had worse attacks than this one, and he knew that if he lay quite still it would ease off. He remembered the tablets the doctor had given him, with the warning that he was to carry them with him at all times and keep them by his bed at night. Very carefully he turned his head and looked at the night-table. The little round box was not there.

For the past two weeks he had been feeling particularly well, and when he was better he always grew careless about the pills. He groaned as his eyes wandered about the room searching for the box. He lay very still, breathing hoarsely and painfully, not daring to move for fear the pincer would press closer.

His clothes hung on the chair at the end of the bed: a hunched, headless scarecrow. A few nights ago he had balanced a few books on the back of the chair, put his hat on top of them, climbed into bed and looked at the crouching figure through half-closed eyes. Now in the half-light the hanging jacket, limp, motionless, blurred, with the back of the chair outlined under the shoulders like skeletal limbs terrified him. He turned his head warily towards the window. As in most country houses the curtains were not drawn. It must be about eight o'clock, and a pale putty-coloured light seeped into the room from the bottom of the window. Outside he knew the

December dawn was rising like a wraith over the black rim of the horizon.

The pain eased a bit, and Willie leaned forward a few inches and stared at the top left-hand drawer of his dressing-table. The light crept up the window, as if an unseen hand were slowly lifting a blind. And suddenly after a few minutes the pain stopped. He raised his hand slowly to his forehead and felt his cold sodden flesh. He leaned forward again, a little further this time. The pain did not return. He lay back against the pillows and waited for a while, trying to regain a little strength. Then slowly, with infinite care, he drew back the clothes and began to move his body towards the edge of the bed. A sudden twinge in his arm made him catch his breath in terror; and he sat rigid and damp with sweat listening to the rapid, frightening thumping of his heart. The twinge of pain disappeared. Gently he drew his legs in their baggy striped pyjamas over the edge of the bed, and lowered them on to the floor. He sighed and closed his eyes with relief as he felt the rug under his feet. He waited for another few minutes before he rose carefully and stood on his feet, raising his shoulders and clasping his hands against his sides. He could smell his own perspiring warmth rising from the rumpled sheets. He took a step forward; and then another. He grasped the top of the chair on which his clothes hung. The journey was already half completed. Four more steps and he would have gained the dressing-table drawer where he had left the pills for the past couple of days.

In the yard below a cock crowed. Hollow steps sounded on the cobbles; and a door opened and shut with a creaking groan. A bucket rattled. Beyond the roof of the outhouse the horizon flickered, the sky paled, and the plain stirred and reared its broad back as another day dawned.

Willie grasped the handle of the half-open drawer and began to pull it out. In the darkness a grey-brown shadow moved. Intent on his search for the box of pills he leaned forward and groped with trembling fingers in the drawer. Suddenly the shadow whipped about; something swift and slimy brushed against Willie's hand and hip, dropped to the floor, with a thud, and scuttled across the carpet. With his fingers closing over the box Willie looked in the mirror, and saw the rat disappear under the bed.

He ran out of the room, dropping the box from his nerveless hand, and clutched the railing of the banister. His weak voice cracked and rose, died away in a toneless sob, and rose again. He fell to his knees, pressed his face against the railing like a man imprisoned, and screamed again and again. The thin sound echoed through the house like the cry of a tortured animal.

Chris in the outhouse heard nothing. He was lulled and comforted as always by the soft swish of the warm blue-white milk flowing into the bucket between Mick Brien's knees – the man he had taken on to do the work since he broke his wrist.

It was more than an hour afterwards that he discovered his uncle in the kitchen, in his pyjamas, huddled over the range, shivering and moaning to himself, like a man bereft of reason. He ran outside and shouted to Mick to go for the doctor.

' In the name of God, what happened?'

Kathleen had arrived to find Dr Wilson just leaving, and Chris pale and ashen-faced drinking whiskey by the kitchen fire.

Chris put more whiskey into his cup, added a little hot water and sugar and stirred the punch jerkily before he answered. He squatted down on the stool which Billy Graham had repaired with many a hearty chuckle only the day before.

' He says he saw a rat in the drawer of his dressing-table. He wouldn't go back to his own room, so I had to put him in mine after I sent for Wilson.'

' What does he say?'

' He'll have to be kept in bed. He gave him something to quieten him down. He was in a terrible state.'

He raised the cup to his lips and sipped his hot whiskey noisily.

'Jesus, Mary, and Joseph,' said Kathleen, filling the kettle and putting it on the range to make tea for herself.

'Chris,' she said in a low voice, 'did you ever see a rat here?'

He wiped his mouth on the sleeve of his jacket and frowned.

'Of course I did. There's plenty of them out behind the sheds. Wherever there's pigs, there's rats. Toby is killing them every day of the week.'

Kathleen shivered, and pressed her arms against her breasts.

'If I saw a rat I'd go out of my mind,' she said in a small voice. 'I'm afraid of my life of them, honest I am.'

'Well,' said Chris irritably, 'you'd better get used to them. They're far more frightened of us than we are of them.'

'But Chris, I'd never get used to them,' Kathleen's voice rose shrilly, and she flung out her hands in the theatrical gesture she used when agitated. 'A cousin of mine had a little girl who was bitten by one in her pram. She was scarred for life, the Lord save us and protect us.'

'People get drowned from time to time,' snapped Chris. 'Are you afraid of water?'

'Oh, it's not the same thing, it's altogether different, Chris. Rats are horrible, horrible. I always heard my mother say they're a sign of death when you see one.'

'Yes, and if you hear a cock crowing during the night, or if a bird flies into the room. A lot of damned nonsense, and that fool Brien hasn't the cows milked yet.'

Kathleen sat down in the armchair. She folded her arms over her breast and stared at Chris with frightened, angry eyes.

'Well, I'm not setting foot in any of them outhouses again until you put down traps or something. If I see a rat in this house I'll go out of my mind. I'm warning you now. It's a nice thing for you to have the place swarming with them and never to tell me a word about it, especially since I told you about my cousin before.'

'Oh, for Christ's sake!' Chris stood up and banged down his empty cup on the table.

Kathleen jumped to her feet also and faced him, wild-eyed, and shaking with self-indulgent hysteria.

'Supposing that rat is still in Willie's room! Did you kill it?'

Chris mumbled something and made for the door.

'Come back here, Chris Ryan,' shouted Kathleen. 'You didn't kill it. That rat must be in the house still. I'm not staying here another minute.' She ran to the door and took down her coat.

Chris closed his eyes, and sighed deeply as he turned from the door.

'All right,' he said with a martyred expression. 'I'll go into town' – he broke off and looked at his wrist – 'No, I'll send Mick into town when he has the cows milked, and he can get as many traps as would catch a herd of elephants.'

'And poison,' insisted Kathleen, holding her coat poised halfway between her and the nail.

'No, no poison,' said Chris firmly. 'Too dangerous. Traps.'

Kathleen hung up her coat, and turned round slowly to look at the kettle, which was boiling.

'Maybe you'd bring a cup up to Willie,' said Chris, opening the yard door.

Kathleen rounded on him.

'I'll do no such thing. I won't put one foot on that stairs until the rat is caught. I don't care if Willie is on his last breath. And what's more, you'll bring Toby in here and leave her with me while you're out. And keep that back door open.' She poured boiling water into the pot, spilling some of it on the range where it spat and sizzled like a live thing. 'It's all right for Willie to see a rat. But I have my life to lead, and I'm not coming into this house with death staring me in the face at the beginning.' She threw tea wildly into the pot. 'And that's that.'

11

HALLORAN LOOKED at the crucifix over the mantelpiece
and walked over to the window. Chris's room also overlooked a
yard; and the big man looked out over the view of the great
plain and the wide curve of the river, which Willie could see
all day long as his bed faced the window.

'Is it possible that they really think you're in this state
because you saw a rat, and got hysterical?' he asked, slowly,
leaning towards the glass with his hands clasped behind his
back.

'I don't know what they think,' said Willie, plucking at the
sheet with his pointed fingers. His voice was weak and throaty
and his colour ashen, but Halloran's visit had brightened him
up. He seemed almost animated. 'Kathleen at any rate is con-
vinced of it, which is a mercy in a way, because if she thought
I had had an attack she'd have Mannix in like a flash. And that
would be awkward.'

'How about Dr Wilson?'

'Well, you know what fools doctors are . . .'

'I'm not supposed to,' Halloran chuckled. 'I'm a nurse.'

'I didn't say anything about an attack, and he didn't
examine me. Chris told him I'd had a fright, and he gave me
something to keep me quiet. Since then I've had two more
attacks, oh, slight ones, Peter, don't worry. I'm not off yet.
I keep the tablets by me all the time now, and they're a great
help.'

'Did you tell Wilson about the other attacks?' Halloran
turned from the window.

'No,' said Willie with a sudden puckish grin, 'I did not.'
He shook his head. 'You know I had this thing for two years

in the asylum before I went to the doctor, and he thought the last attack was the first one.' He tapped his knuckles lightly against his chest. 'When it comes to the old ticker the doctors know just as much about it as Toby below.'

'All the same you find the pills help,' said Halloran with a sly smile.

'Yes, as far as the pain goes. After that . . .' Willie shrugged.

Halloran laughed and looked around the room.

'This is a nice room, bigger than your old one. Doesn't Chris mind moving out?'

'Well, he was very nice about it. I really am terrified of rats, you know. The very thought of sleeping in that bed again . . .' he broke off and shuddered.

'I was talking to that young woman as I came in. Quite a change I must say, since I was last here.' Halloran sat down beside the fire and held out his big raw hands to the flames.

'Kathleen?' Willie leaned towards him, supporting himself on his elbows. 'Yes, she's back again. I always knew she would.' He stopped and bit his lip. 'Poor Susan, I was very fond of her.'

Halloran took out his handkerchief and blew his nose loudly

'Miss O'Neill seems to have changed a bit,' he began in a hoarse voice. 'She seems quite upset about you.' He pushed his chair back from the fire which had flushed his ruddy face to a deep scarlet. 'I suppose the Mass must have gone off well.'

'Very well,' replied Willie lightly. 'A gathering of the clans for the return of the prodigal.'

'I see.' Halloran's cold-clouded voice was grave. 'So you thought discretion was the better part of valour.' He looked about the room again, avoiding Willie's eyes. 'It certainly seems to have paid dividends.'

'It usually does.' Willie drew his knees up under the clothes and clasped his hands about them. He looked at the window. It was a bright frosty day. The river glittered; and between the edge of the plain and the curving blue-white sky a chasm seemed to yawn, so that every object on the horizon, trees, roofs, bushes, were thrown into sharp, lonely relief, like figures on the top of a cliff.

'I hadn't much choice, had I?' he went on, turning away and meeting Halloran's eyes. The big man blinked and looked away. He looked up at the ebony Venus, which together with the hour-glass and Willie's books had been brought in from his old room.

'And what is your friend Mannix going to say to that?' he said pointing to the figurine.

'He won't be seeing it,' said Willie quietly, stretching out his legs again and leaning back against the pillows. He wriggled his toes under the sheets and raised his shoulders, in one of those frivolous gestures he was apt to make at unexpected moments.

'You mean . . .' Halloran turned heavily on his chair and stared at him.

'I did what they wanted me to do. I suppose it means something to them. It meant nothing to me.'

'Didn't it?' said Halloran quietly.

Willie covered his mouth with his hand and raised his eyebrows.

'And Mannix knew, I suppose, or suspected something?'

'No, he didn't,' Willie's voice was muffled as he spoke behind his hand. 'I told him.'

'What if he tells the others?' Halloran planted his hands on his knees, allowing his broad shoulders to slump tiredly.

Willie took his hands from his mouth, and put them under the bedclothes against his side, to keep them warm.

'He won't,' he said firmly. 'And he knows now, in a way he never knew before, that you can't force anybody to do anything they don't really want to do. No, Father Mannix will keep his silence.'

Halloran stood up and walked over to the window again. He

grasped the red curtain and crumpled it in his fist, swinging the cloth slowly to and fro.

' Are you shocked, Peter?'

Halloran did not reply for a few moments.

' Yes,' he began in a voice hoarser and more muffled than before. He stopped and cleared his throat again. ' Yes, I suppose I am. It's horrible that you should have to hide behind the priests like that. The whole thing from beginning to end is horrible, especially if you ask yourself how many people all over the country are doing the same kind of thing because of pressure like this. How can they expect any kind of honesty ' – he broke off, sneezed and fumbled in his pocket for his handkerchief.

Willie took his hand out from under the sheets and thumped the pillows behind him with unexpected vigour.

' Yes,' he said, ' and if I hadn't told Mannix I suppose I could have gone on playing this farce with him.'

' You could have told him you made an act of contrition.' Halloran turned from the window holding his handkerchief in front of his nose. His big frame blocking the light threw a shadow over the sick man's paper-white face.

' I could have, yes. It would have been easy to think up something. He would have been only too glad to believe it. But I didn't want him to believe a lie. I wanted him to know.'

Halloran blew his nose, put his handkerchief back in his pocket and plucked his lower lip thoughtfully with his thumb and forefinger.

' So you really wanted this to happen, did you?' he said at length.

Willie sat bolt upright in the bed. His shoulders were high and rigid and he crumpled the sheet with his hands.

' It was forced on me,' he replied shrilly. ' I didn't know they were going to have it. Oddly enough it was Susan's idea. She did it to keep Chris. Everybody wanted it for the wrong reason. Mary and Michael because it was one up on the neighbours to have a private Mass . . .'

'Yes, yes, I know all that,' broke in Halloran impatiently. 'But you'd have done this anyway. You wanted to do what you thought Roger Dillon had to do. Has anybody or anything else ever meant a tinker's cuss to you? I've never met anybody so single-minded in my life. You didn't really give a damn about anything except what happened thirty years ago.' He snorted, and made a rumbling inarticulate sound in his chest.

'I never . . .' began Willie, pulling up the crumpled sheets over his hollow chest.

Halloran took two steps which brought him back to the fire-place again. He picked up a book from the mantelpiece and began to flick through it nervously. Willie bit back what he was going to say, and rubbed his eyes wearily with his wrist.

'I'm sorry,' said Halloran quietly, putting the book back on top of the pile. 'I shouldn't have said that. After all you hadn't much else to think about, had you, all these years?'

'It's all right,' said Willie weakly. 'It doesn't matter. Things repeat themselves in life. I suppose there's something in what you say. But I didn't make this situation. It's just that people here haven't changed at all.'

Halloran leaned an elbow on the mantelpiece and stared down at the fire. Above the crackle of the wood the silence of the room was broken only by the breathing of the two men: Halloran's deep and bronchial; Willie's quick and laboured. Suddenly Halloran became aware of it, and drew himself up with his hand against his heart. He looked anxiously across at the bed.

'Here,' he said, his hoarse voice taking on a brisk professional tone, 'let me take your pulse. It's time for you to have a little nap.'

Willie looked up in surprise; and then held out his hand. Halloran took off his watch; grasped the proffered wrist between his thumb and forefinger, and cocked his head sideways as he listened to the quick, irregular beats.

'It's a small thing, isn't it, that regulates all the splendours

and miseries of the world?' said Willie when the nurse relin-
quished his hand.

'What?' said Halloran with professional vagueness.

'The pulse.'

12

KATHLEEN HUNG the lustrous ocelot coat reverently over the back of the chair and stroked it tenderly before turning round to see if Mrs Ryan was comfortably seated in the arm-chair. But the older woman was still standing up with her back to the range watching the disposal of her coat. Her hollow eyes darkened and narrowed as she observed the girl's flushed face. Then she turned away and sank gracefully into the old leather chair.

'Well,' she said after a pause during which she looked commandingly from her husband to Chris and back again to Kathleen, 'what does the doctor say?'

Chris, leaning on the ledge of the back window with his injured hand thrust into his jacket, straightened up and turned his head to meet his mother's searching gaze.

'You know what doctors are like,' he muttered uncomfortably. 'It's hard to get anything out of him.'

'Oh, come now,' said Mary briskly. 'Dr Wilson is an old friend. Michael or I would have asked him except . . .' her voice softened and she fingered the pearls at her throat, 'that one doesn't want to interfere.'

'Interfere in what?' demanded Chris.

She smiled blandly at him and touched her goitre gently.

'Well, naturally Dr Wilson would assume that we knew all about it – from you,' she murmured. 'He might think it strange if we enquired behind your back, Chris dear.' She crossed her legs and smoothed her pink tweed skirt with a jewelled hand.

Chris fumbled in his pocket for the cigarettes which he had taken to smoking since he broke his wrist but could not find them. Kathleen took a packet from the table, opened it and put a cigarette in his mouth. She reached up on her toes and took matches from the ledge over the range, lit one for him, and went back to her place at the end of the kitchen, crossed her arms, and began to nibble her lower lip with her small white teeth.

Mrs Ryan turned towards her with raised eyebrows, and twitched the corners of her mouth in a faint mirthless smile. Kathleen blinked and looked away.

' I thought you were talking to him, Daddy,' said Chris, looking at the back of his father's white head. ' At least he told me you were.'

Michael Ryan started, flashed his wife an enquiring look, and half-turned in his chair to answer his son.

' I ran into him outside the shop the other day, Chris. He told me Willie had had a very bad turn. I didn't tell your mother because I didn't want to upset her. But we came out as soon as we could.' When he had finished his explanation he puffed out his soft lips and looked at Mary again.

' I was wondering why you were so anxious to come,' she said smoothly, ' these last few days. You might have told me sooner. Naturally we thought everything was all right, and with Christmas coming on we simply haven't a minute to ourselves. Otherwise we'd have been out long ago.'

Kathleen, who had been watching Mrs Ryan intently, lowered her eyes, and the other three carefully avoided looking at her. It was the first time Mary and Michael had visited the house since her return.

Chris took the cigarette out of his mouth and looked at it.

' Willie saw a rat,' he said almost apologetically.

' A rat!' Mary threw up her long yellow hands and wriggled her fingers in a gesture intended to denote disgust and horror. As with most of her movements it was exaggerated and a little bizarre, so that it was impossible to tell whether she was lying.

Michael moistened his lips and glanced sideways at his son.

' Yes, I know,' he said, ' but I didn't tell your mother. The main thing is – how is Willie now?'

'Not good.' Chris blew smoke through his nose and tilted his head back.

'Dr Wilson seems to think that the great danger now is pneumonia,' went on Michael.

'How could anybody get pneumonia from seeing a rat!' exclaimed Mary, wriggling her fingers again. 'I wish people would tell me things.'

'Rats are bad luck,' said Kathleen in an excited voice. 'A sign of death.'

No one heeded her, and she tossed her hair back with a gesture so defiant that one of her shoulders jerked up.

Chris looked at his mother impatiently.

'Of course he didn't get anything from seeing the rat,' he said sharply. 'It's simply that he got hysterical and I think it must have brought on a heart attack. Dr Wilson wouldn't say. That's over a week ago now, but Willie seems to be getting weaker. Sometimes he's bright enough, other times he's hardly able to speak.'

Michael sighed heavily and shook his head. Mary grasped her little finger and cracked a knuckle. Kathleen winced and closed her eyes.

'I see.' Mary got up suddenly and peered through the window behind her. 'Look, it's beginning to snow.'

'Maybe we'll have a white Christmas,' said Michael, leaning sideways and peering over his wife's shoulder. 'It's been threatening snow for the last two days.'

'You'll have a cup of tea?' said Kathleen looking enquiringly at Chris. He gave a little nod and she started for the range.

'The chimney isn't finished yet,' said Mary, turning from the window, and looking narrowly at Kathleen bustling with the kettle and teapot.

'No,' said Chris firmly. 'It is not.'

'What a pity it wasn't finished for the Mass,' went on his mother kneading her hip-bones with her fingers. 'Thank God the wind was in the right place that day.' She sat down again and stroked the diamond brooch on her lapel. 'I suppose Father Mannix has been out to see Willie.'

Kathleen put down the kettle and looked at Mary with a brisk decisive air.

'Now, isn't that a funny thing?' she said. 'I was just thinking about it the other day. He must have heard that Willie is sick.'

'They're such friends,' murmured Mary, looking up at the girl with a faint smile. 'Willie and he used to talk for hours.'

'Maybe Father Mannix has a cold,' said Chris. He was leaning again on the window ledge, looking out at the slow tentative white flakes dissolving on the cobbles in the yard.

'No, he hasn't,' said his mother quickly. 'I saw him in town this morning.'

'Has Willie asked for him?' said Michael.

'No,' said Chris and Kathleen speaking at the same time. There was a pause as the speakers gave each other time to continue. Kathleen rinsed the teapot and remained silent.

'I suppose he doesn't want to admit anything to himself,' said Chris. 'Or maybe he doesn't know.'

'In that case the priest should be sent for,' said his mother sharply.

'That's what I was just going to say,' said Kathleen, going over to the dresser and taking down the cups and plates. 'If Father Mannix is such a friend, Willie won't mind him calling. What I can't understand is that he hasn't come out sooner.' Her voice was aggrieved, as if she thought the priest's absence was meant as a snub to her. 'It's very queer, that's what it is.'

Mary and Michael exchanged glances before the girl turned round, holding a tray against her stomach.

'Well, I think that's just the point – that they are such good friends,' said Mary with a kind smile. 'It's a delicate situation and Father Mannix is a very sensitive man. And of course he knows how highly-strung Willie is. I know that priest as well as I know my own hand, and I'm perfectly sure that he's waiting for Willie to send for him.'

She got up and motioned towards the tray.

'Do let me help you with that,' she said.

'No, no,' said Kathleen in a shocked voice. 'Sit down and rest yourself. It's not a bit of bother.'

Mary tucked her skirt against the back of her knees and subsided gracefully.

'I must say I'm looking forward to a nice cup of tea on a cold afternoon like this,' she remarked affably.

Kathleen bustled happily about the range, while Michael drew his chair back out of her way, crossed his feet and looked at the floor. Chris tapped on the window with his fingernail. The snow was thickening; and the roofs of the sheds were already streaked with white. Mick Brien crossed the yard and went into the barn.

Chris made for the door.

'I'll be back in a minute,' he said as he went out. 'I forgot to tell Mick about the new time for the creamery. It has to be in at eight now instead of nine.'

Kathleen took the kettle off the boil.

'There's no use in wetting the tea until he gets back,' she said crossly. 'When he gets talking to that Brien . . .'

Mary stroked her goitre gently and looked up at the girl.

'Well, I doubt if Chris will spend all his time farming,' she said softly. 'At least I hope not.'

'You bet he won't,' said Kathleen, staring out at the whirling snowflakes.

'It's such a hard life,' went on Mary, watching the girl's pouting, protruding profile closely.

'Sure, Chris isn't able for it at all,' complained Kathleen. 'He has himself killed.'

Michael pushed his chair further back from the range and left the two women in possession. He clasped his hands over his belly and twiddled his thumbs.

'He was always very susceptible to colds,' went on Mary in an intimate voice. 'And it's so cold out there, don't you think, and damp?'

Kathleen nodded sulkily.

'And now he's given up his bedroom to Willie,' she said, snapping her fingers irritably.

'Oh dear,' sighed Mary, 'changing beds in this weather. It's a wonder he hasn't got his death. Why on earth did he do that?'

Kathleen told her.

'It's very silly of Willie to want to change his room because of that,' said Mary severely. 'Of course he's very highly-strung.' She sighed again and closed her eyes. 'Men are so difficult.'

The silent old man on the other side of the range might not have been there.

'About Willie – ' began Kathleen thoughtfully.

'Yes?' Mary smiled up at her, and twisted her sapphire ring.

'Do you think I ought to mention Father Mannix to him?'

'Now, I'm very glad you mentioned that, Kathleen, I really am. It's all very worrying. Poor Willie probably doesn't realise – ' she broke off and was silent for a few minutes. 'Perhaps you could, well, give him a hint. I know it's difficult, but after all, it's something we've got to face.'

'We're bound to do it,' said Kathleen sternly. 'It's our duty, if we're to be good Catholics.'

'Quite, my dear. And of course we must all pray hard for him.'

'I'm lighting a sixpenny candle every day.'

'And I'm saying the rosary.'

Michael coughed and stirred on his chair. The women fell silent. After a decent interval Mary leaned forward with an expression of deep concern on her long yellow face.

'Oh, and by the way, how is poor Miss White? I knew I had something to ask you. She's gone a week now, isn't she?'

Kathleen lowered her voice, turned her back to Michael, and bent over her prospective mother-in-law confidentially.

'Cancer,' she whispered, tapping one breast and then another significantly. 'Both gone.'

'The Lord preserve us,' said Mary clasping her hands and exchanging a look of perfect understanding with Kathleen. A pact had been sealed. Miss Pinkie White had not lost her breasts in vain.

Suddenly Michael started up and looked at the front window.

'I hear a car,' he said.

Mary sprang to her feet and looked through the window.

'Thanks be to God, maybe it's Father Mannix,' exclaimed Kathleen.

'I can barely see,' said Mary kneeling on the chair and holding her nose against the glass. 'The snow is awful.'

'That's not Father Mannix's car,' said Michael, peering over her shoulder.

'My goodness, it's Mrs Whittaker,' said Mary, twisting round and standing up. 'She must be coming to see Willie. They were always such friends.' She tugged at the hem of her jacket and touched her hair with her fingertips. Her yellow face was slightly flushed and she looked about the kitchen with glittering eyes. 'It's a good thing you got out the best china, Kathleen. We must – you must give her tea. Such an old friend.'

'Great God almighty, isn't it awful that the chimney in the parlour isn't finished yet,' cried Kathleen, looking at her grubby hands.

'And it won't be while you have those two villains pretending to work at it,' said Mary quickly, as she searched in her bag for her pocket mirror. 'I'd see about those two if I were you, Kathleen.' She scanned her flushed face in the glass. 'Michael, run to the door and open it. Don't keep her waiting in the snow.'

'Look at the appearance of me,' said Kathleen, throwing out her hands in despair.

'Run upstairs and tidy yourself, dear,' said Mary, dabbing

her cheeks with her powder puff. 'I'll hold the fort until you come down.'

'Oh, will you?' said Kathleen, running out of the kitchen. 'I won't be a minute.'

The knocker sounded. Mary touched her hot cheeks with her palms, before turning eagerly to greet her visitor.

⟨⟨⟨ 13 ⟩⟩⟩

WHEN CHRIS had shown Mrs Whittaker into Willie's room and settled her comfortably in the chair by the fire, she waited until his footsteps had died away on the stairs before getting slowly to her feet again and looking at the window. It was now quite dark and the snow was falling thickly.

'Yes, I've been looking at it too,' said Willie. 'It mesmerises you, like running water.'

The ghostly flakes drifted lazily down, swirling now to the right and now to the left as the wind coiled about the house. The light in the room lit them up, softening the gleaming white to a pale amber. Blobs blown against the panes shimmered for a moment like glow-worms, then flattened, faded and dissolved into water. The window was alive with luminous specks of reflected light.

Mrs Whittaker turned away and sat down painfully in her chair.

'That's pretty,' she said pointing to the ebony Venus.

'Yes, I think so. They don't approve of it much here, though. Sometimes I cover it modestly with a handkerchief.

Mrs Whittaker chuckled.

'Your brother and sister-in-law are downstairs,' she said. 'They very kindly gave me tea. Which is why I'm late.'

'I heard voices. I was wondering.'

'How are you, Willie?' Mrs Whittaker folded her gloves neatly over her handbag and settled it on her lap.

'Alive.'

'I heard you weren't well. But you look . . .' she hesitated, and flicked the clasp of her bag with her misshapen thumb.

'I look like death,' said Willie calmly. 'At least I did three days ago, which was the last time I looked at myself in the mirror. All eyes and nose. I won't be looking again.'

'Oh, come now,' the clasp clicked again. 'It's been a hard winter.'

'I'm not dying of the winter, Mrs Whittaker. I'm dying of my life.'

The old woman looked up sharply. Her wrinkled face was still flushed from sitting in the overheated kitchen. The unnatural colour staining her parchment skin gave her a flustered, unhealthy appearance.

Willie glanced at her and smiled.

'Don't look so startled,' he said. 'After all it's quite true. It's not death that kills us, but life.'

Mrs Whittaker took up her left glove and began to pull it on her mottled hand. She looked at the fire abstractedly, shook her head and peeled off the glove again.

'It's just that, well . . .' she bit her lip and slapped the glove against her bag. 'Well, Roger said the same thing to me,' she went on in a shaky voice.

'When he was dying?' There was a harsh note in the weak voice.

'It was almost the last thing he did say to me.' She sniffed and brushed her nose with her knuckle. 'I have a bit of a cold. He spoke about you a lot. Poor Roger.'

'He was always very kind to me.' Willie turned his head on the pillow and looked at the drifting petals of light outside.

'Well, he was very fond of you. We all were. Those were good days.' She drew herself up, gripped her bag firmly and stared up at the shifting hour-glass.

Willie's slanting eyes closed, and he drew his blue lips tightly together before he spoke.

'Were they?' he whispered. In the silence that followed Mrs Whittaker looked at him anxiously and sat very still in her chair, fiddling with the clasp of her bag.

Willie opened his eyes and looked sideways at the door. The sound of laughter could be heard faintly from the kitchen.

Mrs Whittaker raised her eyebrows and turned down the corners of her mouth. Willie smiled faintly.

' A family reunion, Mrs Whittaker.'

' I gather there was a bit of trouble. Or so one hears.' The old woman coughed. ' Ah, well, these things happen. I'm glad they've got together – family quarrels are always so stupid.'

' Mary is doing the sensible thing,' said Willie, his eyes flickering with something of their old restlessness. ' If you can't lick 'em, join 'em.'

Mrs Whittaker smiled back.

' For Chris's sake, it's a good thing, isn't it?'

' I hope everything turns out well for him. He's a nice boy.' He lifted his hand from the quilt and pointed at the light. ' He plugs his electric shaver into it every morning, so that I can tidy myself in bed. Also it means I don't have to look in that mirror ever again.' He grinned suddenly and felt his chin. ' Of course it doesn't give you as good a shave as the old razor, but it'll do me.'

' You look very smart, Willie.'

He smiled and closed his eyes again, opening them after a few seconds to look at the window. The ledge was white with snow.

' It was very nice of you to call, Mrs Whittaker,' he murmured.

' Oh, for heaven's sake, Willie,' exclaimed the old woman, tugging at her shapeless felt hat. ' I would have come ages ago, but my old aches and pains have been really bad this winter.'

' I'm sorry to hear that.'

' I'm much better now, much better,' said Mrs Whittaker gamely, squaring her shoulders.

Willie looked at her sideways. She was staring into the fire, her gnarled hand, covered with liver spots, tightly clenched on top of her shabby leather bag.

' What did Roger say about me?' Willie asked suddenly in a clear strong voice.

Mrs Whittaker started and looked at him in surprise.

'Oh, lots of things,' she replied slowly, as if she were playing for time. 'He talked a great deal about the old days.'

'Tennis parties, tea on the lawn, Chopin in the drawing-room.' The husky voice was still strong, but a note of bitterness had crept into it.

'Yes, all that, of course.' She paused and held her head down. 'But he worried too that you might not forgive him. I can see that you haven't.'

Willie stared at the window. Snowflakes blown against the glass were glittering steadily in the light. It was beginning to freeze.

'I have nothing to forgive Roger for, Mrs Whittaker. I suppose Father Mannix insisted on that too.'

'Father Mannix insisted on nothing, Willie,' said the old woman quietly.

'Not even on your coming to see me at this time?' The blue lips curled in a tired smile.

'No.' Mrs Whittaker's voice was firm as she turned heavily on her chair and faced Willie who was looking at her intently. 'I think I'd better tell you that I know what you mean.'

'You know.' The voice was flat, it asked no question.

'Yes, I've known for a long time. Ever since you stopped coming to the house.'

'Who told you?'

Mrs Whittaker's mouth twisted with distaste.

'A kind neighbour. For my own good. The usual.'

Willie stirred in his bed and a faint colour crept into his livid cheeks.

'I think I know who she was,' he said. 'Am I right?'

Mrs Whittaker was silent. There was a sudden tiny sound at the window. A robin fluttered on to the snow-covered ledge, chirped, pecked at the wooden frame, and flew away. The faint lacy imprints of its claw-marks were obliterated by the falling snow.

'I thought perhaps you had sensed something without understanding, as people do.' He propped himself up with his elbow, and groaned. ' Now it's much worse. It's horrible.'

' In a way it isn't, Willie,' said the old woman gently. ' Sometimes good can come out of evil. You see, if I hadn't known I wouldn't have been able to help Roger.'

' You mean . . .' Willie lay back and held out a wasted hand in supplication.

' I didn't understand. I still don't. I suppose it was the way I was brought up.' She sighed and moved her swollen feet into a more comfortable position. ' But women are not so unsympathetic as men like to think, even women of my generation. And Roger was my only brother. He gave me a home when my marriage broke up. I was the only one he had in the end. I did my best.'

' So it wasn't necessary for him to deceive you in the end?' Willie's voice was low and calm, but his fingers dug into the quilt, and a thin line of saliva crept down his chin.

' No. There was no one left to deceive. Our mother was paralysed. I tried to let him know that – well, that he could talk to me. I knew how horribly lonely he was. And of course he understood at once. He never asked me how I found out. But I think he was glad, because I noticed a change in him, particularly after he became ill. When you live with a person for a long time you sense when they're lying and when they're not. Women do, anyway. Roger wasn't lying in the end. The only thing he worried about was you. He blamed himself a great deal.'

Willie looked down at his arched, scrabbling fingers, and flattened them out, smoothing the quilt with a fan-like movement on either side of his body; so shrunken now that he seemed almost a legless trunk propped up in the narrow bed.

' Why didn't you say something about this when I was staying with you – you know, the time I was sick?' he asked pettishly.

' Well, you gave me no opening, my dear. I don't suppose

234

I'd have mentioned it even today, if it hadn't sort of come up of it's own accord.'

'You were talking to Halloran,' insisted Willie.

Mrs Whittaker looked shocked and sniffed loudly.

'Now that's hardly the sort of thing one would bring up with somebody one has met for the first time,' she said stiffly. 'My own brother!'

The colour had drained from Willie's face and his cheeks were as white as the pillow behind him. His black eyes and his wide mouth might have been painted on the linen.

Mrs Whittaker looked at him anxiously and tightened her grip on her handbag.

'You were the last person he spoke about,' she went on, speaking quickly and nervously. 'I hope for the sake of the dead that you will forgive whatever there is to forgive. And not only Roger, but all the others too.'

She looked away and fumbled with her gloves. Willie stared at the falling snow.

'I was never much of a chess player,' he whispered. 'Roger always said so.' He turned his head slowly and painfully and looked at his old friend with a smile. 'But don't worry, I have one last move to make.'

Mrs Whittaker looked puzzled for a moment, but as Willie continued to smile she relaxed and smoothed her gloves as gently as she might the back of a cat.

'And I was never much of a one for riddles,' she replied. 'But I hope everything is all right.'

'Yes, Mrs Whittaker, everything is all right. You have been very kind.' The dark eyes closed and the mouth fell open a little. Mrs Whittaker waited for a few moments before she pulled herself to her feet as quietly as she could. Moving stiffly, she tiptoed past the bed and reached the door.

Willie opened his eyes and smiled again. A curiously sweet and youthful expression flitted over his mortally tired face.

'Goodbye, Mrs Whittaker.'

'Goodbye, Willie.'

235

When she was gone the room was very silent. The fire had settled down; the sick man seemed hardly to breathe; outside the falling snow muffled the earth. And the old weep quietly.

⸙ ⸙ ⸙ 14 ⸘ ⸘ ⸘

IN THE PARLOUR a cosy fire burned. No wind blew above the white Christmas landscape outside, and the smoke from the chimney drifted lazily under the peacock blue sky. A great peace lay over the plain, whiteness mantled the horizon, and the stilled and frozen river melted into the slumbering land. The beast-black bog slept under its shimmering mantle. Bells tinkled over the hushed fields and voices rose clear and hopeful in the sparkling air.

The funeral sherry was placed upon a silver tray in front of the sofa and the four mourners gathered about it were untroubled by bothersome smoke.

'But wasn't it a terrible big funeral,' said Kathleen in an awed voice, sitting up straight and dignified in her smart new black costume. 'Who'd ever have thought that so many people remembered Willie?'

Mary tightened her lips, and looked the girl up and down.

'It was a tribute to the family,' she said sharply.

'All the same,' Kathleen blundered on, 'seventy-six cars, and for a man that only a few old people remember.'

'Seventy-seven,' corrected Mary. 'I counted them.'

'The last one was a Dublin car that got caught up in the line,' retorted Kathleen stubbornly. 'He turned off for the main road at the bridge.'

'Fifty-six, or seventy-six or seven, what does it matter?' broke in Chris impatiently. 'Most of them owed us a funeral anyhow. Don't we go to all of theirs?'

Mary and Kathleen exchanged glances and remained silent.

'All the same,' said Michael, refilling his empty glass and

237

drinking it as if it were lemonade, ' the place won't be the same without poor Willie.'

' Lord rest him.' Kathleen clutched her breast. ' I'm not over the shock of it yet. To think that he might have been dead when I went up to see him after Mrs Whittaker left. I wanted to bring him up his tea, but he seemed to be sleeping so peacefully, the poor old thing, that I hadn't the heart to wake him. Sure, he was like a little child, lying there with his hand under his cheek.' She looked at Chris appealingly.

' Don't worry,' he said definitively. ' Dr Wilson said he was only a few hours dead when I called him. He must have died in his sleep at about eight o'clock in the morning. Or thereabouts.'

' Ah, sure it was a blessing,' said Michael, holding his empty glass and looking longingly at the bottle.

' Well, thanks be to God I didn't find him anyway,' said Kathleen, sighing with relief. ' If I did I'd have gone out of my mind.' She looked at Mary and bit her lip. ' Only . . .'

' Only what?' asked the older woman sharply.

' Only that we should have got a priest in sooner. I mean to say . . .'

' No one can stay the final hand of God,' said Mary severely. ' And thanks be to God and His Blessed Mother, Willie made his peace with the Lord the day of the Mass. Everybody in town and country knows that. And what wrong could a harmless old man like that do between then and the end? No Kathleen, he had somebody's prayers.'

' All the same,' persisted Kathleen, ' it must have been a great disappointment to that young curate Chris got, to be anointing him, and he as stiff as a door-nail.'

' He gave him conditional absolution,' snapped Mary.

' And then the way Father Mannix acted at the grave,' went on Kathleen inexorably. ' I never saw a priest to act like that, swaying and muttering like he was going to fall in, and nobody could hear a word he said. You'd think he was drunk, the Lord save us.'

Michael snatched the bottle from under his wife's disapproving eye and refilled his glass.

'That fellow, is it?' said Mary scornfully, 'don't talk to me about him. I was shaking in my shoes until the last spadeful was thrown up on the grave that he'd make an exhibition of us all.' Suddenly with a sharp glance at her husband's glass she pulled herself up, sipped her sherry, and looked up with a smile to meet Kathleen's bewildered stare. 'Of course they were great friends,' she went on quickly, 'and everybody knows that Father Mannix brought him back to his duties. It was a bond between them. No wonder he was so upset. It was plain for the whole town to see how attached he was to Willie, and how highly he thought of him.' She paused and then pronounced final judgement. 'He's gone to God, I'm sure.'

'Do you know what?' said Michael, his bleary eyes lighting up as he looked fondly at Chris, 'You and Kathleen ought to get married before Lent.'

'This is a nice time to be talking about a thing like that,' snorted Chris, glaring angrily at his father.

Kathleen covered her mouth with her hand and closed her eyes modestly.

'Oh ho,' said Michael tipsily, 'many's the good and true match I saw made at a wake. It used to be a right place for them long ago.' He stopped and his puffy face sagged. 'Only poor Willie didn't have a wake.'

'And a good thing too,' declared Mary, putting down her glass on the tray. 'That's one new Church regulation that I thoroughly approve of. You die before three in the afternoon, and you're in the church that night before eight. In the old days people were killed with those ghastly wakes – drinking and roaring and carrying on at the very foot of the corpse. It was downright pagan.' She frowned and pursed her lips. 'All the same there's something in what your father says, Chris. Nobody expects you to go into mourning for your uncle – that's all done away with too. And in the meantime people might talk.'

She cast down her eyes and twisted her ring pensively.

'What do you mean, people might talk?' demanded Kathleen, all coyness forgotten.

'Well dear,' replied Mary sweetly, 'I'm only telling you for your own good. You know what a pack of busybodies and hypocrites they are in this town. I can hear them saying that it's not proper for you to be out here alone with Chris all day long when you're not married.'

'Well, the dirty faggots!' exclaimed Kathleen hotly, looking at Chris with flaming cheeks. 'Did you ever hear the like of that?'

'I did,' replied Chris, looking at his mother with cold angry eyes. 'It doesn't surprise me a bit.'

'It never entered my mind,' cried Kathleen. 'Never, never, never!'

'Don't worry,' said Chris with a little smile. 'I'll make an honest woman of you.'

'Now look here, you,' shouted Kathleen furiously, 'I won't be talked to like that. If my mother only knew, and the dead not cold in their graves. And while we're on the subject I want to talk to you about this place . . .'

Mary stood up and looked at her watch.

'I'm exhausted,' she said in a faint voice, but with an encouraging look in Kathleen's direction, 'I'm going home to lie down.' She gave another meaning look at Kathleen and smiled gallantly. 'And for heaven's sake don't start arguing about your problems before your marriage. You'll have quite enough of them to face afterwards. Offer up whatever little troubles you have for those that are gone.'

'Gone, gone,' muttered Michael tearfully, grasping the bottle and pouring himself a final sherry. He gulped it down and belched. 'Poor Willie, when all is said and done he didn't get much out of this life. Not even a wake.'